DISCARD

GUADALUPE CANYON

GUADALUPE CANYON

PAUL COX

THORNDIKE PRESS
A part of Gale, a Cengage Company

GALE
A Cengage Company

GALE
A Cengage Company

LIBRARY OF CONGRESS CIP DATA ON FILE.
CATALOGUING IN PUBLICATION FOR THIS BOOK
IS AVAILABLE FROM THE LIBRARY OF CONGRESS.

ISBN-13: 978-1-4328-9120-6 (hardcover alk. paper)

Published in 2022 by arrangement with Paul Cox.

Printed in Mexico
Print Number: 1   Print Year: 2023

GUADALUPE CANYON

CHAPTER 1

For the last two months I had been working cows down along the Mexican border and in that rugged desert country, I was lucky to cover five miles in an hour on the back of a horse. Admittedly, I made much better time riding on the long, dusty road from Sasabe to Tucson, but by the time I got to town, I was looking forward to driving something that could eat up the miles and put wind in my face. At Richardson and Company, however, the only automobile available to me was a battered 1911 Oakland Roadster. Having no other choice, I left my horse at the livery and reluctantly rented the humble two-seater. The next day, still dressed in my range clothes, I sped out of town an hour before sunup, heading southeast toward Arizona's San Bernardino Valley.

Thinking like the greenhorn Easterner I was, I had telephoned the Slaughter ranch the evening I arrived in Tucson and told them I would easily make it to their ranch before supper. But at the time of the phone conversation I was naïvely thinking of the streets in and around the city of Tucson. I hadn't counted on country roads that were little more than game trails, dubious routes winding through the brush that, all too often, were peppered with potholes or scarred with deep wagon ruts.

When I approached the border town of Douglas, the sun was already setting. Trying to make up for the hours I lost on the bad roads, I had not stopped for lunch and all I had eaten since daybreak were a few sticks of jerky I found stuffed in my shirt pocket. So, knowing full well that I had missed supper at the Slaughters, I stopped in Douglas, pulling up in front of a grocery store on Tenth Street. There, I bought a cold bottle of Coca-Cola and then went next door to a restaurant that was just getting ready to close. After bribing the proprietor with an extra fifty cents, he hurriedly threw a ham and cheese sandwich together and wrapped it in brown paper. Then, with the soda wedged between my legs and eating as I drove, I headed out of town, pushing the roadster to an impressive fifty miles per hour. But in less than a mile, as the twilight dimmed into darkness, I ran out of good city road and once again found myself bouncing down a brush-lined dirt road.

The Oakland Roadster may have been an older model automobile but when I switched on the bulbous brass-encased headlamps, I was pleasantly surprised. Both lamps flashed instantly and cast a brilliant beam of light, illuminating the road ahead for at least one hundred yards. But then I soon discovered the headlamps left the potholes filled with black shadows, the jarring depths of which were impossible to estimate.

It was late September and yet the daytime temperatures in the Southwest often still reached ninety degrees. But, unlike Tucson, the land around Douglas was high desert and after sundown the air cooled quickly. I soon decided it was that sudden drop in temperature that somehow had affected the damned rabbits.

The first to lope across my lighted path was a gangly long-eared jackrabbit. Its sudden appearance startled me and I instinctively swerved, almost running off the narrow road. The second and third rabbits that darted out of the brush were chubby-looking cottontails. Both times I slammed my foot on the brakes, skidding to a stop amidst a rolling cloud of dust. But after a dozen more close calls and realizing I still had thirty miles to go, my compassion for the diminutive and furry desert fauna began to dissipate. Bewildered and irritated by such an inexplicable phenomenon, I set my jaw and drove on through the night, doing my best to ignore the frequent flashes of white and the occasional dull thud.

As the death toll rose, I repeatedly asked myself why an animal, ordinarily in possession of superb survival instincts, would suddenly bolt from the security of the desert and run directly in front of a monstrous, roaring machine. It made no sense to me then, nor has it ever, but the moment I caught a glimpse of light that was coming from the Slaughter ranch, an amusing, if not illuminating thought occurred to me.

It had only been six months since I graduated from Harvard University. I could have waltzed from my college dormitory straight into the family business and become an important member of Weston Shipping, a centuries-old company that commanded respect around the world. Instead, I had defied my parents' wishes and decided to become a news reporter. My grandiose plan was to acquire my own newspaper within five years, expand its circulation, and eventually rival the news empire of William Randolph Hearst. And to prove to my parents just how capable I was, I confidently informed them I would accomplish my lofty goal without requiring the least bit of assistance from anyone, friend or family.

To demonstrate my point, I decided to enter the world of business not using my real name of William Cabott Weston III, but adopting the moniker of Billy Cabott. Shortly after graduating I landed a job with the *Chicago Tribune* and within days had eagerly accepted my first assignment, which was to travel to the city of Columbus, New Mexico. There, as a subordinate to a seasoned reporter named Floyd Gibbons, I was to cover General Pershing's Punitive Expedition, a military mission of which I knew absolutely nothing.

However, tutored by Gibbons on our long train ride from Chicago, I learned that, days earlier, a Mexican named Pancho Villa had crossed the border of New Mexico and attacked the small and isolated town of Columbus, killing eight soldiers and ten civilians. In response to that outrage, President Wilson was sending General "Black Jack" Pershing and virtually the entire United States Army after Villa.

The assignment sounded quite exciting

but I had no sooner stepped off the train in Columbus than Gibbons snubbed me and partnered up with a former acquaintance, Robert Dunn, who was a reporter for the *New York Tribune.*

Standing dumbfounded on the busy train platform, Gibbons advised me to "keep an eye out for a good story" and then disappeared with Dunn. I glanced at the people around me, most of whom were soldiers, and then out past the crowded platform. Everywhere I looked I saw nothing but dust and chaos. South of town a vast city of military tents was springing up, and all along the train tracks, there seemed to be nothing but mass confusion. The soldiers nearest me, in sweat-stained uniforms, were hurriedly unloading several autotrucks and even some automobiles. Farther down, men were unloading dozens of horses and covered wagons. Among the wagons and parked autotrucks, in fact, wherever the men could find room, they were stacking bulky wooden crates of every conceivable shape and size. North of the tracks was the pocket-sized town of Columbus, at the center of which several buildings lay in ruins. Surrounding the rubble, a dozen or so structures stood unmolested; yet, to my dismay, I quickly surmised those few stores and scattered houses were all that constituted the village of Columbus, New Mexico. The half-dozen streets the town did have, though, were packed with bustling soldiers, heavily loaded hay wagons, and, here and there, a few civilian onlookers.

With Gibbons and Dunn off on their own, I wandered around Columbus and the burgeoning military camp for days on end in the sweltering heat. But in all that time not once did I see a gallant column of United States Cavalry galloping off to punish a foreign invader. What I witnessed, a story not worthy of reporting to the general public, was an army struggling just to establish a rudimentary semblance of order.

Eventually, though, Pershing did cross the border. He took four thousand troops with him and a few select news reporters, including Gibbons and Dunn. As time passed and conditions in Columbus did not improve, I became more and more disenchanted with my assignment and with the *Chicago Tribune*. And after enduring a twenty-four-hour dust storm, I was even ready to abandon my grandiose plans of becoming a newspaper tycoon.

Spoiled as I was, it had only taken two weeks of sweat and boredom to convince me that it was time to give up my cherished dreams, humbly go home to Father and Mother, and accept my anointed role as a proud member of Weston Shipping. So, the day after the storm I dejectedly packed my bags and plodded off to the train station. But it was there, on that sun-beaten platform, that I met Monte Segundo, a man destined to become a legend throughout Northern Mexico and, in time, my closest friend.

That fortuitous day, the El Paso and Southwestern train arrived from the west heading east. Waiting my turn to board, I was standing in a jostling throng of disembarking passengers when I first spotted Monte Segundo. At five-foot-ten inches and two hundred pounds, he appeared to me to be a walking brick. Like so many others, he was dressed in an army uniform but I noticed that on his left side, instead of the standard army issue automatic pistol, he wore an old-style six-shooter in a cross draw. On his right was a menacing-looking hunting knife sheathed in a beaded scabbard. And then I noticed the ominous expression in his eyes, eyes that were dark, unwavering, and deadly serious.

Out of everyone scurrying about on that crowded platform, I often wonder why, of all people, Monte walked up to me and asked where the camp's headquarters were located. He could have asked anyone but, as fate would have it, that was not to be.

That meeting changed my life forever. Some might say it was simply my dreary state of mind that caused me to do what I did that afternoon, but, looking back, I rather think my actions were directed more by providence than by blind chance. For instead of boarding the train for home that evening I imprudently and, quite impulsively, chose to accompany the reckless and totally unpredictable Monte Segundo across the Mexican border and then into the very bowels of the Mexican Revolution. A few weeks later, after narrowly escaping death at the hands of the Villistas, evading the Carrancistas, and then facing a United States military court-martial and possible firing squad, I still felt no compulsion whatsoever to return to the safety and comfort of my native New York City. On the contrary, both Monte and I eventually took a job as ranch hands in Sasabe, Arizona. There, instead of living at home enjoying the peaceful comforts of Carnegie Hill, Monte and I were soon embroiled in a running battle with murderous cattle thieves.

Chuckling as I neared the front of the sprawling Slaughter ranch house, I realized that I wasn't much different than the fool rabbits. They likely had no idea why they left the security and comfort of the desert to dart across the road in front of my automobile just as I had no idea why I had chosen to ride a horse, carry a gun, and become a cowboy. All I knew for certain was that the borderland, along with the wild and rugged expanse of the Southwest, contained the last remnants of our untamed West, and I instinctively, almost desperately, knew I wanted to be a part of it.

Seeing another automobile in front of the house, I pulled up alongside it, turned off my lights and then my engine. Expecting someone to exit the brightly lit ranch house, I sat and listened. A cool breeze brushed my cheek as my eyes drifted to the car next to me. To my surprise, even in the dim light I could see that it was a sleek, brand-spanking-new Cadillac touring car, a vehicle that could carry seven passengers.

No one, however, came out the front door of the ranch house and, oddly, I saw no movement through the many illuminated windows.

Even as green as I was, I had quickly learned that it was dangerous to go unarmed anywhere along the border. However, being only five-foot-six and slight of build, I preferred to carry a compact thirty-eight Smith and Wesson in a shoulder holster instead of hanging a big six-shooter on my hip. And, too, feeling a bit uneasy carrying a weapon of any sort, I habitually wore a vest to conceal my pistol. Now, I adjusted my lapels, pulling the vest forward. Taking one last glance over my shoulder, I grabbed my hat and stepped out of the roadster.

Standing motionless, I listened for a moment, my eyes searching the shadows around me. Being cautious, especially at night, was something I had learned by observing Monte Segundo, and it was a lesson that had saved my life on more than one occasion in the previous six months.

Tugging on my hat, I glanced down and was astounded to see that I was standing not on packed desert sand but a lawn of freshly cut grass. I stooped down and rubbed my hand over the lawn. I could smell the sweetness of it. Then, in the darkness off to my right, I heard the deep croak of what sounded like a frog. In seconds, I heard another croak and then another. Soon, the unmistakable chorus of a dozen bullfrogs echoed through the night air.

I came to my feet and swore softly. "Water!" I muttered. "John Slaughter has water! Lots of it."

The frogs abruptly went silent. I heard a laugh, the sound of which seemed to have come from behind the ranch house. I waited and then heard more laughter, the laughter of women. Seconds later, I heard the voice of a man.

Feeling more at ease but not wishing to interrupt anyone, I went to the front door of the ranch house and knocked. There was no answer. I knocked more vigorously but still no one came to the door.

Left with no other choice, I started around the edge of the house toward the rear. As I cautiously rounded the first corner, I could see firelight flickering across the lawn and on the wall of what appeared to be a long, low-roofed bunkhouse a short distance off to the right of the ranch house. I heard more voices, now more distinct. The tone was cheerful if not jovial.

Before I rounded the second corner and stepped into the light, I paused in the shadows and raised my voice. "Excuse me. I'm sorry to intrude but no one came to the front door. I am Billy Cabott. I work for Señor Cruz over in Sasabe. I'm here to drive some breeding stock back to his ranch."

There was a moment of silence and then a man spoke. His words came slowly, lazily. "Come on back, Billy Cabott. I've been expecting you. Come out in the light so's we can get a good look at you."

I eased around the corner and into the amber light of a blazing campfire. In one sweeping glance I took in five people, four seated on wooden chairs that had been arranged around the fire and one kneeling next to the fire adding sticks of wood as sparks swirled upward into the black sky.

Two of those seated were women. Across from them, two soldiers sat erect with their campaign hats perched neatly on their laps. The man feeding the fire, dressed in range clothes, was an elderly-looking Negro. All eyes locked on my face for a moment but then, in unison, everyone but the Negro began looking me over from head to toe.

"Mistah John," said the Negro, "was done called to away on sheriffing business, but he had the boys get your stock ready, nohow."

"My apologies for interrupting," I said.

I knew I was an unimpressive sight but the way the others were staring and sizing me up made me feel as if I were standing there in my underwear. "Am I the first to arrive? The first from Sasabe, I should say. Two of my friends, Monte and Rosa, are due any time."

One of the women leaned to the other and whispered. Both of them giggled.

The women, one blond and one brunette, appeared to be in their thirties. They were well dressed in riding skirts, long-sleeved blouses, and lace-up boots. Both had their hair pulled back and tied with a ribbon. To me, except for a vague hardness around their eyes, both women were a few shades better than average looking, the blonde being slightly more attractive.

"So," said the brunette seated on the left, "you are an honest-to-goodness cowboy?"

I noticed a hint of derision in her tone. I hadn't been working with cows for more than two months but I was wearing my range clothes. I knew that I looked like a cowboy, but still, I wondered if the woman could somehow sense something about me was out of place, something that told her I was nothing more than a city-born green-horn.

"The cows seem to think I am," I said forcing a smile.

The Negro laughed and came to his feet. "Them cows ought to know, sure enough," he said and then hobbled over and shook my hand. "They call me Tin-Pan. That's on account I used to do all the cooking when me and Mistah John drove cattle and chased after Apaches. We still go after a bandit from time to time, and when we do I still do all the cooking. Mistah John is mighty good at keeping the law but he can't cook a lick.

"But Mistah John and Mrs. Viola was called off to Bisbee on business this morning. Important business, it was. He left me in charge but all the cows is ready for you to take. It's all set. Him and Señor Cruz got it all worked out. They talked yesterday over the telephone."

Tin-Pan turned toward the two women and pointed. "Let me do the introductions, Billy. That lady sitting yonder on the right is Miss Marzel Appleton. The one on the left is Miss Ada Thorndike. They been here a couple of days visiting with the Slaughters. They're from back East."

Both women smiled flatly. I tipped my hat but, since I wasn't planning on staying, did not remove it.

Turning and pointing at the soldiers, Tin-Pan said, "That's Cap'n Miller over there and Lieutenant Jones. They's in charge of a garrison of soldiers that's camped up on the ridge above the pond. They's up there to watch out for Mes'cans that might cross the border like they been doing over Texas way and like that bandit Pancho Villa done last spring in Columbus."

Neither soldier stood to shake my hand so I merely nodded in their direction. "Pleased to meet all of you."

Feeling like the unwanted guest, I glanced at Tin-Pan. "Is there somewhere I can wait for my friends? They should arrive tonight but I have no idea when."

"Mr. Cabott," said Ada Thorndike, "I must say, you don't speak at all like a cowboy."

Marzel Appleton snickered. "And I'm a bit disappointed. He looks nothing like William S. Hart or Tom Mix."

Both women possessed a very familiar aristocratic air about them and both had similar accents. My guess was that they were from Massachusetts. And the names Appleton and Thorndike were familiar to me, names well-known in the city of Boston as well as New York.

I had grown up around blue-blooded women, and their sarcasm and condescending antics were routinely accepted and considered nothing more than harmless, frolicsome behavior. In that regard, these two women were nothing out of the ordinary, and yet I found myself taking an immediate dislike to them both.

"I must say," offered Lieutenant Jones as he cast a flirtatious smile toward Miss Appleton, "that I too am a bit disillusioned with his appearance."

"Sorry to disappoint you," I said. "I don't know a William or Tom. Do they work for Mr. Slaughter?"

Both women and the two soldiers burst into uproarious laughter. I looked at them for a moment and then glanced at Tin-Pan for some explanation. Tin-Pan, as perplexed as me, merely shrugged and shook his head.

When the guffaws began to subside, Lieutenant Jones wiped a tear from the corner of his eye. "Tom Mix and William S. Hart are stars of the cinema," he said, then took a deep breath. After hesitating for several seconds, he blurted, "That could possibly be the reason you haven't met them!"

More laughter exploded. Realizing I was being played for the fool, I felt my face flush with heat. I could excuse the women for such silliness but I suddenly wanted to pistol-whip the lieutenant. However, instead of trying to think of some clever remark to make in my defense, I clenched my teeth and waited for the mirth to run its course.

Tin-Pan started for the ranch house. "I'll fetch you a chair, Billy Cabott. And I'll fetch that marshmallow cream while I'm at it. And like I said, folks, I got us all some willow switches, too."

Catching her breath, Ada Thorndike said,

"Speaking of the cinema, I recently heard that the movie producers are moving out of New York and Chicago. The entire industry is relocating to a small rural community near Los Angeles, California."

"Yes, that is true," agreed Miss Appleton. "They say the weather is better in California for outdoor filming. I'm told that it hardly ever rains there. The town they chose, though, is hardly on the map. It is called Hollywood."

Lieutenant Jones nodded. "I heard that the film industry is growing by leaps and bounds. Not long ago I went to the cinema and saw Charlie Chaplin playing in *The Tramp.* He was quite the clown and very entertaining. I can see how it's catching on."

Miss Thorndike huffed, "That *'clown'* as you refer to him is now being paid ten thousand dollars a week by the Mutual Film Corporation! For merely acting in front of a camera. Can you imagine? Ten thousand dollars *a week*!"

"Are you certain it is so much?" Captain Miller asked. "Surely not that much. Not a week."

Marzel Appleton flashed a patronizing grin, "Oh yes, Captain. Let's just say that Ada and I have that information on good authority. No doubt the stars of the cinema will soon become the nouveau riche, a prospect I find to be perfectly dreadful."

"My word!" muttered Jones. "I can't imagine that much money."

"And you, Billy Cabott," taunted Thorndike, "how does that strike a genuine cowboy? Ten thousand dollars a week just for acting?"

This time I knew not to take the bait. I was a Weston, a member of one of the wealthiest families in the country and well-acquainted with incomes far greater than half a million dollars a year. I was also aware, thanks to my recent experiences, that by itself, money meant nothing. And, besides, Ada Thorndike and Marzel Appleton needed a good verbal kick in the buttocks.

"How does that strike me?" I repeated slowly. "It sounds good in a way." I paused for effect and then gazed up at the stars. "But to me, all that really matters is what all the folks are going to say about you when they gather around your grave. That's the test, right there, what they're going to say. The way I see it, in the end money's got nothing to do with what's really important."

I lowered my head and glanced over at the two women. For a moment they were speechless, each no doubt attempting to grasp a sentiment that, for them, was ut-

25

terly incomprehensible.

"Well said," agreed Captain Miller. "Well said."

Tin-Pan stepped back into the firelight. He carried a wooden folding chair in one hand and a jar in the other. Under his left arm was bundle of straight branches four to five feet long.

Walking over to me, Tin-Pan handed me the chair. "Now I'll show you folks what I was talking about earlier this evening."

I unfolded the chair and set it back from the fire, opposite the women and across from the soldiers. Being in the presence of ladies, I took off my hat and then dropped it on the grass next to my feet as I took a seat.

Tin-Pan handed me a branch and then gave one each to the women and the soldiers. He kept one for himself. "Now this is how it's done, folks," he said, taking a butter knife from his shirt pocket and then unscrewing the lid from the jar of marshmallow. "You scoop up some cream with this here knife and then you wipe it onto the tip of your switch like this," he said, dabbing a blob of thick white cream on one end of his branch.

Holding up his switch, Tin-Pan turned toward the fire and held the marshmallow over the flames. "You roast it and then eat it. It's like candy only it's hot and creamy smooth. Kind of sticky, though, so watch out so you don't get burnt."

Miss Thorndike held out her hand. "Oh, let me try. I love to try new things."

Tin-Pan handed the jar and knife to Miss Thorndike but kept an eye on his marshmallow. "Don't hold it too close to the flames or it'll catch fire. If it does, just take it out and blow out the flame. It won't hurt it none too much if it catches fire. I favor it being a little burnt, myself."

I watched Ada Thorndike dab marshmallow on the end of her stick, but from the corner of my eye I saw the lieutenant glance at me several times. As she passed the jar and knife to Marzel Appleton, Jones broke his silence.

"Mr. Cabott, you look quite familiar to me. Were you ever in the military?"

A jolt of fear shot through my body. I don't think I flinched but in that instant, I realized the lieutenant had almost certainly been present at the military court-martial in Colonia Dublán. As yet, though, he wasn't sure I was one of the two defendants who had been accused of treason. I had only played a minor role in the trial and for the most part had kept my back to the onlookers. However, I had no doubts Jones would recognize Monte Segundo if he were to arrive before the officers left and then come anywhere near the fire. Even if Jones didn't recognize Monte, I knew he would instantly recognize Rosa Bustamonte. No soldier at the court-martial, or for that matter, any man who had ever seen Rosa Bustamonte, would be able to forget such a beautiful woman.

"No," I answered easily. "Never been in the army. But I get that sort of question all the time. I just have one of those faces, I suppose."

"Yes," agreed Jones, seemingly satisfied. "That must be it."

Rosa and Monte had left the ranch at Sasabe a few days ahead of me but they were on horseback heading east along the border. On their way to the Slaughter ranch, they had planned to stop first in the border town of Nogales and then Agua Prieta. In doing so, they hoped to locate Rosa's family, it being one of many that fled those cities when Pancho Villa attacked them the prior year. Rosa was looking forward to contacting her relatives so they could all be present for her upcoming marriage to Monte, a ceremony to be performed in a matter of weeks.

Monte, having been orphaned at the age of six, had no family but Rosa had more than enough to fill the San Xavier Mission. It was in that old Spanish church, just south of Tucson, that Rosa wanted to have their wedding. And despite being terribly abused at the hands of some Carrancista soldiers, she desired a traditional Mexican wedding in which she would proudly wear a white dress. She wanted the whole affair to be a joyous celebration with family and friends, an occasion filled with music and dancing. And she had made it abundantly clear to all concerned that then, and only then, would she and Monte share the enchantment of a proper honeymoon.

Rosa had made up her mind about the wedding. She had her heart set on how it should be but to a man like Monte Segundo, it made no difference how, when, or where they were married. In fact, as far back as Monte could remember, he had never cared much about celebrations of any kind, much less dates or places. And, if the truth be known, until he met Rosa, Monte Segundo had never cared much about anything or anyone.

As the women tried their hands at roasting marshmallow cream, they ventured into a lively conversation with Miller and Jones regarding President Wilson and the merits of national women's suffrage. I had no interest in the matter and was pleased that no one included me in the discussion or bothered to ask my opinion.

Watching the fire, I tried my best to think of all of the things that might go wrong if Monte arrived before the officers went back to their quarters. I wanted to anticipate any difficulties and hopefully avoid trouble. However, I was tired from my long drive and the dancing flames of the campfire proved hypnotic. In minutes my mind began to drift, my musings lazily skirting the more uncomfortable issues at hand.

I pictured Monte and Rosa standing in front of a priest, a thought that a month earlier had seemed wholly unnatural. However, over time, the more I thought of a man like Monte Segundo being wed to the fiery Rosa Bustamonte, a former officer in Villa's army, the more the idea started to grow on me.

Rosa was undoubtedly different from any of the women Monte had known but she had also arrived at a crucial point in his life, a time when fragments of his childhood memories were escaping from an emotional abyss where they had remained buried for thirty years. At that particular time, Monte was starting to remember bits and pieces of a day that he, as a tormented six-year-old child, had desperately tried to forget. And for the first time in thirty years, he was beginning to feel twinges of sadness and grief, emotions completely foreign to him. However, and more importantly, he was also experiencing vague sensations of longing and, at times, even loneliness. And that, perhaps by design, was when Rosa Bustamonte was abruptly thrust into his life.

I was there when that happened, sitting in the darkened corner of a cantina in Las Palomas, a village two miles from Columbus and just across the Mexican border. Less than an hour had passed since our initial encounter on the train platform, and yet, remarkably, there I was in a foreign country sitting with a man I knew nothing about and getting my first taste of tequila from a dirty shot glass. And make no mistake about it, I was having the time of my life.

Why Monte, a North Idaho lumberjack and dyed-in-the-wool loner, had adopted me as a companion remained a mystery to me, and yet from the moment we met at the train station, there seemed to be an unspoken understanding between us, an acceptance that we, as complete opposites, were in fact a natural fit.

It had only been a few months since that fateful day when the two of us walked into Las Palomas, but in that short span of time my life had been turned upside down and inside out. I was fresh out of college and well traveled before I stepped off the train in Columbus, but I had never ridden a horse or even seen a dirt road. Nor had I built a campfire, slept on the ground, or fired a weapon of any kind.

I learned later that it was on an impulse that Monte had left Idaho determined, for reasons he poorly understood, to join President Wilson's so-called Punitive Expedition. More specifically, as a member of Idaho's militia, Monte had traveled to Columbus in order to join the Apache scouts that had recently been recruited by General Pershing.

Joining the scouts made perfect sense to Monte, for as a young boy he had lived several years with the Kootenai Indians of Idaho and could track as well as any Indian. When he heard about Pershing calling up the Apaches to locate the elusive Pancho Villa, he was overcome by a sudden urge to volunteer for the expedition. His intention was to work alongside the Apaches and help track down the illusive Bandit General.

That was Monte's plan, but as fate would

have it, his offer to volunteer and join the Apache scouts was rudely rejected. When Monte crossed the train platform and asked if I knew where headquarters was located, I offered to show him. I knew the headquarters tent was pitched only a short distance from the busy train depot, but I also wanted to know more about a soldier who carried a six-shooter in the twentieth century.

When he stepped into the open-flapped tent, I was close enough to see and hear what happened.

Monte explained to the attending officer that he was a member of the Idaho militia, Company A, and ready to volunteer his services and join the Apache scouts. The lieutenant in charge of running Camp Furlong on that particular afternoon was apparently overworked, hot, and irritated. Instead of accepting Monte's offer, he proceeded to insult the militia as a whole and, as fate would have it, referred to Monte as one of the "damned weekend soldiers," soldiers that were, in his professional opinion, inferior even to the Boy Scouts.

Monte's fist sent the unwary officer ass over teakettle and landed him in the back of the tent sprawled out in a complete state of unconsciousness.

Then, turning as if nothing unusual had

occurred and still determined to join the Apache scouts, Monte looked at me and asked if I knew how to get to Mexico. Even though the headquarters tent was surrounded by other tents and soldiers were scurrying about in every direction, inexplicably, no one but me seemed to have seen anything unusual.

And that's how it all began. At that instant, I knew without doubt I was standing in the presence of someone the likes of whom I had never encountered. Suddenly, Carnegie Hill was of no importance. Even my suitcase, which I had left on the train platform, was forgotten. My dreams of becoming a reporter reignited and burst into white-hot flame. This man was like no other. He was going to make news and I was going to be the one reporting it to the world.

Enthralled with what I had witnessed and feeling a resurgence of enthusiasm, I offered to personally show Monte the road to Las Palomas. He accepted and off we went, the two of us strolling casually through the middle of Camp Furlong and then on across the border to Las Palomas. It was there we were to soon meet the one-of-a-kind Rosa del Carmen Fernandez Bustamonte.

I had just finished taking my first scalding sip of tequila when five drunken Carrancista soldiers entered the cantina. The men then pulled Rosa inside by jerking on a rope that was tied around her neck. That day, covered in dirt and with her hair a frightful mess, it was impossible to see her incredible beauty. In fact, she reminded me of a witch.

Monte took one look at the situation and casually got up from his chair. Before I knew what was happening, he had pummeled four of the Mexicans while the fifth ran out the door leaving Rosa behind. And that was how Monte met Rosa. It was as unlikely a beginning for the two of them as it was incredible.

It was also the beginning of a myth that spread like wildfire across Northern Mexico. Fueled by Monte's lethal temperament along with his unusual abilities and a healthy dose of Mexican superstition, reports of Monte's vengeful exploits, when told and retold, quickly evolved into stories of *El Muerte,* a living legend.

Weeks later, after Monte, Rosa, and I had ventured hundreds of miles south of the border, Monte and I were arrested at Ojos Azules after a battle between the United States Cavalry and a ragged band of Villistas. In the coming days near the settlement of Colonia Dublán, we were accused of joining forces with Villa and then tried as traitors in a military court-martial. Very fortunately, however, during the court-martial General Pershing was convinced by an incredibly astute Catholic priest that releasing the captured *El Muerte* would, at the very least, diminish the escalating tensions between Mexico and the United States. According to Padre Marco, that single act of leniency, along with the effect it would have upon the Mexican population was, in essence, a strategic military maneuver, one that in all likelihood would prove instrumental in preventing an all-out war between the two countries.

As a result of Padre Marco's intervention, the charges against Monte and I were dropped. At the time, General Pershing's decision was an unpopular one. In fact, most of the officers at the court-martial preferred that Monte and I face a firing squad. Instead, under armed guards, we were escorted back to Columbus and put on a train to parts unknown.

Sitting there by the fire, I recalled the afternoon Monte and I had been taken back to Columbus. We both thought our entanglements with the United States military were finally over, and since that time, with more urgent matters to attend to, both of us had put the entire affair out of our minds. But it appeared that Lieutenant Jones might be on the verge of resurrecting a contentious issue that was better left alone.

Jones leaned toward me, resting his palms on his knees. Breaking into my thoughts, he said, "I'm certain I have seen you somewhere, Mr. Cabott."

"Could be, you have," I answered. "I get around quite a bit."

Watching Miss Appleton place the marshmallow cream on the end of her stick, I tried to think. Trouble seemed to follow Monte Segundo wherever he went, and for that matter, Rosa Bustamonte's life had been no bed of roses, either. Calloused by lifetimes of toil and hardship, even under the best of circumstances neither of them suffered fools lightly. And I knew that by the time they arrived at the Slaughter ranch they would be tired and in no mood to deal with the likes of Lieutenant Jones. Before Monte returned, I needed to know for certain if the lieutenant had been present at the court-martial.

I glanced at Jones, hoping what I was about to say was the right thing. "I was in Columbus, New Mexico, a few months back. There were lots of soldiers there. Maybe we passed by each other."

Lieutenant Jones eyed me closely. "Maybe. What were you doing in Columbus?"

37

I thought for a moment. If he was at the trial, I wanted to discover just how much of the proceedings he remembered. "I was there to help a friend of mine. He had some legal matters to clear up."

Marzel Appleton stuck the knife in the jar and set it down beside her in the grass. She held up her stick. "What do we do now, Tin-Pan?"

Tin-Pan pointed at the tip of his stick that he held over the flames. "Just like this, Miss Appleton. Just roast it ever so slight for a minute or two. Just like I'm a doing, see."

I got up from my chair and picked up the jar of marshmallow. Scooping out a glob of cream, I wiped it onto the tip of my willow branch and then, taking a step in the opposite direction, handed the knife and jar to Jones, who had not taken his eyes off me.

As he accepted the jar his eyes flared with recognition. "It wasn't Columbus," he burst out. "It was in Mexico!" Pointing at me with the butter knife in his hand he said, "It was Colonia Dublán, wasn't it? That's where I saw you."

I shrugged and then sat back down. "Could've been."

"You were the subject of the court-martial," continued Jones. "You and that hayseed from Idaho. The two of you were being tried for horse theft and treason! And your accomplice was also charged with murder and attempted murder."

Casually extending my stick, I passed the marshmallow through the flames and said nothing. As a matter of fact, I didn't know what to say.

Miss Thorndike glared at me with a raised eyebrow. "So, Billy Cabott, how does a cowboy from Arizona end up being court-martialed for horse theft and treason in Mexico? Were you in the army?"

"Oh do tell, Mr. Cabott," chided Miss Appleton. "We've heard all of Tin-Pan's campfire stories so now it's time for you to entertain us. And, please, don't leave out a single sordid detail."

Staring at the fire, I tried to think. "With all due respect, ladies, I'd rather not go into it," I said, but then an urgent question crossed my mind. How much did the lieutenant actually *know*?

Casually, I muttered, "Maybe Lieutenant Jones can fill you in."

Captain Miller nodded. I could feel his eyes boring into me. "Yes, Lieutenant. I would like to hear more about it myself . . . now that I've actually met one of the traitors, one of the two Americans General Pershing allowed to walk away from a firing squad."

Pershing's decision to release Monte and me was a calculated risk designed to avert a war with Mexico. It was the right decision and, as a result, the Mexican armies that were poised to attack Pershing's army had balked and then backed down. But that fact had apparently been kept from some, if not all, of the officers under Pershing's command. Only now did I fully realize the negative impact his decision had on the officers present at the court-martial. And, judging from Captain Miller's comments, news of the court-martial proceedings had spread to the soldiers stationed along the border.

"Now, folks, we don't want no trouble," said Tin-Pan easily. "You's all invited guests here at the ranch. Ain't nobody here that Mr. Slaughter ain't invited. And we get all kinds. All kinds of folks come to visit. Mr. Slaughter ain't one to judge a man just on hear-say."

Anxious to hear what Jones had to say, I took my marshmallow out of the fire and inspected it. "There'll be no trouble from my end," I said and then swung my stick back into the flames. "I've got nothing to hide."

Captain Miller shifted his weight, sitting

more erect. "I'll have you know, Tin-Pan, that Lieutenant Jones and I are West Point graduates. I can assure you we are not troublemakers."

Miss Appleton wiggled back in her chair as if she were huddling into a warm blanket. "Please go on, Lieutenant. I dearly love a good story! And I must say that I am intrigued already."

Jones set down the marshmallow jar but held onto his willow branch. Flicking the branch in my direction as if he were a schoolmaster, he began with, "Until two weeks ago, I was with General Pershing in Colonia Dublán, which is about forty miles south of the border. However, I was in his cavalry column from the beginning, from the very first day we left Columbus and rode into Mexico searching for that murdering Mexican, Pancho Villa."

"Wait, wait," exclaimed Miss Thorndike. "Why did the army go into Mexico and who is Pancho Villa?"

"Oh, you know," said Miss Appleton. "Remember we were talking about this with Mother several weeks ago when we informed her of our plans to come here. Villa's army attacked a city somewhere, a dreary little border town as I understand it. President Wilson is up for reelection and, of course, like most men he only understands one way to respond to any crisis."

Miss Appleton paused and with a smile announced, "No offense to you, Captain, or to you, Lieutenant, but that is why we must and will have national women's suffrage, to put an end to men's wars once and for all. Women, as everyone knows, are not prone to physical violence."

The recollection of Rosa Bustamonte standing with a bandolier of bullets over her shoulder and a rifle in her hand flashed through my mind. If my predicament had not been so dire, I would have laughed out loud at the irony. But had Rosa been sitting next to me, I was quite confident that Ada Thorndike and Marzel Appleton would presently be the subjects of a blistering barrage of Spanish profanity.

Jones was clearly taken aback by the woman's comment but quickly recovered. He responded with a cordial smile and a gentlemanly, "I take no offense, Miss Appleton. None whatsoever."

"Nor do I," said Miller. "I find a woman's point of view very refreshing, especially out here in this desert."

"Now I recall," Thorndike said thoughtfully. "It was last March or April. We invaded Mexico because some bandits misbehaved.

It was in a miserable little hamlet, wasn't it? One with an Italian name?"

"Villa," Jones responded politely, "attacked Columbus, New Mexico, with his army on March ninth. He killed eight soldiers and ten civilians, one a woman with child. We crossed the border on March fifteenth."

"But that was six months ago," scowled Thorndike. "Didn't we catch him?"

Jones squirmed a bit. "Not yet. But we pushed him so far south he won't be any more trouble. And we considerably weakened his forces."

"I see," Miss Thorndike said and then shrugged indifferently. "Now that I am up on current events, please continue with the story."

"As I was saying," nodded Jones, "we entered Mexico in mid-March. We were proceeding according to plan but along the way we had many obstacles to overcome, not the least of which was the cooperation of the Mexican people. We had no decent maps to guide us and the villagers we approached constantly lied to us about the terrain of the country and the trails that coursed through it. And, even though they knew the whereabouts of Villa's army, they lied about that also. After a while, General

Pershing had had enough of such treachery and decided to send for two dozen Apaches that were already enlisted as army scouts. Some of those scouts had been with the Geronimo campaign years earlier and, as a consequence, knew the country we were in better than the Mexican peons themselves."

Miss Thorndike's eyes flashed with excitement. "You mean actual Indians? Real Apaches? You don't mean to tell me that we still have Indian scouts in the army?"

"Yes, we do," assured Captain Miller. "Even after Geronimo surrendered there were all sorts of renegades still on the loose. The bands were smaller and less organized but still very lethal. And as they say, 'It takes an Apache to catch an Apache.' So, in order to hunt down the renegades, the army decided to keep a couple dozen Apache scouts on hand even though Geronimo was long gone. And, from what I am told, they still hunt down an occasional criminal Indian, one that commits a crime and then jumps the reservation."

"I saw Geronimo several years ago," said Miss Appleton, almost swooning. "He was in Teddy Roosevelt's inaugural parade. On that cold and windy day, I was standing on Pennsylvania Avenue when the great Indian chief rode by on a magnificent dark horse.

He rode so close to me that I could have reached out and touched him. As he passed, even though I was quite bundled up against the cold, I shuddered at the frightful sight of him. However, looking more closely I saw that he had a well-shaped head which assured me that he was certainly not a bloodthirsty savage as some claimed, but a man of considerable intelligence. And in his steady black eyes I saw an abundance of wisdom, understanding, and boundless courage.

"As he passed by, people began to shout 'Hooray for Geronimo' and 'Public hero number two.' What a brave and noble Red Man he was. I'll never forget that day."

I glanced at Miss Appleton out of the corner of my eyes, marveling at the profound ignorance of the woman. I knew that among countless other killings, it was some of Geronimo's band that had murdered Monte Segundo's father and mother. Monte was only six years old when he saw his father tortured to death and then, after witnessing that atrocity, had been thrown into a patch of cactus and left to die a slow and agonizing death.

In fact, Monte's experience was so horrid he had somehow succeeded in erasing most of that tragedy from his memory. For years,

45

the only demon that had escaped from his gruesome past was one that stalked his nights in the form of a recurring nightmare. Only in the last few months had a few fragments of actual memory returned, and even those haunting remnants were oftentimes cloudy and distorted.

And, as far as the Apache soldiers were concerned, while in Mexico I had personally seen what some of Pershing's scouts had done to two Mexican wire cutters, defenseless men they had captured and then tortured to death. I found nothing "noble" about pulling a man's entrails out while he was still alive and then stretching them out in the sand in front of him to see.

Jones hesitated for a moment and then continued. "Well, yes, Geronimo may have been a noble Red Man but the army did have to subdue him in order to end the Apache wars. And we needed Apaches loyal to the United States to find Geronimo for us, which they did. That is how peace was restored to this area we are in now. The army's Apache scouts, you see, played a pivotal role in writing the last chapter in the Indian Wars.

"But as I was saying, twenty or so scouts were with us as we drove deeper and deeper into Mexico. Eventually, with the help of the scouts, Major Howze caught up with two hundred of Villa's men at a place called Ojos Azules. He defeated them handily with a brilliant cavalry charge and suffered virtually no casualties in his ranks. It was a wonderful victory. However, it was also there that a deserter from our own forces tried to kill one of our Apache scouts, an Indian named Norroso. And it was also at Ojos Azules that his partner in crime, Billy Cabott, was captured."

Jones paused. The only sound heard was the crackling of the fire. All eyes, including those of Tin-Pan, turned and locked onto me.

I brought my marshmallow close and took a bite of the melted cream. It was sweet and tasted like hot sugar. I chewed a bit and then swallowed.

"Go on," I said easily. "I like a tall tale as much as the next person."

Jones huffed disgustedly. "I'll bet you do!"

"So they court-martialed the two of them?" questioned Miss Thorndike. "Is that it?"

Glancing back at the women, Jones answered, "Yes. The trial was held in camp Colonia Dublán, with all of the officers present. Two classmates of mine were involved in the legalities: Hugh Johnson for

47

the prosecution and good ole Georgie Patton for the defense. Both of them are lieutenants. General Pershing, Major Howze, and Colonel Dodd were the presiding judges.

"After the initial formalities, George Patton, always the blowhard, pompously called his first witness, a woman, for the defense. But Hughie blew her out of the water with a single question. After that debacle Patton even got the deserter, a private named Segundo, to admit he tried to kill the scout, that he shot and wounded him. Thanks to Georgie, who was arguing *for* the defendants mind you, it was an open and shut case. Both were clearly guilty of treason."

"Wait now," said Miss Appleton, holding up her hand. "You referred to the witness as 'her.' Who was she? Who was that witness?"

Jones cleared his throat. "Let's just say she was an unmarried Mexican *companion* of Segundo's, one who traveled with him wherever he went. And other than her obvious lack of virtue, she was also an admitted liar. So, her testimony was immediately dismissed as fabrication." Jones paused to snicker, then continued. "Only someone like Patton would think she was going to make a good witness for the defense. What a fool.

"Mark my words, ladies, George Patton will never amount to anything!"

I took another bite of marshmallow. "That would be Rosa Bustamonte you're talking about. She was a captain in Villa's army."

Captain Miller snorted derisively. "A captain? A woman?"

"So she claimed at the trial," said Jones. "We all just laughed at her when she said that."

After sucking the last bite of marshmallow off the tip of my stick I asked, "Is that all that you remember about Rosa Bustamonte, Lieutenant? Are you saying that nothing else about her comes to mind? Nothing at all?"

Jones was too sure of himself and I wanted him to squirm a little. Rosa was a stunning beauty. When she walked into the court, no doubt every man in the room felt his pulse skip a beat. I looked at Jones and smiled. "Was there anything . . . unusual . . . about her?"

The lieutenant knowingly glared back at me. "Nothing of importance. All that interested me was her testimony."

Tin-Pan had been squatting by the fire calmly roasting his marshmallow. Satisfied that it was cooked to perfection, he took it out of the flames. Sitting back cross-legged he asked, "What all did that woman say,

Lieutenant?"

Jones frowned. "She claimed that Segundo rescued her from some Carrancista soldiers, soldiers she said had been abusing her. This accusation, of all things, coming from a woman who traipsed around Mexico with a traitor the likes of Segundo.

"How naïve did she think we were? No doubt what really occurred was that she had been *entertaining* the local soldiers when Segundo happened along and offered her, shall we say, more incentive. Clearly, she found American dollars more persuasive than pesos and she simply rode off with Segundo and Billy Cabott. Perhaps there was a drunken bar fight in a cantina somewhere but there was no heroic rescue as she claimed."

Having been present when Monte thrashed the Carrancistas, I had never given any thought to how reports of such an event could be so grotesquely distorted. Despite my nearness to the fire, I felt my face flush with heat.

I wanted to say that I was there in the cantina that afternoon, that I knew exactly what had happened. I wanted to tell them how Rosa, a captured Villista, had been drug into the cantina with a rope around her neck, how she was treated worse than an animal. Most of all, I wanted to tell everyone how Monte had beaten the Mexicans with his fists and tossed them around as if they were rag dolls.

But I knew Jones would call me a liar. Then I would try to defend myself, an argument would ensue, and trouble would follow, not only for me but also for Monte and Rosa. If that happened everything would be ruined. Everything.

Taking a deep breath and swallowing my pride I said evenly, "That's one way to look at it, I suppose. But you forgot a few details."

"What details?" snapped Jones.

"Like the fact that in the court-martial Monte Segundo was charged with killing one of the Carrancistas that day in the cantina, killing him in a fight with his bare hands."

"Killed a man?" gasped Miss Appleton. "My word!"

"You say with his bare hands," said Tin-Pan. "How'd he do that?"

I shook my head. "I don't know. Looking back on it, I think it was when he threw one of them into the wall. Must have broken his neck. Or maybe Monte just punched him too hard."

Jones scoffed. "I don't believe a word of it."

"But," asked Thorndike, "was there at least an actual fight between this Segundo and the Carrancistas?"

"Yes," admitted Jones. "It happened in a cantina in a village called Las Palomas."

"So, what were they fighting about?" asked Miss Thorndike.

Jones merely shrugged. "Maybe the soldiers didn't like the fact the woman was changing her allegiance. Maybe the soldiers were jealous. Who cares what they fought over? Segundo supposedly killed a Mexican soldier, one of our allies. That was the charge. But like I said, I believe that charge was based solely on rumor or purposeful disinformation."

The conversation stalled. Even the bullfrogs fell suddenly quiet.

I tried to maintain my composure but inwardly I was appalled with the way the night was going. Jones and Miller were portraying Monte Segundo as a criminal and the Misses Thorndike and Appleton were making a saint out of Geronimo. And worst of all, I could say nothing about either issue. Presenting the truth, which would not be believed anyway, would very likely lead to an argument or worse. And, after all, my only purpose for being at the Slaughter ranch was to get cattle, breeding stock desperately needed back at the ranch in Sasabe.

Señor Cruz and his daughter, Angelina, had lost most of their stock to borderland rustlers and were in danger of losing the ranch. Since the ranch shared a border with Mexico, the banks in Tucson had refused to loan money to Señor Cruz until the revolution was over, and without that capital he had no way to restock his range and recover his losses. That's when he contacted John Slaughter and worked out a deal.

As difficult as it was, I held my tongue. I didn't want to disappoint Señor Cruz and I certainly didn't want to jeopardize my budding relationship with his daughter, Angelina. I had to be careful and say as little as possible.

Chewing some of his marshmallow, Tin-Pan broke the silence. "So it sounds like this Segundo fella might have killed a man fighting in a saloon. I've heard of that sort of thing. It happens from time to time."

"Even if he did," conceded Jones, "he didn't do it with his fists. He might have clubbed one of the Mexicans with a chair or hit him over the head with a tequila bottle."

Addressing the women, Miller gloated, "The lieutenant knows a thing or two about fisticuffs. He was a champion pugilist at West Point. Those that saw him in the ring compared him favorably to the great John L. Sullivan."

Ignoring his boastful smirk, I took a closer look at Jones. Even sitting down, the lieutenant appeared to be at least six feet tall and I could see he had a stout build. As I sized him up a sense of foreboding engulfed me. He was arrogant and overconfident. It was more than likely he would relish a chance to challenge Monte Segundo.

"I seen John L. fight once," offered Tin-Pan. "He come to Tucson back in eighty-two or three. He had him a wicked right hook and he was mighty dangerous in the ring. But they's a big difference 'tween a boxing match and a fistfight. A mighty big difference."

"That's true to a point," agreed Jones, "but according to the tale spun at the court-martial by Rosa Bustamonte, Segundo fought all five men at once and, according to her, emerged unscathed. If he were in the ring with me for even one round I guarantee you he would not escape unscathed. He would receive at least a few good blows, blows that I assure you would leave his face adorned with a goodly number of angry welts."

Under the circumstances, I tried hard to keep a straight face but I couldn't help myself. I lowered my head, chuckled, and then began to laugh. It was all so absurd. The only one around the fire that seemed to have any sense at all was Tin-Pan. How, I marveled, could educated people be so pompous and arrogant when, in fact, they were such buffoons?

"You find that amusing, do you?" drilled Miller. "Perhaps we should arrange an exhibition match when your friend arrives. Lieutenant Jones could use the exercise and my men could use some entertainment."

Monte's fists were like sledgehammers. Thinking of what I had seen him do to a man's skull with a single blow, I began to sober up. "I saw what happened in the cantina, Captain. I was only a few feet away. Believe what you want, but there were five of them and it was over in a matter of seconds."

"Your bedtime stories," Jones said derisively, "are better suited for children. In case it has escaped your observation, we here are adults."

I glared at Jones, feeling the blood starting to pulsate through my veins. My eyes focused on his big, pompous chin. Envisioning what Monte's fist would do to such a vulnerable target, I said too much.

"When you were at West Point, Lieutenant, did you ever go toe-to-toe with a five-foot-ten-inch, two-hundred-pound bull-of-the-woods lumberjack? Did you ever fight a man who had been orphaned since he was six years old, a man who had lived with the Kootenai Indians for years and had killed his first man when he was only fifteen years old? Did you ever square off with a man who could kill you with his fists, do it without breaking a sweat, and not think twice about it? In your military academy boxing matches, did you ever face anyone that even came close to a man like that?"

Before Jones or Miller could even think of a response, a horse whinnied from the darkness. It was answered by other horses in the Slaughter corral.

Indicating the horses, I said, "That's likely Monte Segundo and Rosa Bustamonte coming in. If it is, they'll be here in a few minutes. I will say this and say it only once. Neither of them puts up with foolishness."

Miller leaned forward. "That sounds a like a veiled threat, Mr. Cabott."

I shook my head. "No sir. With all due respect, it's not meant to be a threat. It's simply a warning. As we all agreed, none of us want any trouble."

Jones, seemingly lost in thought, glared into the campfire, saying nothing.

"My word," giggled Miss Appleton, "how wonderfully dramatic. This is better than the cinema, isn't it, Ada? Enter the anti-hero."

"But, Billy Cabott," objected Miss Thorndike, "how is it that you and your friend were released from custody? How was it that you escaped the court-martial? You haven't explained that part."

I settled back in my chair, wishing I had kept my mouth shut and not stirred the pot. "I think it's best to ask Lieutenant Jones that question."

Jones looked up from the fire, his eyes focusing on the women. "What was that?"

Thorndike repeated her question. "How did Billy Cabott and Segundo avoid the firing squad? You never told us the reason."

Clearing his throat, Jones said, "We were never told the reason. But it was the general consensus of the officers that it was to appease the Mexican peons. The idea being to win the approval of the people residing in Northern Mexico and perhaps make them more cooperative.

"You have to understand that the people

57

resented us being in their country the entire time we were there. It didn't matter if they were Villistas or Carrancistas, you could see the hatred in their eyes. To them we were invaders, plain and simple. We all assumed the general was playing politics."

"And do you agree, Billy Cabott?" asked Miss Thorndike, her voice tainted with scorn. "Is that why, instead of being shot as traitors, you were set free . . . for political reasons?"

I didn't like being referred to as "traitors," especially since Monte and I were nothing of the sort. At that moment, however, I clearly understood that General Pershing had not explained to any of the subordinate officers the strategic reasons behind his decision to release us. And now that lack of communication and the resentment that followed was starting to cause problems. I was suddenly worried that if the present tensions escalated, Captain Miller might even be tempted to interfere with what should have been a simple business deal, a purchase of cattle that was vitally important to the Cruz ranch.

Trying to think of a way to get out of the mess I had created, I answered with a feeble, "Not exactly."

"No?" badgered Miller. "Then why don't

you enlighten us. What *was* the exact reason?"

I swore under my breath. Why hadn't I just walked away from the fire and waited in the automobile? Had it been necessary, I could have even slept in the driver's seat. Then, I wouldn't be sitting around a campfire with a foursome composed of hostile army officers and arrogant Eastern bluebloods. Now I was in a tight spot. Feeling cornered, I felt my only hope to diffuse the situation was to offer a brief defense, an explanation of what actually occurred.

"It is a long story but I will have to be brief."

"Go on," encouraged Miss Appleton. "This is so intriguing."

I took a moment and gathered my thoughts. "Only a few miles from where we're sitting tonight, Monte Segundo's parents were murdered by Apaches. Monte was six years old at the time and saw what happened, yet for the next thirty years he had no real memory of it. But he did have a recurring nightmare, a dream he never understood. In that nightmare he was thrown into a fire by a man with a dark, unrecognizable face. But that face bore a distinct scar.

"A few months ago, not long after Monte

59

saw a photograph of one of the Apache scouts in a newspaper, he was overcome with . . . with a . . . let's call it a drive . . . to join up with the Apaches and hunt down Pancho Villa. That's why he left North Idaho for Columbus and volunteered to join the scouts.

"But the officer involved in recruiting volunteers made the mistake of insulting Monte. So, Monte floored him with a single punch. He started walking toward Mexico, determined to find the scouts on his own. That's when I joined up with him."

"The two of you *walked* to Mexico?" questioned Appleton.

"Sure. Las Palomas is only two miles from Columbus. We were there before any of the soldiers knew what had happened.

"Anyway, it was there in a cantina that Monte freed Rosa. She was a Villista and ready to head south to rejoin Villa's army. Since Monte wanted to find Pershing and the scouts, we all went south together. We protected Rosa from Carrancistas and, in turn, she guided us through the country on our way to find Pershing's forces.

"On our way south, Monte made a name for himself by dispatching a number of bandits and vile Carrancistas. So many, in fact, that his fame spread throughout all of northern Mexico and he became known as *El Muerte.* The Mexicans, especially the peons, are very superstitious and some began to believe Monte was an angel, some thought he was a demon. But they all feared *El Muerte.* All, including the Villista and Carrancista soldiers."

"El Muerte?" scoffed Miller. "What kind if a sobriquet is that?"

I wasn't sure how far out from the ranch Monte was but I knew I had to hurry. "In Mexico, Villa is known as *El Jaguar.* One of his bloodthirsty officers is called *El Carnicero.* The jaguar and the butcher. They like names like that down there much like here in the West we like names such as Billy the Kid, Wild Bill Hickok, or Three-Fingered Jack."

"And, *El Muerte?"* asked Tin-Pan. "What does that mean?"

I hesitated and then said, "The death."

I ignored Miller's snorting scoff and continued. "As we went south, more and more of Monte's buried memory came back. Finally, he could clearly see the face of the man in his nightmare. It was one of Pershing's scouts, one of the older ones by the name of Norroso. Once he figured out who it was in his dream, Monte naturally assumed it was Norroso who had killed his parents. So, Monte understood why, after seeing Norroso's picture in a newspaper, he had been so dead set on joining the Apache scouts. But after recognizing Norroso, he then set out to kill him. And word eventually got out to the Mexicans that *El Muerte* was in Mexico *hunting* Apaches."

Tin-Pan chuckled. "Hellfire! That would have made them Mexicans stand up and listen!"

"Why would doing such a thing concern the Mexicans?" asked Miss Appleton.

"Because," answered Tin-Pan, "the Apaches have been killing Mexicans for hundreds of years. The Mexicans is more afraid of an Apache than anything in this world or the next. Any man going hunting for Apaches by his own self, would sure enough strike them Mexicans as being some kind of demon."

I nodded. "That's right. And, like I said, the Mexican people are very superstitious. Add that to the fact Monte killed some bandits that were attacking a village called San Miguel and you get the avenging angel part of his reputation. The stories grew as they do with the telling and retelling. By the time of the court-martial, *El Muerte* was legendary."

"So, then," said Miss Thorndike, "General

Pershing let the two of you go because of an overrated reputation, a myth? He was attempting to appease the peasantry? That hardly seems appropriate."

Ada Thorndike's suspicions were quite correct, but if General Pershing had chosen to keep the rationale for Monte's release a secret, I wasn't about to divulge his reasoning now. "Well, Monte didn't intend to kill that Carrancista in the cantina and we never fought with the Villistas. As for Monte attempting to kill the Apache scout, that turned out to be a matter of mistaken identity. So, we really weren't guilty of treason at all.

"All things considered, releasing *El Muerte* was a good move by the general. You should have heard the people cheer when they got a look at Monte Segundo. There were thousands of them waiting outside the camp at Colonia Dublán that day. Who knows what would have happened otherwise?"

"We weren't there to please peons," snapped Jones. "As far as I'm concerned, the general violated army regulations. We should have gone by the book. Regulations and orders, spit and polish. That's the army way. No exceptions. And let's not forget he shot one of our scouts."

Leaning forward on her elbows, Miss

Appleton was mesmerized. "And what happened to the poor Indian who was shot. Was he badly injured?"

I waited for the lieutenant to answer, wondering if he knew the trap he had just fallen into. Jones appeared to be close to my age and just as cocky and self-assured as I was a few months earlier.

Jones's eyes narrowed thoughtfully and his left knee began vibrating as he nervously pumped his heel up and down with the ball of his foot. "The wound was minor."

"It was an earlobe," I added dryly. "Monte Segundo shot it off."

Miss Appleton cringed. "Oh, how awful!"

"So, Lieutenant," I taunted, "what became of that poor wounded Apache scout? What was his rank? Wasn't he enlisted as a private?"

Glaring at me with eyes full of contempt, Jones said nothing. I stared right back at him.

"Oh, that's right," I said. "He deserted, didn't he? Right after the court-martial was adjourned he and two other army scouts hightailed it. But as I recall, no one went after them."

"Deserted?" stammered Miller as he turned toward Jones. "I didn't hear about that. Why on earth would he desert?"

Watching Jones's fidgeting knee, I let the captain's question hang in the air for several seconds before answering. "Because when Monte finally tracked down Norroso it was at the battle of Ojos Azules. Monte found Norroso hiding behind an unarmed Mexican woman and holding a knife to her throat. That woman was Rosa Bustamonte."

Miss Thorndike held up her hand. "Hold on. What was this Rosa woman doing at the battle of Ojos Azules?"

"As I mentioned before, Rosa was a soldier. By the time of that fight she had left Monte and me and was back fighting with the Villistas. When the battle turned against them, dozens of the Villistas discarded their weapons and ran to the nearby mountains to hide."

"They threw away their guns?" questioned Thorndike. "Why do that?"

"That's because," broke in Tin-Pan, "the Villistas don't wear uniforms of no kind at all. Lots of 'em don't even have shoes to wear. Without a gun they look just like any old peon, so if they get away and into a village, ain't nobody can tell 'em from nobody else."

"That's right," I continued. "But the Apache scouts followed close behind those retreating peons, killing any they caught.

65

Any man, that is. Monte caught up with Norroso in a ravine. Just the three of them were there.

"Monte shot at what little he could see of Norroso and then, to escape, Norroso stabbed Rosa in the back and sprang into the brush.

"Monte had a choice. He could go after Norroso or try and keep Rosa from bleeding to death. Monte stayed with Rosa and that's how both of them were captured by the army.

"So, to answer your question, Captain, Private Norroso deserted because he knew Monte was going to be set free by General Pershing. And, for stabbing Rosa, he knew that Monte would kill him if he ever got the chance. Norroso figured he was better off in the rugged mountain ranges of Mexico than pigeonholed on an army base.

"If anyone doubts what I am saying, I'm sure you can ask Lieutenant Patton about what happened. He'll back up every word."

"How exhilarating!" squealed Miss Appleton. "Such a dramatic and exciting climax."

"Yes," I agreed, "Monte and I were freed and Private Norroso took to the hills. All's well that ends well."

Jones knew the point I was making. Norroso was a soldier in the United States

Army. He had deserted and no one had so much as saddled a horse to go after him. For the Apache scout, the army had tossed its "spit and polish" regulations out the window.

Scowling at me, Jones grumbled. "He was an Indian."

"By the book, Lieutenant," I said evenly, "he should have been arrested and jailed, maybe even shot."

The leg stopped bouncing. Jones leaned forward and rested both palms on his knees. His eyes, conveying a poorly veiled threat, locked on me. "I say he left to get back to his own people because he had his fill of the white man's justice. Segundo tried to kill him and got away with it. As an Indian, Private Norroso saw that injustice as another betrayal of the trust his people had placed in the white man, just another version of a whole host of broken treaties."

Miss Appleton sighed sympathetically, "The poor Red Man. How we've mistreated them. And all because of the injudicious pursuit of Manifest Destiny!"

"The poor Red Man?" I said but then glanced at Tin-Pan. Our eyes met and almost imperceptibly, he shook his head "No."

Understanding I was to let the issue drop,

I immediately thought of Pancho Villa. He was a cold-blooded murderer, but to most Mexicans he was a hero of the revolution. But the few Mexicans who had witnessed him murder both men and women, and those that were directly affected by his brutality, all hated him. Their reports of his atrocities, however, were ignored, excused, or, worse, labeled as out-and-out lies by the majority of Villa supporters.

I realized that when it came to Apaches, the women, the lieutenant, and perhaps even the captain were not much different than the peons of Mexico. But the peons desperately needed a hero. Exalting Villa as a great general who was fighting to give them a better life was at least understandable. To me the idea that renegade Apaches were worthy of sympathy was pure fantasy. It might have been a very fashionable notion in the East but in the Southwest the people knew all too well such a sentiment was complete and utter nonsense.

At times, killing was unavoidable. In times of conflict it was an acceptable act of war. But the harsh reality was that even cold-blooded murder could not hold a candle to the horrors of Apache torture. And yet, like Pancho Villa and his henchmen, it appeared that Easterners, including the likes of Teddy

Roosevelt, were well on their way to idolizing Geronimo and justifying the deeds of his ruthless band of renegades.

I nodded to Tin-Pan and changed the subject. "It was dark when I drove up. How close are we to the border?"

Tin-Pan thumbed over his shoulder. "Come morning, go out on the front porch. You'll be looking south right into Mexico. It's only a quarter mile away. But that land on the other side of the border belongs to the ranch here, the San Bernardino ranch. We got acres of corn planted out that way."

"Corn?" I asked. "In the desert?"

Taking a bite of his smoldering marshmallow, Tin-Pan talked while he chewed. "There's water down that way and ponds built to irrigate. That's why old Pancho Villa come by last year when he was getting ready to attack Agua Prieta, the town right across from Douglas.

"Fact is Agua Prieta and Douglas is really the same town. They even got one street that goes down the middle. South side of the street is Mexico and the north is us. Kind of funny when a body thinks on it."

"Pancho Villa was here?" I asked.

"Yep. Him and his whole army. We all saw the dust cloud coming a long time before he got here. He holed up not a mile from here and started feeding his army on Mistah John's beef and corn.

"Now, understand, Mistah John and Pancho knowed each other already. Mistah John saw they was after his cows and such and he says to me, 'Saddle up my horse, Tin-Pan. And saddle yours, too. We're going down there!'

"I was praying hard 'cause I knew Mistah John was serious and we was both about to die. But I got our horses and my pistol and he fetched his shotgun and we rode lickity-cut toward them thousands of starving Mexicans along with Pancho Villa hisself.

"Mistah John, he rides right up to ole Pancho and says to get off his land. Ole Pancho says 'I don't think I'm going to do that, Mistah Slaughter.' So, Mistah John looks that bandit straight in the eye and says, 'Then pay up for them beef you're killing and the corn you cut.' "

Tin-Pan, as it turned out, was a master storyteller. Increasing the suspense, he paused and took several bites of his marshmallow.

"What happened?" demanded Miss Thorndike.

"Well, Mistah John and me rode back to the ranch all peaceable-like. Nobody got shot and Mistah John had his saddlebags full of twenty dollar gold pieces. Ole Pancho paid up."

Appleton huffed. "Pancho Villa sounds like an honorable man to me. Why would someone like that attack Columbus . . . unless we provoked him somehow?"

I have to admit that my pride had been bruised a bit with all that had been said so, to impress them and perhaps regain some of my credibility, I spoke up. "He wasn't provoked exactly, but to his way of thinking he was in the right."

"You would say something like that," sneered Jones.

"You're defending Pancho Villa?" demanded Miller.

"Not at all. But you know, Captain, that when the revolution started President Wilson had a neutrality policy. We couldn't favor or help either side."

"That's correct," agreed Miller. "What's your point?"

Studying the captain, I guessed he actually didn't know the answer to his own question.

"Just before Villa attacked Agua Prieta, Wilson threw his support behind Carranza and then, unknown to Villa, allowed our railroads to ship hundreds of Carrancista reinforcements across American soil, through the back door of Douglas and secretly into Agua Prieta.

"Villa attacked at night but the Carrancistas *miraculously* had brilliant searchlights that lit up the battlefield and allowed Villa's forces to be cut to pieces. The Villistas claim the lights and electricity came from the U.S. side of the border.

"Villa found out Wilson had double-crossed him and he was irate. You combine that with what the Germans are up to and you get an idea why Villa hit Columbus, both the military camp and the town."

Skepticism was imprinted on the faces of both Miller and Jones but neither of them had anything to say.

"What do them Germans have to do with anything?" asked Tin-Pan. "We hear stories that they's all over Mexico. And some of them Japanese, too."

I glanced at Miller and Jones and then turned to the women. They were clearly reevaluating their opinion of me. "Ladies?" I said. "Any ideas about the Germans and Pancho Villa?"

"You're no cowboy," snipped Miss Appleton. "Who are you?"

I shook my head. "I'm nobody special but I do read a lot. And I've been to Mexico and seen the revolution up close. That's all."

"Go on," encouraged Miss Thorndike.

"As for the Germans," I said, trying my best not to sound like a Weston, "they want us to go to war with Mexico so we'll stay out of the fracas in Europe. They likely goaded Villa to attack Columbus, to get back at Wilson for the double cross. After what Wilson did, having the Germans whispering in his ear would be just enough to tip the balance of Villa's judgment. And look what we've got as a result. Our entire army is in Mexico and the National Guard is strung out all along our border.

"The way things are, we couldn't join the fight in Europe even if we wanted to."

The frogs suddenly fell silent. I heard an owl hoot in the direction of the pond and then seconds later I heard another round of hoots coming from behind me. "It sounds like we have company," I said.

Everyone turned and peered expectantly into the blackness. Nothing moved. There was no sound but the fire popping.

"Your friends don't take no chances, do they?" commented Tin-Pan. "Reminds me of the old days when me and the boys rode with Mistah John. A man couldn't be too careful back then, no sir."

"For heaven's sake," scoffed Miss Thorndike as she turned back and faced the fire. "This is the twentieth century. Your friends are being overly dramatic and I, for one, am not impressed in the slightest."

Slowly, catching the faint rays of amber light, a ghostly figure appeared in the direction of the pond and began coming closer. It was Monte but, except for his campaign hat, he was dressed in range clothes. Since he was not wearing his Idaho militia uniform as he was in the court-martial, I assumed it would be several seconds before Jones recognized him.

Fifty feet from the fire, Monte stopped. "Everything alright, Billy?"

"It is."

Monte started walking again, his bulky features becoming more and more distinct as did the Colt forty-five and hunting knife buckled around his waist.

"That's him, isn't it?" Miss Appleton gasped. "That's Monte Segundo."

Jones came to his feet. "It is him, alright. I'm sure of it."

"Come on in, Mr. Segundo," invited Tin-Pan. "We been waiting for you. Come on in and make yourself at home."

Jones swore softly as Monte circled behind the chairs until he came to stand next to me.

Without taking my eyes off of Jones, I

asked, "How long have you been here?"

"Long enough."

"So where is Rosa Bustamonte?" snipped Jones.

"She's holding a bead on the captain's head," Monte said flatly. "The house looked empty and we saw no ranch hands. Things didn't look right to us."

Miller uneasily turned back around in his chair. "You can see nothing is wrong here."

Monte looked from Miller to Miss Appleton and Miss Thorndike. Without saying a word to them he raised his hand and then signaled with a flick of his wrist. The frogs began to croak again. In seconds Rosa stepped out of the shadows and stood beside him.

She was dressed as always, wearing a Mexican skirt, cotton blouse and jacket, a sombrero, and sandals. Her long black hair, woven into two braids, hung down in front of her shoulders. But this night she also had a bandolier of cartridges buckled around her waist and a Mauser rifle in her hand.

"Where is everybody?" asked Monte.

Tin-Pan got to his feet and shook hands with Monte. "All the hired hands is out on the range. We been losing a few head of stock lately and they're out to see what's the matter. Maybe some rustlers have showed up or a mountain lion. Maybe even a jaguar.

"Mistah John, he and his wife are off to Bisbee. It's on account of some law business. With him still being a deputy sheriff of the county, he gets called in from time to time."

"We were told," said Monte, ignoring everyone but Tin-Pan, "there was a room for Rosa in the ranch house."

"Sure enough is. Mistah John and Miz Viola said Miss Rosa was to stay in the guest room. It's right across the hall to Miss Thorndike and Miss Appleton."

Miss Appleton raised an eyebrow. "But our luggage is in that room."

"I done stacked your bags real nice and neat in a corner. Miss Rosa can get around just fine."

Batting her eyes and flashing a counterfeit smile in Rosa's direction, Miss Thorndike said, "Well that is very thoughtful of you, Tin-Pan. We'll just need to make certain our bags are locked up nice and tight. We wouldn't want anything to spill out in the middle of the night. Would we, Marzel?"

Glancing down at Rosa's sandal-clad feet, Miss Appleton replied innocently, "Oh, absolutely. My shoe bag is constantly overflowing and shoes get scattered everywhere.

We wouldn't want Rosa to sprain an ankle wandering around in the dark."

I heard a disparaging huff come from Jones. I held my breath, hoping Monte and Rosa didn't recognize the insults that were swirling around them.

"Las mujeres," said Rosa as she looked impassively at the two women, *"son pendejas."*

Tin-Pan choked a bit and then cleared his throat. "Are you folks taking the cows tomorrow or the next day?"

"Not tomorrow," answered Monte, still paying no attention to anyone but Tin-Pan. "I'm riding farther east tomorrow but I'll be back before dark. We'll leave first thing the next day if that suits you."

"Fine with me. You had supper?"

"We ate. We're done for the day and ready to turn in."

"Aren't you going to introduce us, Tin-Pan?" Miller asked, with a taunting edge in his voice.

"No need for that," Monte said flatly.

"Mi cuarto, por favor," Rosa said as she shifted the heavy Mauser in her hands.

Tin-Pan seemed relieved. "Sure thing," he said cheerfully as he extended his hand toward the rear door of the ranch house. "Follow me, *señorita,* and I'll show you where you can bunk."

Tin-Pan took a step and then turned back. "Breakfast for all the guests is right at sunup, that means six o'clock sharp. Monte and Billy, you two get the bunkhouse. That's the building right behind you."

Rosa followed Tin-Pan as they walked past Miss Thorndike and Miss Appleton and then disappeared in the darkness.

"Hardly a social butterfly, is she?" quipped Miss Appleton.

"She was up long before sunup and she's very tired," I said coming to my feet. "And so am I. I'll be saying good night."

Pointing off to his left, Monte glanced at me. "That the bunkhouse?"

"Yeah. You ready to turn in, too?"

"Before you go," announced Jones, "I'd like to meet you, Mr. Segundo."

Monte's eyes, void of expression, slowly shifted to Jones, who had puffed out his chest and already started toward Monte.

With a crooked smile, Jones said sarcastically, "It's not every day that I get to meet a legend."

When Jones was within reach he extended his hand. "*El Muerte,* isn't it? That's what the humble peons call you?"

Monte grasped Jones hand but did not shake it. Instead, Monte's grip closed like

78

the steel jaws of a vice. Jones was helpless as Monte increased the pressure. The lieutenant's mouth flew open and his legs began to fold.

"Billy's not a liar," Monte said softly. "You damned well better remember that."

"Alright!" grunted Jones. "Alright!"

When Jones was halfway to the ground, Monte let go.

Jones staggered and then regained his balance.

Miller, his face a mask of uncertainty, slowly rose from his chair but stood where he was.

"My, my," grinned Miss Appleton. "He *is* an ill-bred brute, isn't he?"

Miss Thorndike giggled. "Can you just imagine a brawny rube like that strolling down the streets of Boston?"

Jones's eyes blazed with instantaneous hatred as he opened and closed his right hand. "I wasn't ready for that. But it won't happen again. I'll be ready next time."

Completely unimpressed, Monte turned and headed for the bunkhouse. I started to follow but hesitated. "Lieutenant, remember the things I said. Please do yourself a favor, do all of us a favor, and make sure there is no 'next time.' "

CHAPTER 2

Six months earlier I could hardly get out of bed in time to make my first class at Harvard, but over the last few months I had learned, amongst other things, to wake up at first light. But I had yet to wake up before Monte Segundo.

I cracked my eyes open and, in the lantern light, saw Monte stretching as he sat on the edge of his bed. With the bunkhouse empty we could have had any bed we wanted, but Monte wanted one close to the door and I took the one next to his. There was a chill in the air because the night before, Monte had propped the door open. When he explained that he wanted to hear if the frogs stopped croaking, I took the hint and hung my pistol on the bedpost within easy reach.

The cool morning air began to stir. "I smell bacon," Monte said. "Tin-Pan's up and at it."

Being as tired as we were the previous

night, Monte and I had turned in minutes after entering the bunkhouse and soon fell asleep, neither of us having said a word about the lieutenant, the captain, or the two women.

I yawned. "I can't wait to see this place in the daylight. John Slaughter's got water, lots of it. His San Bernardino ranch was built on an Arizona oasis."

Bending over, Monte shoved his foot into a boot. "Out where I used to live, I don't remember anything but a spring, a small one. That must have been our only water."

I knew Monte was referring to his childhood home, a place that had almost been erased from his memory. I was aware that he could recall a corral for it was there the Apaches had tied his father and then tortured him to death. But this was the first I had heard anything about a spring.

"I don't recall you ever mentioning a spring. Do you remember anything else? Are more things starting to come back?"

Finished with his boots, Monte sat up. His brow wrinkled in thought. "No. That's about it. But maybe when I get there . . . have some time . . . maybe then some things will come back to me."

I threw off my blanket and sat up with my sock feet resting on the floor's smooth-worn planks. "How far do you think it is from here?"

Shrugging, Monte came to his feet and belted on his Colt and hunting knife. "Half a day's ride, I'm guessing, off to the northeast up near the base of the hills. Last time I was there, I came in from the north so the landmarks will look a little different from this direction. It may take a while but I'll find it."

It was during the court-martial, in a bizarre twist of fate, that Colonel Dodd divulged the approximate location where Monte's father and mother had been killed. The massacre, he said, had occurred very near the junction of the Arizona and New Mexico state lines and the Mexican border.

After the court-martial, Monte and I had split up for a while. Needing to take care of some family matters, I left Columbus on a train to New York and Monte had taken a train heading west toward the massacre site. There, he hoped to find answers to questions that had haunted him for thirty years.

When he arrived in the Arizona town of Rodeo, Monte met an old cowboy who remembered the Apache raid of 1886. He also recalled the exact location down near the border where a husband and wife had been murdered. Provided with detailed directions, Monte followed the western edge of the Peloncillo Mountain Range until he was within sight of the Mexican border. Then, next to a small arroyo, he found the charred remains of the abandoned homestead and the neglected graves of his murdered father and mother. But, once again, as fate or perhaps providence would have it, Monte Segundo's graveside reunion had been abruptly interrupted by circumstances beyond his control.

But now Monte was only a few hours away from his childhood home and this day promised to be different.

"Is Rosa going with you?" I asked. "Or would you rather go alone?"

Monte walked to the open door and looked out toward the ranch house. "She's coming. And you can come, too, if you want."

The invitation stunned me and for a moment, I was speechless.

Monte Segundo did not have what one might call "friends." Enduring what he had as a child had all but cauterized his emotions and then growing up a mistreated orphan had hardened his very soul. As a result, he had never felt the need to have a "friend" and likely never would. I sensed that coldness about Monte when we first met in Columbus, and yet, he had at least accepted my company.

At first, Monte tolerated me like a man would a stray dog but over the weeks that followed, as we rode through Mexico together, I realized that I had gradually earned his respect. And for me, a complete neophyte, gaining that respect was a monumental achievement. But, now, being invited to accompany him on what could be the most important day of his life, I realized I had also earned his trust.

"That sure beats staying here," I said, suppressing any sign of being overwhelmed. "I don't care much for those two women."

Monte turned and glanced at me curiously. "Those two aren't spring chickens but neither one of them is hard to look at. It seems strange they would be here without their husbands."

"I don't think they're married, at least not Miss Appleton," I said. "When I first got here I could see right off that Lieutenant Jones was making eyes at her."

"Must be widows," Monte said.

I started putting on my boots. "So, how much did you hear last night?"

"Rosa and I got here just after dark. We went to the pond to wash up about the time the captain was comparing the lieutenant to

84

John L. Sullivan."

I felt my stomach roll with anxiety. "You heard all that?"

"We did. We heard it all. It's rotten luck to run into the army like this. Too bad we didn't know they were stationed here. If we had, maybe Señor Cruz could have found credit somewhere else."

"Rotten luck and my big mouth," I confessed. "I wish I would've just walked away from that fire. If I had, the lieutenant wouldn't have recognized me. It turns out he was at the court-martial."

Monte thought for a moment and then nodded slowly. "Bad luck, that's for damn sure."

"Once Jones recognized me I didn't know what to do. I tried not to say too much but one thing led to another."

"He and the captain were after you, Billy. And then they went after me and Rosa. You did fine by us. It's just the way it turned out. We'll steer clear of the army today and get our cows tomorrow. Then we'll get the hell out of here and that'll be the end of it."

Pulling on my shoulder holster and then my vest, I went to the door and stood next to Monte. Suddenly the crisp and peppy notes of a bugle cut the morning stillness.

"The garrison's blowing reveille," Monte

said. "They're just now rolling out of their blankets. I guess they're not too awfully worried about Mexicans crossing the border."

Shaking the sleep out of my head, I muttered, "I wish we would've known they were here. And so stinking close. Their outpost is only a couple of hundred yards east of here."

"Less than a hundred," countered Monte.

Out across the green lawn, the rays of the rising sun were just hitting the rooftops of the ranch house and several nearby outbuildings. Now, in the light of day, I could see that all of the adobe structures had been covered with a neat layer of white plaster and the ranch house was lined with several varieties of flowers.

Tin-Pan stepped out the back door, rang a dinner bell, and then went back inside.

"I could eat a horse," Monte said. Starting for the ranch house he added, "There's a privy in back of the bunkhouse. There's a two-seater behind one of those other outbuildings but I figure it's for them that live in the house."

I circled the bunkhouse, made a quick visit to the outhouse, and then went to the rear door of the ranch house. Opening a screen door, I stepped into a small room that had a door to my left. Next to the door was a table. On it was a washbasin, linen towel, and a folded copy of the *Daily Dispatch.* As I washed and dried my hands, I glanced at the newspaper. An article on the front page read, "Brits use Tanks in Battle of Somme."

Hearing the voices of Monte, Rosa, and Tin-Pan, I stepped through the door and passed through another small room, its only piece of furniture being a sheet-metal bathtub. The tub had no plumbing and, without legs, it sat flat on the floor.

Exiting that room, I walked through the kitchen and then into a spacious dining area. To my left, Rosa and Monte were seated at one end of a table that was capable of seating twenty people. Near the table, a polished china cabinet had been built into the wall and across from it on an adjacent wall there was a massive stone fireplace. Against the far wall I was surprised to see an ornate piano and a Victrola. Several feet from the dining table, in the center of the combination dining-living room, a comfortable-looking sofa and easy chair were nestled on top of a large rug.

Tin-Pan appeared near the Victrola, having come down a hallway that connected the bedrooms to the living area. "Them two women heard the bell, good enough," he said. "They's just taking their sweet time."

As Tin-Pan made his way back to the kitchen, I took a seat opposite Monte and Rosa. With my back to the china cabinet, I sat facing the open room and fireplace. Wincing a bit, I asked Rosa, "How did you sleep?"

Rosa huffed. "Probably better than the two *gringas*."

Tin-Pan came out of the kitchen with a stack of plates, three coffee cups, and a handful of forks. He set them down in front of us, and as he returned to the kitchen we each grabbed a plate, cup, and fork.

"You don't think the captain and lieutenant will show up, do you?" I asked.

Monte shook his head. "No. They'll be with their men."

"Good," I said, "Something tells me Jones could be looking for trouble. Maybe the captain is, too."

Next, Tin-Pan brought out a large bowl filled with scrambled eggs and a platter stacked with steaming biscuits and sizzling bacon. Setting the breakfast down in front of us, he said cheerily, "Coffee's a-coming."

When Monte reached for the eggs and Rosa for the bacon, my impulse was to suggest that we wait for the two women. But then, I realized there was no point. The food was hot, the women were late, and Monte

Segundo and Rosa Bustamonte were not the least bit restrained by a punctilious list of sophisticated table manners. Most of their lives they had struggled to survive from one day to the next, which left little time to memorize Victorian rules of etiquette.

I, on the other hand, was not so unencumbered. However, my loyalty was to Monte and Rosa, not to Ada Thorndike and Marzel Appleton. So, taking a deep breath, I forked some bacon onto my plate and then gingerly picked up a biscuit with my fingers. Glancing at the fireplace, I caught sight of a clock on the mantel. It was four minutes past six o'clock.

Knowing at that moment there was no turning back, I crossed the Rubicon and took a bite of biscuit. Chewing the warm bread, I uneasily shifted my attention to the hallway where Miss Thorndike and Miss Appleton would soon make their predictable and fashionably late entrance. I was adrift in a cloud of anxiety and guilt when a question pierced the fog.

"Are you going today or staying?" asked Tin-Pan as he set a coffee cup in front of me and filled it with black coffee.

I shifted my attention to Tin-Pan. "Me?"

"Uh-uh."

"I'm going with Monte and Rosa."

"Alright. I'll be packing five lunches, then," Tin-Pan said. "And I'll make a stew so you all can eat whenever you get back, early or late. I'll be leaving it on the stove in the kitchen so it'll stay hot."

Suddenly curious and somewhat distracted, I asked, "Five lunches? Where are the women off to?"

"They're riding over to Guadalupe Canyon to look for birds. I told 'em it was a ride of fifteen miles or so and I should go along but they told me, no. Said they didn't need no man to show 'em the way, especially since there's a wagon road that leads up to the canyon.

"That's true enough about the road, I s'pose, and it'd be hard to get lost in the canyon since they's lot of sand where they'll be riding. I figure they can follow their tracks back out of the canyon or just let the horses have their head. Them horses they'll be riding are Mistah John's and they'll know where home is."

I glimpsed a flicker of movement and felt a stinging jolt of panic shoot down my legs. I looked up as Miss Thorndike and Miss Appleton entered the dining area and found myself staring at two flushed and sneering faces.

"Good morning," I said cheerily, feigning

90

innocence the best I knew how. Dropping my eyes, I noticed Miss Thorndike was clutching what appeared to be a large book.

Miss Appleton flashed a malignant smile as the two women approached the table. "So good of you to start without us," she said indignantly.

Tin-Pan took two plates from the stack on the table and started to place them next to me.

"Don't bother," Miss Thorndike said as she and Miss Appleton worked their way around the table and up to the china cabinet. "All we need is cold milk. Tin-Pan, would you be so good as to get us some from the icehouse?"

Appleton opened a glass door of the china cabinet and removed two bowls. She then opened a drawer, closed it, and then opened another. From the second drawer she removed two silver spoons. Then, an arm's length from me, Miss Thorndike placed a cardboard box, which I had originally mistaken for a book, end up on the table. Miss Appleton put the bowls and spoons near the box and then both women smugly took their seats, deliberately leaving two vacant chairs between me and them.

"I'll get your milk," Tin-Pan said. "Want it for your coffee?"

"Hardly," moaned Appleton. "We enjoyed the experience of your breakfast yesterday, Tin-Pan, and we're certain that such sustenance is quite suitable for ranch hands and laborers but our delicate systems are not accustomed to . . . to such wonderful frontier cuisine.

"This morning Ada and I prefer to indulge in a much lighter breakfast, one with a bit less grease."

Thorndike pointed to the box, which was about the size of a large dictionary. On it "Wax-tite" was printed in large blue letters. "We will be eating toasted corn flakes. They are newly marketed by a man named Kellogg. Very new, you understand. Fortunately for us, we brought a number of boxes with us from Boston."

Tin-Pan eased the plates back down. "Flakes of corn?" he asked suspiciously. "I never heard of such a thing. Corn flakes sounds more like something you'd feed a horse or pig maybe."

"Oh," assured Miss Thorndike, "I'm certain that you are not alone, Tin-Pan. I doubt anyone in Arizona has even heard of Kellogg's flakes. It's a fanciful dish, you understand, one that only appeals to those with more refined tastes."

I glanced at Tin-Pan as he strode back

toward the kitchen and then at Monte and Rosa. The insult seemed to have slipped by Tin-Pan and, as far as I could tell, Monte and Rosa were busy eating and ignoring the women all together.

As Miss Thorndike peeled open the top of the cereal box, I said, "Tin-Pan said you two are going to look for birds today."

"I don't suppose," sighed Miss Appleton, "that you are familiar with the works of Louis Agassiz Fuertes?"

I shrugged. "No. Is he a Mexican?"

Tearing a hole in the wax paper inside the box, Miss Thorndike huffed scornfully, "Hardly! He is America's greatest bird painter. Marzel and I are students of his and we're here to observe, for the first time, the brilliant red *Piranga rubra* or, to non-birders like yourself, a bird known as the summer tanager. And, since we have finished with our suffrage meetings in Tucson, we're free to explore Guadalupe Canyon, which is said to be an excellent location for sighting the tanager in its native Sonoran habitat."

"Back in the old days," said Tin-Pan as he reentered the dining area with a pitcher in his hand, "Guadalupe Canyon was a mighty dangerous place. Apaches, bandits, rustlers. All using it to go back and forth from the territories into Mexico."

Tin-Pan set the pitcher of milk down in front of the women. "Yep, I recollect the time Old Man Clanton got hisself killed in there by Mexican federales. He stole some Mexican cows and those Mexicans came across the border after him and killed him and his gang right there in the canyon. And nine or ten years ago, the Apache Massai come through there on a raid. And he got killed not long after. That was over near San Marcial, New Mexico."

Pouring corn flakes into her bowl, Miss Thorndike said, "Thank you, Tin-Pan, for reciting more of your quaint frontier stories. However, even if some of them were actually true, they all transpired years ago. We'll be perfectly safe. After all, this *is* the twentieth century . . . even in Arizona."

Tin-Pan shook his head. "The Apache Kid is still out there somewhere," he grumbled. "They ain't never caught him." Turning back toward the kitchen, he added in a near whisper, "And the Kid ain't the only one, either."

"Señor Tin-Pan," called Rosa, *"por favor, tiene pimientes, pimientes picantes?"*

"Yes'm. I'll fetch you some."

Miss Thorndike's eyes flickered with a wicked light as she handed the box of corn

94

flakes to Miss Appleton. "Mr. Segundo," she began with a smirk. "I was told that you used to live near here. Do you, like dear old Tin-Pan, have any *hair-raising* stories about Guadalupe Canyon?"

Monte Segundo was nobody's fool but he didn't know what to make of Ada Thorndike and Marzel Appleton. Throughout his life, the women he had come across were men's sweethearts, men's wives, or prostitutes, and he treated them all with the same respect. In fact, if any woman was ever harmed, he, like many western men, took it personally and acted accordingly. To Monte, women of every stripe were sacred, to be protected at all costs. But the women Monte knew lived on the edge of civilization and appreciated the respect men gave them. The Misses Thorndike and Appleton, on the other hand, were unlike any women he had ever encountered.

Monte chewed on a piece of bacon. Saying nothing, he studied Miss Thorndike as if she were a two-headed snake.

"Well," said Miss Thorndike, a bit unsettled by Monte's silence, "do you care to make a comment? Do you have anything to say about the dangers of Guadalupe Canyon?"

"I came here to get cattle," Monte replied

flatly. "You came here to look at birds. It's best to let sleeping dogs lie."

Miss Thorndike's face went blank and then flushed red. After a moment, like a hungry lioness searching for easier prey, she shifted her attention to Rosa. "So, Rosa," she taunted with a sarcastic smile, "Do you herd cattle along with the men? Are you also a *cowboy*?"

I saw Rosa's eyes harden when her name was mentioned but she continued to eat as if she had heard nothing.

Filling her bowl with corn flakes, Miss Appleton raised an eyebrow. "Now, don't be silly, Ada. You can see she is much too attractive to be a cowboy. I should think she accompanies the men to do their cooking."

Gazing haughtily at Rosa, Miss Thorndike inquired, "I'm dying to know, Rosa. What, precisely, is your *occupation*?"

I felt like grabbing the pitcher of milk off the table and emptying it over the women's heads. Such impudence was outrageous and yet there I sat, unable to do or say anything. These were the kind of women that, as children, would have enjoyed pulling the wings off insects.

My only hope was that the thinly disguised insults had once again gone unnoticed.

Nervously, I glanced at Rosa, expecting any second to see her reach across the table and rip out a handful of hair. Instead, I saw her smiling at Miss Thorndike and nodding agreeably.

Miss Appleton grinned slyly. "Ada, I don't think she understands a single word you are saying."

Returning Rosa's friendly smile, Miss Thorndike nodded, "Do they have Kellogg's flakes where you live, *Señorita*?"

Rosa nodded again. She smiled and then took a bite of her eggs. As she chewed, she glanced innocently from Miss Thorndike to Miss Appleton and back again. Smiling agreeably, she said, *"Estas mujeres son pendejas."*

"Poor thing," sighed Miss Appleton, "she doesn't speak our language."

I had no idea what Rosa had said in Spanish but when she didn't object to Miss Appleton's declaration, I knew trouble was on its way. Rosa could speak English almost as well as she spoke Spanish. Her only weakness came when she chose to swear. Then she reverted to Spanish and, with blistering speed, would flawlessly deliver an unbroken string of profanity that would rival any sailor on the high seas.

Hoping to head off a disaster, I attempted

to steer the conversation in a different direction.

"Tin-Pan said the two of you were planning on using horses to get to the canyon," I said, not caring which woman responded. "Have you been riding long?"

Miss Appleton huffed and then poured milk into her bowl. "I studied dressage in Austria and Ada attended an equally prestigious academy in Portugal. I assure you, we ride as well, if not better, than any run-of-the-mill cowboys."

"I got you ladies two fine horses," said Tin-Pan as he rounded the table and set a bowl of red peppers in front of Rosa. "And I got three fresh mounts for you other folks and put your saddles on them this morning. All five are tied out front of the corrals."

Tin-Pan grabbed a plate. He pulled out a chair across from me. When he took a seat, Miss Thorndike and Miss Appleton stiffened. Their lips puckered involuntarily as their cheeks flushed rosy pink.

"How *nice* of you to join us join us, Tin-Pan," said Miss Appleton, her tone carrying only the faintest hint of contempt.

As Tin-Pan filled his plate, Rosa leaned toward Monte. *"Cuchillo, por favor,"* she said softly.

Monte casually reached down with his left

hand and pulled out his hunting knife, a Bowie with a staghorn grip and twelve-inch blade. He handed it to Rosa.

Picking up a bright red pepper, Rosa began slicing pieces from it and allowing them to fall onto her eggs. When she was finished she smiled at Miss Thorndike and Miss Appleton. *"Fruta,"* she explained. *"Muy buena fruta."*

Recovering from the audacity exhibited by Tin-Pan when he dared sit at the table, the women started to eat their corn flakes. And for a moment there was an uneasy lull in the conversation. Moments later, however, Marzel Appleton was at it again.

"One might divine," she muttered, "that paring knives are unknown to Mexicans."

"Speaking of Mexicans," Tin-Pan said, "them rustlers that's giving all the ranchers fits might be Mexicans crossing the border. Now if they was Americans you two ladies would have nothing to worry over. No white man would ever harm a woman. But Mexican bandits is different. Not as bad as Apaches of course, but bad 'nough."

Miss Appleton took a dainty mouthful of corn flakes, chewed, and then swallowed. With a patronizing smile she said, "With the soldiers all along the border, Tin-Pan, I doubt we shall see any Mexicans. And as far as Apaches go, Ada and I share a modern, more enlightened view of their history and culture than many of you Westerners. In fact, we both made it a point to study the works of John Bourke before coming to the West."

"Did you ever meet Captain Bourke, Tin-Pan?" asked Miss Thorndike. "He was with General Crook."

Tin-Pan lifted a piece of bacon and bit into it. Chewing, he said, "Sure, I knew the captain just like Mistah John knowed him. When it came to dealing with the Apaches, Cap'n Bourke wasn't worth much."

Miss Appleton gasped. For a moment she was speechless. Catching her breath, she strained to control her anger. "Why, Captain Bourke was a recipient of the Medal of Honor in the Civil War. He was a prolific writer and a respected ethnologist. He is recognized as having been a renowned authority on the Apaches and their customs."

"Is that a fact?" sighed Tin-Pan. "What did the cap'n write about them Apaches?"

Clearly disgusted, Miss Appleton shook her head. "Let's just say that if you people had not stolen the Apache's land and broken your treaties there would have been no Apache reprisal, none of the so-called

Apache wars.

"He said he trusted the honesty of an Apache more than he did white men. And he described them as intelligent, courageous, and good-natured. Physically, he said they had bones of iron, sinews of wire, and muscles like India rubber. But, once aroused, the Apaches were among the greatest fighters in history."

To my surprise, Tin-Pan calmly reached for a biscuit and said, "Them old-time Apaches weren't great fighters. Mostly they ambushed folks or killed people that was unarmed.

"Now, there ain't no better trackers in the world though. They can see little things that most folks miss, a little thread or sometimes a few little hairs. Even a bent blade of grass and tracks of bugs. A good tracker sees all them things. I learned all I know from friendly Apaches.

"And I'll admit they were tough and could go without water and cover a lot of miles on foot if they had a mind to, but if they didn't outnumber an enemy they always scattered like quail and run off to hide.

"This here desert's like the ocean and back then the Apaches were nothing but sand pirates. Pirates don't care about the seas any more than an Apache cares about the land. And, just like pirates, all the Apaches were after was plunder. Long before the Americans got here, the Apaches learned it was easier to steal corn than to grow it or to butcher somebody else's cow than to raise one yourself.

"Ask the old Papagoes or the Zunis or Pimas about how the Apaches were always raiding them. Or ask the Mexicans south of the border. Them Mexicans care about the land and they work it to grow crops. The Apaches have been raiding Mexican and Indian villages for more than two hundred years and it don't have a thing to do with whose land it is."

"The Mexicans," snapped Miss Thorndike, "invaded the Apache's land just as the whites did. They're nothing but a mongrel race of Spaniards encroaching on Apache land."

"No, ma'am," Tin-Pan replied easily. "Ya see, Mexicans *is* Indians. Only they've had the killing and stealing churched out of 'em. Why, they hardly got a drop of Spanish blood in 'em. Them Mexicans have a right to their land as much as any Indian but the Apaches didn't care. Apaches live to raid. In fact, there's wild Apaches that are still raiding down in Mexico."

"That's ridiculous," scoffed Miss Appleton. "There are no wild Apaches left. We've imprisoned them all on our wretched reservations."

"Is that what Cap'n Bourke wrote down for you to read?" asked Tin-Pan.

"In essence," snipped Miss Appleton. "If one is *able* to read."

Tin-Pan forked a piece of bacon. "I s'pose one man's weeds is another man's flowers."

Miss Thorndike indignantly sucked wind up her nostrils but for the moment she held her tongue. Miss Appleton's eyes narrowed and her forehead flushed bright pink.

Fearful that Monte might be dragged into the disagreement, I did what I could to divert the conversation away from Apaches all together.

"How long a ride is it to Guadalupe Canyon?"

"Three hours, maybe," replied Tin-Pan, completely unmoved by the women's scornful stares and pursed lips. "And where you three are heading is called the Pickhandle Hills. It'll take you about the same amount of time to get to there as it does the ladies to get to the canyon. Maybe a little longer 'cause there ain't no road where you're headed."

As the two women sulked, Monte picked up a pepper and took a bite. But Monte, like Tin-Pan, had been raised with the fiery fruit and ate them with as much relish as Rosa. To my surprise, however, Tin-Pan looked at Rosa and gave her a quick wink. He then innocently picked a pepper out of the bowl and forked it into his eggs.

Rosa mixed her sliced peppers into her eggs, laid the knife down, and then took several bites. Glancing once again at Miss Thorndike, Rosa pointed at the bowl. *"Fruta. Es muy buena, Señora."*

"Is she saying 'fruit'?" asked Miss Appleton.

"Yes'm," answered Tin-Pan, his tone casual. "Fruta is fruit in Mes'can. She's saying it's very good. *Muy buena.*"

As I ate I studied Tin-Pan carefully. His face was poker-player blank, which meant he was an accessory to the unfolding scheme.

I began to eat faster. If what I suspected was about to happen, my breakfast was about to be interrupted and cut short. In between bites I took a gulp of coffee and, with my eyes peering over the rim of the cup, I glanced anxiously around the table.

Before I took the cup from my lips, the inevitable question was asked.

"May I try one?" Miss Appleton asked. "They look delicious."

Chewing with his mouth full, Tin-Pan nodded and slid the bowl of peppers down the table.

Miss Appleton fingered a brilliant red pepper. Looking it over carefully she asked, "What do you think, Ada?"

Not to be outdone, Miss Thorndike selected a large yellow pepper and raised it high. "Damn the torpedoes," she grinned. "Four bells!"

Simultaneously, both women bit off half a pepper and began to chew.

Monte and Rosa came to their feet. Instantly, I scrambled out of my chair and, nodding to Tin-Pan, I said hurriedly, "Thanks for breakfast."

Without so much as a glance at the two women, Monte and Rosa started for the front door. I had only taken a step when I heard the first gasp for air. By the time the three of us were out the screen door, the hoarse pants and agonizing screams were coming in erratic bursts, no doubt voiced between futile gulps of cold milk.

We began tightening our cinches as if nothing had happened. Cutting through the cool morning air, we heard more raspy screeches and then the slamming of the back door. A moment later Tin-Pan sauntered out the front screen door and over to the corrals where the horses were tied.

Picking his teeth with a toothpick, he suppressed a smile. "They run out to the icehouse."

"Serves them right," Rosa said, tying off her cinch.

Tin-Pan grinned, showing an even row of large white teeth. "I figured you could speak American but Mistah John told me I was to be hospitable. That meant for me not to speak my mind one way or t'other to the guests, so I didn't say nothing at the table. But between me and you folks, it seems them fine ladies know as much about this country as they do chili peppers."

Monte swung into his saddle. Peering through the leaves of the cottonwoods and into the rising sun, he said, "We should be back about sundown. We'll head out with the cattle tomorrow at first light."

Tin-Pan nodded as Rosa and I mounted. "I'll have breakfast ready," he said starting back to the ranch house. "Ain't nobody leaving John Slaughter's ranch on an empty stomach."

Throughout the night and most of the morning Monte's thoughts had been focused on visiting the graves of his father and mother but nothing in his life had come easily, and, as a consequence, anticipating trouble had become ingrained in his nature. Sitting in his saddle, Monte took a moment to consider what he knew of Captain Miller and Lieutenant Jones. He accepted the fact that both officers believed he and I were traitors and he recognized Jones for the troublemaker he was. Whether it came from the captain or the lieutenant, Monte was convinced word of our presence would spread quickly to the other soldiers in the garrison. But more importantly, he was keenly aware the previous night he had kowtowed Jones in front of his commanding officer and the two women. At the very least, the lieutenant would want to save face. At the worst, he would try and get even.

Monte glanced at Rosa, then at me. "The sentries up on that mesa will be looking out toward Mexico. So, I figure we'll head out of here to the northwest for a mile or so, circle around behind the garrison, and then angle back to the east. It's best that we keep plenty of room between us and the army. I don't want any problems. Not today."

Side by side, the three of us rode away from the corrals with the warmth of the rising sun on our back. "This is the devil's own luck," I muttered. "Who'd have thought the Slaughters would have an army post a stone's throw from their front door!"

"And those two women!" Rosa flared. "Is that what American women are like? Are they all so stupid?"

I grunted with disgust. "Only the rich ones."

Monte merely frowned and then, spotting a likely looking trail, nudged his horse into the brush and took the lead. A half hour later, after making a wide arc around the outpost, Monte pointed east toward the Guadalupe Mountains, the peaks of which now paled in the hazy brilliance of the morning sun. Continuing to ride, he said, "See that saddle?"

Rosa and I shaded our eyes with the flats of our hands. Rosa saw it first and then, squinting against the glare, I caught sight of a distant hill that indeed resembled a western saddle.

"On this side of the saddle there's a round-top knoll. A mile or so from the base of that knoll is where the ranch used to be."

"Do you know this from your memories?" Rosa asked.

"No. I remember those landmarks from when I was here last June. That day I only had a few minutes to look around before I had to take off. But while I was there, I did seem to remember a cottonwood tree. Then, not far from the graves, I found what was left of an old cottonwood and, below it, what might have been our spring.

"I'm thinking this time, if I look around long enough more will come back to me." Monte paused. "Maybe a few things anyway."

Rosa reined in, allowing Monte to gain some distance between us. Understanding she might want to talk, I nudged my horse and came up alongside her. "He's got a lot to think about, doesn't he?"

"No se," Rosa said, then thoughtfully gazed at Monte. "All that matters to me is that he continues to think of me in a way that he has never before thought of a woman. And I know that is true. For now, that is enough for me. The rest, the love, will come in time."

I glanced at Monte and then back at Rosa. At that moment, bathed in sunlight, she seemed serene, almost angelic. I envied her simple approach to life. And Monte's, too, for that matter. Both took everything in stride. Good or bad, they faced life head-on with a mixture of courage, determination, and optimism that continued to baffle me. Even with all they had endured over the years, each appeared to be free of the gnawing insecurities and doubts that plagued me and so many others like me.

The word "grit" came to mind, a term I had recently added to my expanding western dialect. At first, I assumed "grit" had something to do with an intimate discomfort caused by invasive grains of sand, but once you've heard the term applied to someone like Rosa Bustamonte or Monte Segundo, the meaning of the word, though difficult to explain, becomes perfectly clear.

"When we get there," I asked, "I mean when we actually get close to the graves, what should I do? I think I should stay back and let him go on alone, don't you?"

Rosa nodded somberly. "Yes. Graves are best visited alone. Especially for someone like Monte. Even I must give him room. His whole life, all of it that he can remember anyway, he has been alone. It is all he knows. When he is ready for us, he will let us know."

We rode on in silence for several minutes, the only sound being the clopping of hooves and creak of saddle leather. Monte had not looked back in a long while, which, for him, was unusual. Perhaps that was why I took it upon myself to turn and check our back trail. Straining my eyes, I thought I detected a faint wisp of dust rising far behind us.

Believing the dust was of no importance, however, I turned back to Rosa and said,

"It's only midmorning. Monte will have plenty of time to look around today, and I'd bet my last dollar he's going to start to remember things. I just know he will.

"Just like when he first saw you, Rosa. Remember how you reminded him of his mother and later how he recalled hearing her voice? And that pitoreal back in Mexico, that big woodpecker banging on the dead tree caused him to think of his father."

Rosa shrugged. "But those were bad memories, Billy, memories that were better forgotten and never remembered."

I thought for a moment. "But he said the graves helped him to remember a cotton-wood tree. And then he remembered the spring they had. It's like one memory trig-gers another. I think he'll remember. Things will come back, good things. Maybe even his name or the names of some relatives. Then he would know who he is."

"He knows who he is," Rosa said confi-dently. "Nothing will change that."

We rode on another mile or two, passing over wispy stands of dried grass and through patches of scattered creosote. But then Monte, who was now a good distance ahead, suddenly drew up. He peered over his shoulder and yet, oddly, not directly at Rosa and me. Then, wheeling his horse, he galloped back to us.

"Are we there?" I asked as Monte slid to a stop.

Monte pointed over of my shoulder but off to my left. "We've got company."

Rosa and I turned our horses. The dust cloud I had ignored earlier was closer now and rising higher.

"Rustlers?" questioned Rosa, pulling her Mauser from her saddle scabbard.

"Maybe," answered Monte. "But whoever it is, they're following our tracks. I doubt rustlers would do that. Mexican bandits might, though."

Glancing around, Rosa asked, "Is there any cover around, any rocks?"

Looking back toward the nearby Pick-handle Hills, Monte sighed, "We could get to high ground in those hills but there's no good cover that I know of. If we need to make a run for it, we'll have to ride all the way to the mountains and then find a good place to fight."

"Whoever they are," observed Rosa, "they're coming fast. Mexican bandits are not that foolish."

"Then it must be someone from the Slaughter ranch," I said. "Maybe it's Tin-Pan. Maybe something happened with the cattle."

The three of us watched the plume of dust until we could make out a single-file line of riders as they repeatedly appeared on the high ground and then disappeared into the desert swales.

"They're soldiers," Monte said. "The one riding in front is an officer."

Squinting at the riders that were easily a half mile out, I asked, "How can you tell?"

"Because they're wearing uniforms and the one in the lead rides like he's got a broom handle stuck up his backside."

A few seconds passed and then I too could make out the uniforms. I also noticed the erect, almost rigid, posture of the officer. "But what do they want with us?"

Rosa sneered. "Maybe the *gringas* want us arrested for giving them chili peppers."

Monte squinted and then swore under his breath. "Nope. It's that damned lieutenant from last night. He just can't leave well enough alone."

We waited where we were as the army patrol galloped to within twenty feet and then encircled us. Along with Jones, there were five privates and one corporal. When they came to a dusty halt, Jones was staring us in the face and sporting a triumphant smirk.

"You said you were going to drive cattle

113

west," chided Jones. "Fortunately a patrol ran across your tracks and then discovered you were going north. And here you are now heading east with no cattle anywhere to be seen. So, in light of the fact that one of you is a Mexican and the other two are traitors, and since your tracks were headed in the wrong direction, Captain Miller sent me to investigate."

"So?" returned Monte evenly. "Investigate."

The smile on the lieutenant's face faded. "What are you doing out here?" he demanded.

"That's my business," replied Monte, "and it doesn't concern the army."

Jones straightened his legs. Standing tall in the saddle, he looked to his left and then his right. "Very well. I see no suspicious activity. My investigation is complete."

There was a moment of silence in which no one moved a muscle. Then Jones took off his campaign hat. Handing it to the corporal on his right, Jones announced, "The men understand that the rest of this is off the record."

Stepping down onto a bed of packed sand, Jones unbuckled his cartridge belt and sidearm and handed it to the private on his left.

"Last night, Monte Segundo, there were ladies present," Jones said casually, but then, with his eyes full of contempt, he glared up at Rosa. "But as anyone can see, there are none present today. And you, Billy Cabott, will soon observe that there is a decisive difference between fighting a trained pugilist and a few drunken Mexicans in a crowded cantina."

My stomach turned. I knew this was not going to end well and if worse came to worst, we would soon be hunted by the army as well as the local sheriff. Jones had no chance against Monte and if Monte became enraged, Jones might not survive the next five minutes.

"You don't want to do this, Lieutenant," I said. "You've done what you came to do so why not go back and make your report? We don't want any trouble with anyone."

"It's just like you said, Lieutenant," said a soldier behind me. "Segundo's a damned traitor *and* a coward."

Several other soldiers noisily voiced similar sentiments. One called out, "Show him how it's done, Lieutenant. Give him hell!"

As Jones started unbuttoning his shirt, I glanced at Monte. To my utter amazement, he appeared to be anything but agitated. In fact, he appeared to be somewhat amused.

115

"Ordinarily, Lieutenant," Monte said easily, "I'd be more than happy to step down and knock the snot out of you, but today I have more important things on my mind."

Untucking his army shirt, Jones slipped it off and draped it over his saddle. Covering his wiry but muscular torso was a sleeveless boxing jersey with "West Point Academy" printed on the front.

"More important things," mocked Jones, as he began to punch the air with a series of swift jabs and hooks. "Like not getting whipped in front of your . . ."

Jones threw a few more warm-up punches, paused thoughtfully, and then said, "What is the word in Spanish . . . *puta*?"

"*Chinga su madre, cabron!*" spewed Rosa.

Monte turned to Rosa. "What does that mean? What is *puta*?"

Rosa knew better than to answer truthfully. "Nothing. He is loco. It means nothing."

The corporal laughed. "It means whore, you fool. *Puta* is Mexican for whore!"

Anger has a unique look as does rage. But what washed over Monte Segundo in such moments was neither. It is best described as a rising tide of thunderous wrath.

Monte eased out of his saddle and then gently backed his horse into the circle of

116

army horses. Knowing there was nothing to do but watch, Rosa and I tightened our reins and backed our horses next to Monte's.

"Hell is never full," Monte said as he handed his hat and pistol belt to Rosa.

My heart was racing. I had seen what Monte's fists could do, and for a split second all I could think about was the day Monte demolished the five Carrancista soldiers. It was the day he met Rosa, the day he had unintentionally killed a Carrancista soldier, an ally of the United States. For that, he was later charged with treason. That charge was dropped and yet, as if fate were not satisfied, here we were again. But these soldiers weren't unsuspecting, intoxicated Mexicans. These were sober American soldiers and they were armed and itching for a fight.

When Monte turned to face Jones, I panicked. "Don't kill him, Monte!" I blurted. "Remember what happened the last time!"

Apparently, the desperate tone in my voice had a ring of truth in it. All eyes of the soldiers, including those of Jones, shifted to me. Jones seemed startled but Monte, with his hands at his sides, was already moving toward the lieutenant, taking slow, even steps.

Someone yelled, "Get him, Lieutenant!"

Glancing back at Monte, Jones put up his guard and pranced to the center of the thirty-foot circle. He firmly planted his feet and then struck a classic boxing pose, a picture of athletic perfection.

The soldiers began to cheer. Monte took three more steps, then with his left arm he sent a sweeping backhand into Jones's guard. The blow came so quickly and with so much force that Jones's guard collapsed, his arms slamming into one another as he half spun to his right. Before Jones could react, Monte's right fist thudded squarely against the lieutenant's temple.

Jones's knees buckled. He staggered but he did not fall. Instead, he regained his balance and again threw up his guard. However, when he did so, he found himself facing the muzzle of a horse.

For a moment, Jones glared at the animal, then, in a daze, spun around and tottered forward a few steps. With his head wobbling, he tried to focus on Monte. Unsatisfied, he looked up at the soldiers as if he intended to ask a question. A few seconds later he fell backwards, landing in a seated position with his legs outstretched.

The boisterous onlookers were stunned into silence.

Ignoring Jones, Monte took a quick step. Jerking the corporal out of his saddle, he flipped him in the air and then slammed him flat on his back, knocking the breath out of him.

"Apologize, damn you," demanded Monte, "or I'll break you in two!"

It took a few seconds for the downed soldier to get air into his lungs. He coughed and then coughed again. "Sorry, miss," he managed between breaths. "Sorry. I apologize."

Monte's blood was hot and he was just getting started. He glared up at the soldiers. "Who's next?"

No one moved. The welt that was closing Jones's left eye was already turning glossy blue.

Keeping her rifle level across her saddle, Rosa tossed Monte his pistol belt. I eased my hand inside my vest. Time seemed to slow to a crawl. The soldiers glanced uncertainly from one to the other. None of them, except for the corporal, could have been much over twenty years old.

The corporal slowly got to his feet and then, keeping his distance from Monte, went to Jones and helped him stand up.

"We're going," said the corporal. "You whipped him fair and square."

My thoughts immediately went to Captain Miller and what he might do. Three months earlier Monte had assaulted an officer in Columbus and General Pershing had added that altercation to the long list of charges read at the court-martial. Now, with Monte having flattened Lieutenant Jones and manhandled the corporal, it was happening all over again.

"Jones will have a black eye," I said. "If this is off the record, how will you explain that?"

Helping Jones get his left boot into a stirrup, the corporal grumbled, "We'll think of something. This was 'off the record.' That means it never happened. Because if it did, the lieutenant would have hell to pay."

CHAPTER 3

With Monte again taking the lead, I rode beside Rosa and listened as she first swore in Spanish and then, switching to English, berated the incompetence of the United States military and the pompous ignorance of Ada Thorndike and Marzel Appleton. We had ridden over two miles before her tirade finally ended.

"Feel better now?" I asked.

Rosa turned to me and smiled. "The lieutenant's eye will be black for a month. Every time he looks in the mirror to shave he will see what a fool he is. And he will remember why his eye is black."

I nodded uneasily. "That he will. But I'm wondering if he'll learn from what happened and become a better man or if he's the kind that will let it fester up inside of him. Getting beat is one thing but getting knocked flat on your buttocks in front of your men is another. It would take a pretty big man not to hold some kind of grudge."

Rosa's smile faded. "The sooner we are away from here the better. I want only to think of the wedding, nothing more."

Monte drew up on a slight rise and suddenly dismounted. He didn't signal us in any way so Rosa and I merely reined in and waited.

"I think we are very near," Rosa said softly. "He's looking at something, something that is below him."

Leading his horse, Monte disappeared down an incline. We followed but held our horses to a slow walk. It was midday. There was no breeze and not a cloud was to be seen.

"This will be tough on him," I whispered. "I can't imagine what he must be feeling."

"It is hard for Monte to feel anything," admitted Rosa. "Whatever happens today, I think maybe it will be good for him. Good for both of us . . . as husband and wife."

Rosa was doing her best to be optimistic but I could hear the doubt in her voice.

"The other day," I said, "Monte said he thought he recalled a spring but the last time we talked about this place, all he remembered very clearly was his father's death, the cactus he was thrown into, and the face of Norroso. Has he remembered anything more?"

Shaking her head, Rosa said somberly, "No. All he sees is his father dying. All he hears is the death rattle and all he remembers feeling was pain, pain like he was on fire."

Rosa and I drew up on the crest of the rise where we had last seen Monte. The land below us fell away into a gentle slope and, two hundred paces from us, ended in a level five-acre field of dried grass, a field bounded on the north and south by a pair of shallow brush-choked arroyos. At the upper end of the field, a few blackened timbers jutted skyward, marking the location of what once was a building. A short distance from the timbers we saw a patch of ground where, oddly, nothing grew. In that bare earth we could make out two rectangular mounds of gravestones.

Rosa dismounted and then I did the same.

"We will wait here," Rosa said. "He should be alone when he greets his parents."

Both my parents were living, as were my grandparents. I had never been to a funeral, much less experienced the loss of someone I loved. Uncertain of what Rosa meant, I asked, "Do you think he'll say anything . . . Will he talk to them?"

Rosa glared at me. "Of course he will!

They are his father and mother. And they will hear him just as they do on *Dia de los Muertos.* This is a special day. His parents will be happy that he has finally come home. This is a happy day for them. Who would not speak to his father and mother on a day such as this?"

Such beliefs were completely foreign to me but I could see that Rosa found a good deal of solace in them. I, on the other hand, having no familiarity or faith in the Day of the Dead celebration, was nervous to the point of being jittery. A few feet from where I stood, renegade Apaches had tortured a man to death and killed a woman. Standing there in a moment of solitude, I could almost sense the unspeakable horror the two of them must have felt. Their fear and panic seemed to linger in the stillness of the air.

Was I, I wondered, standing where an Apache had once stood as he looked down upon his unsuspecting prey? Was the ground down below still stained with blood? Was there any such thing as ghosts? Did the tortured spirits of Monte's brutally murdered parents wander about their ranch longing for justice?

I tried to imagine what it was like thirty years before, before automobiles and airplanes. The cabin would have been totally isolated and indefensible. There would be no hope of calling on anyone for help. And the possibility of attack, whether from outlaws, bandits, or Apaches, would have been a constant threat. Here, Monte's family was alone, completely susceptible to any impulse that lurked in the hearts of evil men.

Try as I might I could not fathom why anyone would choose to live under such dangerous conditions. It seemed utterly foolhardy and yet over the years, countless American pioneer families had made the same choice as Monte's parents. And, tragically, many had paid with their lives.

My eyes drifted to the area surrounding the small patch of land that had been Monte's home. I had no special outdoor skills, no training whatsoever in warfare, and yet, had I been present thirty years ago, I knew I could easily have snuck up on the very rise where I stood. With those below hard at work, I would have had no trouble hiding behind any of a dozen nearby bushes or stones. Then I could have taken careful aim. It would have been a simple task to shoot them down, ransack the cabin, and then flee unobserved and unmolested into the Guadalupe Mountains or back into Mexico.

I realized then that the Apaches needed no great skill to massacre ranchers or farmers or even to evade capture. Anyone could see that in the empty expanse of the vast Southwest, settlers and travelers presented no more of a challenge to the Indians than did proverbial "sitting ducks."

How then was it possible, I asked myself, that so many men and women ignored the obvious risks they were taking? John Slaughter and those at the Rancho de la Osa came to the Southwest with small armies, and the haciendas in Mexico were virtual fortresses. But to me, moving to such a place as Monte's parents had done, especially so close to the border, seemed almost suicidal.

For the better part of an hour Monte sat by the graves. Finally he rose and walked to the charred timbers. We watched as he repeatedly circled the ruins of the cabin, each time making a wider and wider arc. The fifth time he circled he stopped, dug in the grass with the tip of his boot, and then reached down and picked something up. He pecked several times at whatever it was with his finger. Then we heard a faint tinkling. Seconds later we realized it was the unmistakable sound of a small bell.

Suddenly, however, the bell fell silent. For

several minutes Monte did not move and both Rosa and I began to worry.

"What do you think he found?" I asked. "He seems to be in some sort of trance. I don't like the looks of it."

"No se," Rosa replied, her tone heavy with apprehension. "Whatever he found must be important. I think he is remembering something. Maybe this time . . . maybe this time the memory will be a good one."

Slowly, Monte turned his head, gazed up at us, and motioned for us to join him. I took a deep, uneasy breath and glanced at Rosa. The fervent, heartfelt concern I saw in her eyes at that moment was, to say the least, soul stirring. She had seen more than her share of tragedy and suffered more hardship than any woman I knew, yet she never expressed even a hint of self-pity in my presence. Rosa could not hope to forget her own past and yet there she stood, worrying about the man she loved and what terrible memory he might have unearthed.

Leading her horse, Rosa started down the incline. Following close behind, I realized all too well that the ground beneath my feet was sacrosanct. The soil had been stained with human blood and was part of a bleak landscape that once heard the frantic shrieks of a panicked mother, the groans of a dying man, and the throaty, agonizing screams of a six-year-old child.

Monte belonged here. Rosa was a victim of the revolution and had earned the right to walk on such hallowed ground. I, however, was William Cabott Weston III and had suffered nothing, had endured nothing. As I neared the graves, I was overwhelmed with a sense of unworthiness, yet at the same moment felt deeply honored for having been granted the privilege to be present.

Stopping a few feet in front of Monte, Rosa tied her reins to a Yucca stalk as I tied mine to a stunted mesquite. I was a step behind Rosa when she asked, "What did you find?"

Monte held out his hand, pinching what appeared to be a necklace between his thumb and forefinger. "This."

Taking the necklace, Rosa examined it closely with me peering over her shoulder. "It is made of braided rawhide," she said, "a ring of braided rawhide with a bell on it."

"I didn't know it was a bell until I dug the sand out of it," Monte explained. "Then I shook it and it rang. After all this time it still rang." Monte pointed to the corroded bell. "If that green is scraped off, the color would come through. That bell is made out of copper."

Rosa respectfully held the necklace up to the base of her neck. "Was it your mother's?"

"No," Monte said and then with a queer look in his eyes slowly shook his head. "It's not a necklace."

"Then what is it?" Rosa asked.

"It's a dog collar," Monte answered solemnly. "I think it might have belonged to our dog."

"You remember a dog?" I said, feeling a wave of relief. "You remembered your dog?"

"When I heard the bell," Monte shrugged, "she just came out of nowhere. I could see her looking at me, panting with a kind of grin on her face. She was yellow and she wore the bell so we could keep track of her. I think she might have been a watchdog or maybe helped with the cattle."

"Is there more?" Rosa asked guardedly and then gently handed the collar back to Monte. "Did you . . . remember anything more?"

For a moment, Monte gazed out into the open desert toward Mexico. "A few things, maybe. Only . . ."

"Only what?" encouraged Rosa.

"I seem to remember the dog's name but

something's out of place. I can't say what but something's not right."

"And the name," asked Rosa. "What is the name you remember? If you think of it maybe other memories will follow."

Monte frowned suddenly. He glanced at Rosa and then at me. "Yeah, I might recall the name but nothing else. I tried but it could be that I don't want to remember much more than that."

Rosa studied Monte for several seconds as both of us waited to hear the dog's name. Finally, she was unable to wait any longer. "Well, what was the name of the dog?"

Monte glared at Rosa for several seconds and then reluctantly grumbled, "Buttercup."

"Buttercup?" I repeated. "It sounded like you said Buttercup."

Monte let out a disgusted grunt. "What kind of a fool name is that? Who would name a dog Buttercup?"

Turning, Rosa looked at me with a question in her eyes.

"Buttercup," I said, "is a flower. A yellow flower."

Rosa's eyes narrowed in thought and then she smiled. Turning back to Monte, she reached out and tenderly placed the palm of her hand on his chest. "Maybe your father and mother were very gentle people,

Monte. If that is true they would have treated you with much kindness. So, when your memory returns you will have many good times to remember instead of just the bad ones."

"I don't know about that," Monte muttered. "Buttercup! That name doesn't make any sense. None at all!"

I have to admit it was difficult for me to imagine a man like Monte Segundo being reared by anything less than a pair of timber wolves. I had no explanation for the name Buttercup but I was convinced that to raise a child like Monte, his parents had to have been, at the very least, strict disciplinarians.

"Anyway," said Monte, his mood darkening, "the Apaches killed the dog the day they came."

Rosa gave Monte a pat and then took her hand away. Going to her horse, she unbuckled one of the saddlebags and took out a small bundle wrapped in linen. "These are not real," she said uncovering two small bouquets of white flowers, "They are silk. I would like to put them on the graves of your father and mother if that is alright with you, Monte."

I glanced at Monte but seeing the expression on his face, I quickly looked away. That moment, that intimate and profound split second, should have been shared by the two of them, shared in private. And there I was standing in the middle of it!

"You brought flowers?" Monte said, struggling to get the words out.

"They are your parents and soon they will be mine. I wish to greet them and let them know about me. And then I will tell them how I plan to make you happy. They have been waiting a long time to know what has happened to their son."

"I didn't bring anything," Monte confessed. "I didn't even think about it."

Rosa shook her head. "You came to them, Monte. After so long, you found them and now you are all together. That is more than enough. You will come many times to visit and then you can bring flowers. Today you bring yourself. For them, there is no greater gift."

Monte was speechless. All he could manage was a nod. When he did so, Rosa clutched the flowers close to her chest and, taking slow deliberate steps, reverently started for the graves.

"She is an extraordinary woman, Monte," I said, "remarkable in so many ways."

Monte hesitated. "Maybe too good for the likes of me," he said matter-of-factly but with a hint of bitterness in his tone that I found unsettling.

I could sense something was bothering Monte and my guess was that it concerned Rosa. I was in no position to offer advice but with the wedding only weeks away, I attempted to intercede with a bit of humor. "You're not getting cold feet, are you?" I asked, ending my question with a weak chuckle.

Monte watched Rosa kneel beside the graves and then his eyes narrowed. "She seems so at home with all of this. It doesn't bother her at all."

"She's been through so much herself," I said, "the revolution, the Carrancistas. She's tough as saddle leather and yet still compassionate and caring on the inside. It's a gift, if you ask me. A kind of miracle, I suppose.

"But what you and your family went through here, Monte . . . it must be terribly hard on you."

Monte took his eyes off Rosa. After taking a quick glance over his shoulder, Monte scanned the hills to the east and then searched the western plane to our left. "Something's not right, Billy. I've got the feeling something's wrong, bad wrong."

Monte was clearly agitated. I couldn't imagine why but having learned to trust his remarkable instincts, I also began to look around. "Do you think someone's coming? Maybe Jones and his men?"

"I don't know," Monte answered. "I don't know what it is. But as soon as Rosa gets through, we should head back. We can make it to Slaughter's by sundown and get a good night's sleep before we start our cattle drive. We need to get out of this country."

Searching the horizon, Monte rested his palm on the grips of his Colt and then began tapping the hammer with his thumb. A minute passed and then he abruptly untied the reins of his bay and stepped into the saddle.

"You stay here, Billy," Monte said, "I'm going to take a look around. I won't be far. Just far enough."

Without further explanation, Monte wheeled his horse, trotted back up to the crest of the rise, and disappeared out of my view. A bit perplexed by Monte's unusual behavior, I started to get nervous. I untied my reins and, checking on Rosa, was relieved to see that she had not noticed Monte's departure. I certainly didn't understand his actions and my gut told me Rosa would be deeply upset when she realized Monte had ridden away and left her alone on such a hallowed and momentous occasion.

Holding the reins of my horse, I kept an eye out for Monte but concentrated my attention on Rosa. It was a beautiful day under a deep blue sky and her kneeling comfortably between the two graves presented a picturesque and touching scene. As the minutes passed, however, I was starting to get nauseous.

This was not the way it was supposed to happen. This was a special reunion, a sacred moment that Monte and Rosa should have shared. But now Monte had inexplicably turned his back on Rosa and ridden away.

At the time I wasn't a praying man but I was desperate. "God," I pleaded, "please get Monte back here before she turns around. She doesn't deserve this!"

I had barely finished my frantic petition when Rosa came to her feet. I could see the white of the bouquets that she had wedged in the stones. Her hair glistened in the sun and I could hear, but not make out, her final farewell to Monte's father and mother.

Her head was bowed when she turned and started walking toward me. I swore under my breath, and at that very instant, she looked up. I could see her glancing about searching for Monte. She kept walking but now her head swiveled from side to side. Slowly, her brow furrowed with confusion.

When Rosa was several steps away I swallowed hard. "He thought someone was coming," I said, bending the truth as far as I dared. "He had one of those feelings that he gets. He went to take a look around. You know how he gets sometimes."

I hoped Rosa would fly into a rage and swear a blue streak. That would have meant everything was as it should be, that everything would be alright. But somehow, I knew she would not react that way. And this time my instinct proved correct.

Rosa's eyes filled with sadness, an emotion I had never seen in her. And then I saw something worse. I saw defeat.

"He's confused, Rosa," I offered. "Maybe this visit was too much for him."

Tears formed in Rosa's eyes but did not fall. "I will get my horse," she said sorrowfully. "We will go now."

As Rosa went to the yucca where she had tied her horse, I mounted so that I could see over some of the taller brush. "Monte, damn you!" I whispered. "Where the hell are you?"

With Rosa trailing behind me, I rode northeast following Monte's tracks. A half hour later and far in the distance, I caught sight of movement. "What are you doing way over there?" I asked myself, watching Monte ride through the brush. A moment passed and then I saw him dismount by a large boulder, a rust-colored stone that jutted up from a dense thicket of creosote. From that point on, I could see nothing but his horse.

Rosa rode up beside me. "Do you see him?" she asked despondently.

I pointed. "See that boulder way out there? That's where he got off his horse."

Rosa peered toward the boulder but said nothing.

Unable to look Rosa in the eye, I said, "We better go find out what's going on."

Rosa sighed heavily. "I don't think I want to know."

"I'm sorry, Rosa," I said feebly, and then retook the lead.

In minutes we came upon Monte's horse at the base of the boulder, a single stone that rose several feet above our heads. Monte, however, was nowhere to be seen.

"There was only one set of tracks," I said. "He didn't follow anyone out here."

Studying the ground below I saw where a bootheel had gouged the sand. Thinking I might be able to make out Monte's trail, I dismounted. I had taken only a few steps when I heard him say, "I'm up on the rock, Billy."

Startled, I looked back at Rosa. Even though she had heard Monte's voice, she made no move to dismount. Instead, she sat in dejected silence.

Making my way to the far side of the boulder, I glanced up and saw Monte sitting and staring at the Guadalupe Mountains. "Day or night," he said, "I can see a lot better than most. And from up here I can see for miles."

"Do you see something?" I asked.

"Not now," he said. "Not then, either."

"What?"

"I remembered something else, Billy."

Looking up at Monte, I could plainly see his face, a face full of regret. "That's good. So things are starting to come back to you?"

Monte took a deep breath and then let it out slowly. "You know that feeling I had a few minutes ago, that something was bad wrong?"

"Sure I do."

"I know what it was now. It's because it was all my fault."

I assumed Monte was referring to leaving Rosa at the graves. I knew she could hear him and she at least deserved an explanation. And I hoped, for both their sakes, he had a damned good reason for what he had done. "What was your fault?"

"I was on the roof," Monte began, his tone distant, "just about as high as I am now. That was my job because my eyes were so sharp. All I had to do was sit there and keep watch."

Monte wasn't making any sense so I asked, "What roof are you talking about?"

Ignoring my question, Monte continued. "I wasn't paying attention that day and I didn't warn them. Ma and Pa died because of me. I should have seen them coming. We'd been warned. That's why they had me go up on the roof. All I had to do was keep watch. But I didn't do it."

It took a moment but then Monte's words began to register. I hung my head and groaned, "Oh, no. Not this, too."

Vaguely, I was aware that Rosa had come to stand next to me. "Monte," she said, her voice now full of compassion, "you were only six years old. Even full-grown men cannot see Apaches coming. No one sees the Apaches coming unless they want to be seen. You are not to blame for what happened."

Monte's unblinking eyes were transfixed on the mountains. "It was up to me to protect them. That's why I was up so high. Six is old enough to keep watch."

"Monte," Rosa said but this time her voice

was more firm, "not three months ago you were here at the graves of your parents. Then, you risked your life to protect an innocent man from the *rurales*. Before that you protected the village of San Miguel from bandits, and before that you rescued the mother of a small boy from the soldiers of Ojo Federico." Rosa paused and then stepped closer to the boulder. "Do I have to remind you," she said sternly, "what you did for me in Las Palomas? No one could protect more people than you have."

A long count of ten passed and then Monte turned his head. Gazing down at Rosa, he said, "Rosa, you deserve better than the likes of me."

Rosa scoffed, doing her best to appear lighthearted, "Maybe it is that we deserve each other. But, now, you and I are together and we are here on this border where there is much danger. I need you to protect me just as you need me. We are meant for each other, Monte Segundo. The Holy Father brought us together for a reason. This I know in my heart. For me, there is no one better than you and there never will be."

Slowly shaking his head, Monte confessed, "Rosa . . . you beat all I've ever seen."

"Yes, I do," agreed Rosa, her voice once again ringing with confidence. "Now get off of that rock and onto your horse. The sun will rise tomorrow and it will be a new day. Then we will be on our way, driving the cattle to the Rancho de la Osa just as we planned. After that, together, we will go to the mission at San Xavier and be married."

Hearing those reassuring words, I heaved a sigh of relief. But that relief was short-lived. Monte had only started to climb down off the boulder when a wave of fore-boding washed over me. It might have been the fact that where Monte Segundo was concerned, nothing ever seemed to go as planned. Or perhaps it was Rosa's invocation of "Holy Father," but for whatever reason, from out of nowhere the ominous saying "Man proposes, God disposes," rumbled like distant thunder inside my head. Not believing in premonitions, I mounted my horse all the while telling myself the incident was simply an example of random and mindless fortuity. However, soon after returning to the Slaughter ranch, I wasn't so sure.

The sun was rapidly sinking below the western mountain peaks when we rode around the back of the icehouse and started for the corrals. Monte and Rosa, side by side, were leading when they abruptly reined in. Wearily, I closed the distance between us and followed their eyes.

Forty paces in front of us, several mounted soldiers were gathered around a single horse that was tied to a hitch rail just outside the fenced corral. I recognized Captain Miller and Lieutenant Jones. Then I saw Tin-Pan come through one of the corral gates leading two saddled horses.

Monte took off his hat and wiped his forehead. "Should we wait here or ride on in and put the horses away?"

"They look excited," Rosa said. "Maybe they will pay no attention to us."

Before we could decide what to do, Tin-Pan gave the reins of his two horses to a soldier and started for us on foot. As he approached, even in the fading light, I could see by the expression on his face that something bad had happened.

"I got stew on the stove for you folks," said Tin-Pan. "I got to go out with the army and won't be back 'til maybe tomorrow. Them cows of yours is all ready for you to take, so you're in good shape. And if I'm not back by morning, there's eggs and bacon in the kitchen icebox. Help yourselves to whatever you want."

Not having the good sense to leave well enough alone, I asked, "What's wrong?"

Tin-Pan sighed. "Them two Eastern women didn't come back like they should have. But one of 'ems horse just come walking in. Captain Miller's going to send out a patrol to Guadalupe Canyon to fetch 'em. But the soldiers don't know the canyon so I'm going along as guide."

"But it will be pitch-black when you get there!" I protested.

"Yeah," agreed Tin-Pan. "There won't be no moon 'til later on tonight but them soldiers has got electric hand lanterns, only they call 'em flashlights nowadays. I suppose they can see good as long as the batteries hold out."

Rosa sneered, "Wait until morning. One night sleeping on the ground will not kill those women."

"They'll likely show up riding double," Monte said. "Why don't you just wait it out?"

Emphatically shaking his head, Tin-Pan said, "No sah! Them two officers, Miller and Jones, won't have it. If you asked me I'd say that Lieutenant Jones is sweet on Miss Appleton. And like most wet-behind-the-ears lieutenants, he's got it in mind to be a hero."

I glanced over at Jones, who was looking our way. "That doesn't surprise me."

"Say, that reminds me," said Tin-Pan, "the lieutenant showed up this afternoon with a shiner the size of a goose egg. Said he rode into a low-hanging branch while he was out on patrol."

"Is that so?" Monte grumbled.

Tin-Pan thoughtfully rubbed the gray stubble on his chin. "You wouldn't know nothing about that, I suppose?"

Monte replaced his hat. "You suppose right."

Eyeing Monte, Tin-Pan mused, "That's mighty peculiar, seeing how there ain't many trees out where he was patrolling. I'd say they ain't a single one out there that's got a low-hanging branch."

"Pendejas!" sneered Rosa. "Those women thought they could ride!"

"That was my mistake," admitted Tin-Pan. "They said they wanted spirited horses, like the kind Mizz Viola rides. So, I give 'em a couple of hers. I'm thinking I shouldn't of done that. Riding in a fancy arena ain't the same as rough country riding, full of wild game and all. Something, a turkey maybe, probably flew up and one of them horses swapped ends and threw Miss Thorndike."

"Why Miss Thorndike?" I asked.

"Because that horse over there is the one

144

I put her on. I'm thinking Miss Appleton's still got her mare and, like you said, they're likely out there riding in double."

Monte turned to Rosa and me. "Well, since we've got nothing to do with tree limbs and lost women, it looks like we can go on in and take care of these horses."

Somewhat impressed with the lieutenant and the cover story that he had presented to Captain Miller, I agreed, "Fine with me. I don't think there'll be any problem."

"Tengo hambre," said Rosa, as Tin-Pan started back toward the soldiers. "Are there peppers in the stew?"

Tin-Pan turned and grinned. "No. But I put 'em out in a bowl as a favor to you, Miss Rosa. Them two women had it coming and I'd say they learned a good lesson."

Nudging his horse, Monte headed for the corral gate closest to us, which was a good thirty paces west of the soldiers. Leaning down, he unlatched the lock and pushed the gate open. Without so much as a glance to our left, we rode into the corral and unsaddled our horses. I tossed some flakes of hay on the ground but all three horses went straight to the water troughs, buried their muzzles, and started sucking up water.

After forking our sweaty saddles and blankets over the fence rails, Rosa slid her

Mauser from the scabbard and then looped her bandolier over her shoulder. "I will sleep lightly tonight," she gloated, "and when I hear the women come in I will get up to greet them. I will say to them in English, 'How was your ride?' and then, after I have enjoyed the look on their *gringa* faces, I will go back to bed and sleep. Or if it is time, I will go to the kitchen and make a noisy breakfast for us."

"I'm worn out," I said, noticing that the soldiers were forming into a column of twos. "I'll be lucky to stay awake long enough to eat."

As the three of us started back toward the corral gate, I counted six soldiers, not including Lieutenant Jones and Tin-Pan who were at the head of the column. Jones gave Captain Miller a sharp departing salute and then the column broke into a gallop heading east into the fading light.

Monte was latching the gate behind us when the captain rode over. "Mr. Segundo, do you still intend on leaving in the morning?"

"Yeah. Before sunup."

Miller shifted his weight causing his saddle to creak. He seemed uneasy. "How much before sunup?"

Rosa rested the butt of her rifle on the

ground. "Why do you ask us this?"

Miller glanced at Rosa, then back to Monte. "Tin-Pan and I had a talk before the troop left," began Miller. "He's a talker so I don't know how much of what he says is tall tales and how much is real. But, in private, he told me that if we didn't find the women tonight, that he wouldn't be of much help come daylight. He said his eyesight wasn't what it used to be and that in order to follow a trail a person had to be able to see up close. He claims a good trailer has to see things, details as small as a single thread or strand of hair, even the tracks of insects. That sort of thing."

"He's right," Monte said.

"Well," Miller admitted, "rumor has it that you can follow a trail as good as the Apache scouts."

"We're leaving an hour before sunup," Monte said. "And once we start with those cows we're not turning back . . . Not for any reason."

Miller stiffened but before he could respond, "Man proposes, God disposes," once again echoed inside my head. Only this time, hearing the maxim caused my pulse to jump.

"And what if it turns out," demanded Miller, "that the women were taken by Vil-

147

listas or Carrancistas, Mexican forces that are attempting to lure the United States Army across the border? If that happens to be the case, Mr. Segundo, and you refuse to help, it would only serve to reinforce the commonly held belief that your allegiance is indeed with Mexico, that you and your friend were . . . and are traitors to your country."

Monte glared at Miller. "I don't have to prove anything to you or anybody else! We're leaving an hour before sunup."

Miller was clearly enraged but he managed to control his temper. "An hour before sunup?" he questioned and then, taking one last look at Monte, spun his horse and trotted up toward the mesa and his garrison.

Rosa hefted her rifle. "What was that about?"

Monte thoughtfully chewed on the inside of his lip. "The captain's worried about those women. He seems to believe Miss Thorndike might not have been thrown from her horse. If she wasn't, that could mean big trouble. And if that's the case, it's going to be up to him to find those two and bring them back. He's the commanding officer and he knows he can't do it with the men he's got."

"You mean," I asked, "he thinks someone

kidnapped the women?"

"His mind is just running wild," Monte said. "He's been listening to too many of Tin-Pan's stories about the old days. And having to guard the border against a Mexican invasion has made him jumpy. Those women are probably halfway home already. Let's eat and get to bed. Tomorrow we'll be five miles from here before the sun hits our back."

Listening to Monte's confident assertion of what the morrow would bring caused me to flinch. I expected the haunting words of the centuries-old maxim to once again rattle my brain, but to my relief, I heard nothing. Feeling a bit foolish for having succumbed to a twinge of primitive superstition, I boldly whispered the last lines of "Invictus," a poem my father often recited for my reassurance and edification.

"It matters not how strait the gate,
How charged with punishments the scroll,
I am the master of my fate:
I am the captain of my soul."

CHAPTER 4

Exhaustion produces a sublime and extraordinarily deep sleep. Thus, the pounding coming from the door of the bunkhouse took several seconds to muddle through the blackness and register as an unsettling noise. I awoke but just barely and did not open my eyes.

Monte stirred. "Who are you," he growled, "and what do you want?"

"Captain Miller sent me," responded a voice that filtered through the door. "I'm Corporal McIntosh."

After muttering a few choice swear words, Monte asked, "Why didn't the captain come himself?"

"He didn't say, sir."

"Sir?" huffed Monte and then rolled over in his bunk.

"Yes, sir."

I forced my eyelids open. They felt dry, almost scraping over my eyeballs. Tossing off my blanket, I lit a kerosene lantern that was next to my bunk. Blinking against the glare of the small flame, I asked, "What time is it?"

McIntosh answered. "Just after four, a couple of hours before sunup."

Taking the lantern, I stumbled to the door and opened it. It took a moment but then I realized McIntosh was the corporal who had been with Jones the day before, the one Monte jerked off his horse and slammed onto the ground.

"We found one of the women around midnight," offered McIntosh, "but she was unconscious when we came up on her."

"So what?" grumbled Monte, as he slowly sat up. "Put her to bed and send for a doctor."

"She's not here yet," replied McIntosh, "but she's on her way. We had to make her a travois. We used yucca stalks. Nobody thought they would work but the old . . . Tin-Pan showed us how. We lashed some together and wrapped our blankets around it. Those stalks worked pretty as you please."

Half awake, I yawned. "How did you get here so fast?"

"I don't know why, but late last night Captain Miller sent a courier out to find us. He met up with us just after we found the woman. That was a couple of hours ago. Once we told the courier that one of the women was still missing and we'd lost the trail, he took out some written orders and handed them to Lieutenant Jones. And you should have seen the look on the lieutenant's face when he read those orders! He was fit to be tied!

"After he read those orders, he sent me here to fetch you. He said I was to get here as quick as I could, that I had to get to you no later than five o'clock."

"An hour before sunup," quipped Monte.

"Yes, sir. Those were the captain's orders. Make sure I got here at least an hour before sunrise."

"Your captain," said Monte, "is a real son-of-a-bitch."

"My sentiments exactly, sir."

Monte sighed and then joined me at the door. "Go on, Corporal."

"There's no sign of the other woman, the one named Miss Appleton. No sign at all."

"What do you mean no sign?" snapped Monte. "She was riding a thousand-pound horse. Even the army should be able to follow her tracks."

"Yes, sir. That's what the . . . that's what Tin-Pan said. There were tracks at first that we followed on up the canyon but then, after a while, they disappeared. There weren't any to be found anywhere. But we did find a button. It was at the spot where we lost the trail. I doubt we'd have seen it in the daylight. It reflected when one of the flashlights hit it."

Monte's obvious irritation vanished. "Whose button?"

"It had to be Miss Appleton's because it didn't match anything the lady we found was wearing."

"That would be the one named Miss Thorndike," Monte said. "When will she get here?"

"At the rate they're going," replied McIntosh, "not 'til after sunup. But the lieutenant still has five soldiers with him. Them and Tin-Pan stayed up in the canyon to keep up the search."

Disgustedly, Monte shook his head. He knew the answer to his next question but he asked it anyway. "And why did the captain send you over here to wake us up?"

"To deliver this message," replied McIntosh as he inhaled deeply and came to attention. "Sir, the captain requests that you volunteer your services and help us find the lost woman."

"Volunteer," scoffed Monte. "The last time I tried that, I got court-martialed. Is that all, Corporal?"

"No, sir. Tin-Pan gave me a message for you, too."

"And what would that be?"

"He said that if you volunteer, you should bring your woman, Miss Rosa, with you."

A grim expression suddenly strained Monte's face. He knew Tin-Pan was an experienced frontiersman and if he wanted Rosa present it meant only one thing. Tin-Pan was convinced the woman was not lost but had been taken by force. And if she were to be found alive, Tin-Pan understood all too well that Marzel Appleton would need a woman to tend to her.

Monte looked at me with a question in his eyes. I shrugged and said, "We have no choice. The cattle will just have to wait a few days. Under the circumstances, Señor Cruz will understand."

"We'll need supplies," Monte said, as he went to his bunk and pulled on his boots.

"Yes, sir. We're loading two pack mules as we speak. The army will supply your mounts and rifles. And we'll have a dozen troopers with us. We'll be ready to leave as soon as you're ready."

"Rosa likes her Mauser," Monte said. "Leave her saddle scabbard empty. And Billy's coming, too."

"I'll get another mount," agreed McIntosh. "We'll meet you in front of the corrals."

With that, McIntosh spun on his heels and disappeared into the night. I, on the other hand, lumbered back to my bed trying to blink moisture into my eyes. Setting the lantern down, I reached for my boots.

"Why would Tin-Pan want Rosa along?" I asked.

Monte shook his head. "Because, for whatever reason, he's convinced Miss Appleton was kidnapped . . . kidnapped and worse."

Not fully awake, I asked, "Kidnapped? Do you really think someone would kidnap Miss Appleton?"

Monte huffed. "I sure as hell wouldn't."

"But," I protested, "Tin-Pan said rustlers wouldn't dare harm a woman."

Monte stood, and was already buckling his gun belt. "He said American rustlers wouldn't. He wasn't so sure about Mexicans. And I'm guessing that's who has her. Maybe it's like the captain said, the Mexicans want to try and start something like they did in Columbus. Kidnapping an American woman, one like Miss Appleton, would kick up a lot of dust in Washington."

Shoving one foot into a boot, I grunted,

"But the Mexicans' chance of starting a war with us has come and gone. They would be wasting their time."

Tossing a serape over his shoulders and then tugging his hat down tight, Monte said, "South of the border they don't know if they're coming or going. There's always die-hards and renegade generals. Who knows what they might do?"

Finished with my boots, I slid into my shoulder holster and then donned my hat and vest. "Do you think she's strong enough, Miss Appleton, I mean. If . . . if she is molested?"

Monte's answer was emphatic. "No, I don't. And I doubt there'll be anything Rosa can do for her, either. But women are a peculiar breed. You never can tell how they'll act."

Following Monte out the door, I said wistfully, "I could use some coffee."

"Me, too," Monte said, "but we've got no time. While I'm getting Rosa, why don't you see if Tin-Pan left any biscuits lying around in the kitchen? Maybe some cheese, anything we can stick in our pockets."

As before, we entered the rear of the ranch house. I veered right into the kitchen and Monte went left. He was on his way down the hall to the bedrooms when he passed by the large dining and living room. A lantern, its wick turned low, was burning on the mantel of the fireplace. Below it in the flickering amber glow, Monte caught a glimpse of John Slaughter's stuffed easy chair. Curled up in it and covered with a blanket, Rosa was fast asleep.

Monte paused. Rosa's hair hung straight and glistened in the light. Her breathing was slow and easy. "I hate to disappoint you," Monte whispered. "But those *pendejas* are not coming."

Stepping softly, Monte crossed the room. He knelt beside the chair and then gently touched Rosa's shoulder.

Though she was still asleep, Rosa said softly, "Monte?"

Smiling, Monte gave her a gentle shake. "Rosa, wake up."

Rosa jerked. She stared at Monte and then blinked. "What is it? Are they here?"

"They're not coming. Something happened. Miss Thorndike is hurt and Miss Appleton is missing."

After rubbing her eyes, Rosa glanced at the front windows. "What time is it?"

"A little after four. But Billy and I are going to help find Miss Appleton."

"What!" said Rosa, flinging the blanket onto the floor. "Why would you do that?

They deserve whatever has happened to them."

"Maybe . . . maybe not. Tin-Pan's still out looking for Miss Appleton and Miss Thorndike was unconscious when they found her. The last anyone heard, she hadn't come to, so nobody knows what happened. Only . . ."

Rosa glared at Monte. "Only what?" she demanded.

"Sometimes Tin-Pan can give the impression he's a brick short of a full load but I can guarantee you he's no fool. He's lived on the border for years and he thinks Miss Appleton was taken, that it was likely bandits that took her. He asked if you would come along . . . in case we find her alive."

Slowly, Rosa turned her head and looked into the shadows. "And he thinks because of what happened to me in Las Palomas, that I could help this woman? Is that what you think?"

"I don't think about that at all, Rosa. That had nothing to do with you and as far as I'm concerned, it never will. Asking you to come along was Tin-Pan's idea and he doesn't know what happened at Las Palomas. He was just thinking of Miss Appleton, that's all there was to it."

After a long silence, Rosa said softly, "I

know you will go to look for her. And I go where you go. What happens after that, we will see."

That was the moment I entered the room with a flour sack full of cold biscuits. Seeing Monte next to Rosa, I said cheerily, "I've got cheese and biscuits for our breakfast."

Without a word, Rosa got up out of the chair, picked up the blanket, and folded it. At that point, I sensed that my entry was ill-timed and yet at that juncture there was nothing I could do. Monte stood up but did not take his eyes off Rosa as she neatly draped the blanket over the arm of the chair.

"I'll be out by the corral," I said and then awkwardly made a quick exit out the front door. Crossing the lawn, I swore under my breath. Monte had obviously just told Rosa what happened to the two women and why Tin-Pan had asked that she accompany us to the canyon. Tin-Pan was merely assuming Marzel Appleton would need another woman's support, but I knew the request for her inclusion in the search had likely opened wounds that, for Rosa, had barely had time enough to heal.

A lantern hung from a sycamore branch that stretched out over the corral fence, its humble light illuminating the drab green uniforms of the army patrol beneath it.

Some of the men were mounted while others were holding their reins and smoking cigarettes. McIntosh emerged from the soldiers and then, with a cigarette between his lips, waved me over.

"I'm leading the troop," said McIntosh. "How about you ride up with me for a while? I've been stuck out here for weeks. I'd like to know what's going on in the civilian world."

Considering the situation, I assumed Monte and Rosa might want to be alone for a while anyway so I welcomed the chance to give them some privacy. "Sure."

McIntosh pinched the cigarette between his thumb and forefinger, inhaled deeply, and then tossed the stub of tobacco onto the grass. As he exhaled he crushed the cigarette under the sole of his boot. "I was a first sergeant before Captain Miller busted me down to corporal. That was on account of a bar fight I had in Douglas. I got into it with some of the National Guard stationed there, the ones from New Jersey."

Surprised by the sudden revelation, I responded with a noncommittal, "You don't say."

"Yeah," continued McIntosh, "I've been in more than my share of knockdown dragouts so I know a thing or two about fighting. But I never saw anything like what happened yesterday with your friend and Lieutenant Jones.

"And you can include what happened to me, too. Sometimes I can be a real ass. I figure I got my comeuppance and so I got no hard feelings about it. None at all. Monte Segundo's alright with me."

"I'm glad to hear that," I said, uncertain where the conversation was headed.

McIntosh pointed at three saddled horses that were tied to the corral fence, and we started walking toward them. "You ever ride with a McClellan saddle?"

"No. I've never even heard of one."

"You'll like it," McIntosh said. "There's no horn like there is on a cowboy saddle but it's got an open seat and, like the Mexican saddles, a high pommel and cantle."

Nearing the horses, McIntosh indicated a small roan. "This one'll go all day for you. I figure you or the woman can ride him."

"He'll do," I said, and catching movement from the corner of my eye, I turned and saw Monte and Rosa coming across the lawn. "I'll adjust my stirrups and then catch up to you, Corporal."

McIntosh glanced at Monte and then his eyes lingered on Rosa and her Mauser. "So,

161

she really is coming along?"

"Looks like it."

"I'll say it does," muttered McIntosh, his tone carrying an undertone of vulgarity. "Does she take that damned rifle everywhere she goes?"

"Yes, she does," I said and then on impulse added, "And she can hit a man-size target at five hundred yards."

McIntosh nodded toward the soldiers that were now forming a column of twos. "I'll meet you up front," he said and then went for his mount just as Monte and Rosa approached.

Indicating the two horses tied next to me, Monte said, "I take it these two are for us,"

I glanced at Rosa but it was too dark to read her expression so I went back to adjusting my stirrups. "That's right, and they're outfitted with McClellan saddles. Have you ever seen a McClellan?"

Monte stepped up to a big sorrel gelding and rubbed his hand down the leather seat of the saddle. "Never have. There's not much to them, is there?"

"I've ridden on them," said Rosa. She spoke matter-of-factly, which put me at ease. Then she went to the remaining horse, a bay gelding only slightly taller than my roan. "They are easy on the back side," she

162

added, shoving her Mauser into the saddle scabbard and then tying a large leather bag onto a saddle ring.

"Corporal McIntosh asked me to ride with him for a while," I offered. "I'm curious to find out why he's friendly all of a sudden, so I accepted his offer."

Tightening his cinch, Monte said, "Watch yourself, Billy. I don't trust him."

"I'll do that," I said and then untied my roan. Not knowing what to expect, I stepped into the stirrup, threw my leg over, and cautiously settled into the flimsy army saddle. The seat was surprisingly soft and the rifle and scabbard under my left leg were hardly noticeable. Shifting my weight left and right, I said, "Not bad, not bad at all."

"If you figure out what McIntosh is up to," Monte said, "let me know as soon as you can."

I hadn't considered that the corporal was up to anything but I was well aware that Monte could read men as well as most could read a book and his hunches were seldom wrong. "I'll do that," I answered and then trotted past the column of eleven troopers and drew up beside McIntosh.

The corporal looked over his shoulder and, seeing Monte and Rosa mount up, waved his hand and voiced a drawn-out,

"Yo-oh!"

To my surprise, instead of a gallop we broke into an easy trot. "How long will it take to get there?" I asked.

"We'll make it right about first light," replied McIntosh. "It's so dark I can barely make out our old tracks and besides, there's no point in getting there before dawn."

Apparently, McIntosh had not heard the stories of how Monte Segundo could see in the dark but since there seemed to be no practical reason to increase our rate of travel, I decided not to mention Monte's unique ability.

"Was Miss Thorndike badly hurt?" I asked.

"All we could see was a bunch of scratches and a big knot on the front of her head. Of course the lieutenant didn't let us look her over all that good . . . if you get my meaning. But the best we could figure from the sign was that her horse got spooked and threw her into some brush. When she landed she whacked her skull on a rock. And then, a while later, she crawled out of the brush and onto the trail that runs up and down the canyon. That's where we found her, right in the middle of the trail."

"Sounds like a concussion," I said.

A metal shoe clanged into a stone and

McIntosh's horse stumbled. The corporal swore as his mount regained its stride. "I hate night rides."

We rode for several minutes, all of the riders rising and sitting in perfect rhythm with their horse's steps. A sliver of a moon high over the mountain peaks ahead bathed the desert around us in a soft silver-blue glow. "You know," began McIntosh, "yesterday the lieutenant had us soldiers convinced that you and your friend were traitors and that the two of you joined up with the Mexicans to fight against the United States. And he told us about the lies you were supposedly telling at the court-martial, especially the one about Segundo whipping five Mexicans in a bar. He got the whole post riled up with his stories. We all made up our minds based on what he told us."

I made no comment so McIntosh continued. "Anyhow, after what Segundo did to the lieutenant yesterday, I changed my mind. I think them stories the lieutenant claimed were lies were mostly true. And I want you to know I don't believe the two of you joined up with the Mexicans. I don't think you're traitors at all."

"I'm glad to hear that," I said.

McIntosh paused and then chuckled. "How'd you like that story the lieutenant made up about getting his shiner from riding into a tree? Wasn't that a good one?"

I tried to get a look at McIntosh's face but it was lost in the moon shadow cast by his hat brim. However, judging from the tone of his voice I assumed he was smiling. "I thought it was an honorable lie, if there is any such thing."

McIntosh sneered. "Honorable, hell! He was covering his own ass. Captain Miller doesn't know anything about that fight. If he did, the lieutenant would be in hot water, but as it is, he got away with it.

"Now me, an enlisted man, I get into a brawl in Douglas and get busted down to corporal and, on top of that, get slapped with double duty. But an officer, let me tell ya, they can get away with anything."

"Well," I said, "at least Lieutenant Jones put it all to rest and there won't be any more trouble."

I heard McIntosh spit. "Don't kid yourself. The lieutenant's still mighty sore. He was claiming he wasn't ready when Segundo slugged him, said the sun was in his eyes."

I shook my head. Knowing full well that Jones was lucky Monte had held back and only hit him once, I said, "What you heard about what happened in that cantina in Mexico, the report about Monte and the

Mexican soldiers, is absolutely true. I was there and I saw the fight from start to finish. Your lieutenant would be wise to consider that fact."

"So you was in Mexico?" questioned McIntosh. "You and him were really down there like the lieutenant said?"

"Over a month. We rode a couple of hundred miles south of the border."

"Huh," grunted McIntosh, "you don't say?"

We rode a few seconds more and then McIntosh asked, "How was it down there? Did you see many señoritas as pretty as Rosa? Damn, I never dreamed a Mexican could be that good-looking. Are the women friendly to whites?"

At first, I found McIntosh's comments offensive but then I remembered that I had had a similar reaction to Rosa when I first saw her. And since he had been isolated on a military post for quite some time, I excused his ungentlemanly question. "I was too busy to pay much attention to the women."

"Well, how did the villagers treat you, knowing you were Americans and all?"

"The villagers," I answered, "treated us alright. But the Villistas and Carrancistas wanted to shoot us on sight."

McIntosh rode in silence for a moment. "But what about that writer fella?" he protested. "He had a name like ambrosia or some such. He went down to Mexico drinking and carousing. It sounded like he had a hell of a time."

At first, I had no idea who McIntosh was referring to but then a name came to me and with it something I had heard. "You mean Ambrose Bierce," I said. "Rumor has it Villa's men killed him after he got drunk and insulted their general. I believe it was near Ojinaga or maybe Sierra Mojada. Either way, the Mexicans say he didn't survive two months once he crossed the border.

"I'd say the only whites that are safe in Mexico are the Germans. They work both sides down there, the Carrancistas and the Villistas, all the while trying to get a war started between us and Mexico. They want to tie up our army so we can't go overseas and fight in Europe."

"You think they can do it?" questioned McIntosh. "Start a war between us and Mexico?"

I shook my head with absolute confidence. "No. They came close a few months back but that time has come and gone. Mexico will never attack us. And now the revolution in Mexico is all but finished. It's dying on the vine."

"You sure about that?"

"Yes, I am," I sighed. "And unlike our Civil War, a lot of good Mexicans will have died for nothing. Nothing's going to change in Mexico, no matter how much blood is spilled. Nothing has changed in hundreds of years."

McIntosh seemed to perk up. "So the revolution's almost over, then?"

"There's some fighting far to the south but Villa is finished. As soon as General Pershing withdraws from Colonia Dublán, this whole border crisis will be over."

"You don't say," chirped McIntosh. "Now, that's good to know."

I was about to mention the hordes of bandits that infested Mexico when a pinpoint flicker of light pierced the blackness ahead of us. "Did you see that, Corporal?"

"Sure did," replied McIntosh as the light began to flash on and off. "That'd be the boys pulling the travois. They must have heard us coming."

Turning in his saddle, McIntosh ordered the patrol to halt. He then reached inside his saddle pocket and removed a flashlight. Turning it on and off several times he signaled the oncoming troopers. "I wonder if that woman has come to yet. I'd sure like to know what the hell happened."

After receiving a return signal, McIntosh ordered his patrol off to one side of the trail. In minutes I could make out four horses and three riders coming toward us in single file. When the leading horse and rider drew to a halt beside McIntosh, I could see that the third horse in line had a travois tied to it.

"Is she still out?" asked McIntosh.

"Yeah," came the reply. "She moaned a couple of times when we went over some rough spots but that's about it."

"Alright," said McIntosh. "The trail's all yours."

"Did you bring supplies?" asked the soldier. "The lieutenant was in such an all-fired hurry that we left the post with nothing to eat."

"We got two mules with us," replied McIntosh. "They're loaded."

"I'm glad somebody's got some brains," grumbled the soldier as he nudged his mount and continued down the trail.

When the travois passed by all I could see was a bundle of blankets. When I glanced up, however, I detected a faint glow in the eastern sky. "How did you lose the trail of Miss Appleton, anyway?" I asked. "Did she ride over some rock or was it too dark to see her tracks?"

"No, her tracks just up and sort of disappeared. At least that's what that old Tin-Pan said. But that's on account he can't hardly see. Towards the end, our flashlights ran low and then none of us could see much of anything. Come daylight, those tracks will be plain enough."

At the time, McIntosh's explanation made perfect sense, and I foolishly concluded that by midday Monte would have located Miss Appleton and before the day was out we would be on our way back to Sasabe. With that confidence, I grew even more optimistic. "Maybe they found her already," I said. "Wouldn't they build a big fire, one that could be seen from a distance? Then if she was lost she could see it and find her own way back."

I heard paper rattling, then McIntosh struck a match and lit up a cigarette. After taking a long puff he asked, "Want a smoke? I got Murads, good Turkish tobacco. Everybody else at the post smokes Fatimas or those new Camel cigarettes. But not me. I'm a Murads man."

"No thanks," I said. "I never took up smoking."

"Suit yourself, but you don't know what

you're missing with these smokes."

"Thanks for offering."

"You were asking about building fires and such," continued McIntosh between puffs. "They'll do that, alright. The lieutenant will have the men firing off shots and yelling all night long. He'll do anything he can to find that woman before we get there. That way he can get all the glory. The last thing he wants is to have Segundo find her.

"Word is going around those two women belong to big-shot families back East. The lieutenant's cocksure that if he finds Miss Appleton it'll get him a promotion and a ticket out of Arizona. But even if it's your friend that finds her, he'll figure out a way to take the credit. You can bet your bottom dollar on that."

I felt a breeze coming fresh off the hills and the sky above the looming mountain peaks was turning lemon yellow. "The lieutenant is welcome to it. Monte doesn't give a tinker's damn who gets credit for that sort of thing."

McIntosh huffed indignantly, "I'll bet he'd care if there was a big reward."

I had learned nothing of importance from the corporal and he was beginning to annoy me so I gathered my reins. "It's getting light," I said. "It's time for me to get out of your way and drop back to the rear."

Determined to make that my final comment, I immediately veered a few feet into the brush and allowed the column to ride by. A long, dusty minute passed before I heard the muffled thudding of hooves. Making out two dingy forms riding toward me, I nudged my horse back out onto the trail and waited. A moment later, Monte and Rosa drew up next to me.

"How'd it go with the corporal?" Monte asked.

"Mostly he just asked about Mexico. But I did learn that Lieutenant Jones isn't happy you're coming to help Tin-Pan. According to the corporal, he doesn't want to share the *glory* of finding Miss Appleton."

Monte swore. "Jones is a bigger fool than I thought he was. If we don't find her he's likely going to be the one that gets all the blame. I wonder if he's thought about that?"

I was startled by Monte's comment. "What do you mean, 'If we don't find her'?"

Pointing down at the trail, Monte said, "What do you see down there?"

It was light enough to make out the trail, especially since a dozen horses had just churned up the sand and rocks. "Horse tracks," I answered. "Lots of them."

"That's right and that's all anybody can

see. If Jones and his soldiers rode up the canyon past where the trail disappeared they'd have trampled all over any sign that was left. If they did that, trying to find that woman will be like looking for a needle in a haystack."

CHAPTER 5

The sun had yet to rise when we entered the narrow mouth of Guadalupe Canyon. However, it was light enough to see color and I was amazed that only a few feet into the canyon, I saw green everywhere I looked. A minute later we rode under a canopy of leaves that clung to the limbs of a massive sycamore tree. A few feet beyond it we passed by a small grove of oak trees interspersed with several large junipers. Willows grew in clumps all along the edges of a dry streambed, many of them draped with the long tentacles of invasive vines. And a few feet above the water line, yucca and prickly pear grew in spiny clusters all along the base of the canyon walls.

I had never seen a desert oasis but I had no doubt that the floor of Guadalupe Canyon qualified in every respect. It was as if we had entered a different world and yet had ridden only a few hundred feet. "Look

at these trees!" I exclaimed. "This is amazing!"

"They are beautiful," Rosa said, clearly as
impressed as I. "There must be water not
far under the sand."

"Look there," I said, catching sight of
some large birds scurrying up the canyon
wall.

"Turkeys," Monte said. "This canyon
must be full of animals. Tin-Pan said the
Apaches used to travel back and forth
through here and now I can see why. If I
was a cattle rustler or bandit this is sure
enough where I'd come. Who would have
thought it could be so different in here?"

Ahead of us on our right was another massive sycamore. Its outstretched limbs grew
high over the trail and merged with the
vertical wall of rose-colored rock, forming a
magnificent natural arch.

Riding under the arch, I exclaimed, "This
is incredible. Simply magnificent."

"Yeah," agreed Monte. "But think of all
that these old sycamores and oaks have
seen. Going and coming, going and coming
for all those years. Imagine all the bad men
that looked at these same trees and very
same rocks. No telling what all happened in
here."

Rosa, suddenly uneasy, slid her Mauser

out of its scabbard and rested it across her lap. "This is a beautiful canyon," she muttered, "but it has the feel of death. Many have died here, died at the hands of others."

I glanced around. Perhaps it was the power of suggestion but for reasons I could not begin to explain, I also suddenly felt uneasy. In fact, I felt the same sense of foreboding I had experienced at Monte's homestead. Only this time I had the distinct sensation that several pairs of lifeless, sinister eyes were watching my every move.

We rode on and the canyon began to meander, the trail gradually rising and then descending gently, only to rise again. I lost count of how many times we crossed and recrossed the dry streambed that, in times past, had cut its way through the entire length of the shadowy chasm. At no place along the way was the canyon more than one hundred yards wide, but everywhere I looked trees grew in abundance. An hour after we had entered the canyon and just before the sun cleared the mountain peaks, Monte, Rosa, and I rode into the encampment that had been set up the previous night by the first patrol.

Smoke rose from a smoldering campfire that had been built in a somewhat rocky but open area. Here and there ropes were stretched tight between trees, and the newly arrived troops were busy tying their horses to the guy lines. Off to the side, McIntosh was speaking with Lieutenant Jones. Tin-Pan, now wearing a pistol and sweat-stained broad-brimmed hat, had seen us ride in and was walking toward us.

Disgustedly shaking his head as he approached, Tin-Pan said, "I tried to tell 'em last night, Mistah Segundo, I tried my best, but the lieutenant wouldn't listen. I'm afraid they done gone and chewed up half the countryside."

Monte swore under his breath and dismounted, and then Rosa, keeping hold of her rifle, also stepped down. I stayed in my saddle and glanced at the soldiers. Most were now busy unloading the pack mules and apparently getting ready to make breakfast. A few, however, stood scowling in our direction.

"Alright, how bad is it?" Monte asked glibly.

Something about Tin-Pan was different but I couldn't put my finger on it. At the time I assumed it was the hat and pistol he wore, or the fact that he was upset. It wasn't until later that I realized it was his eyes. Instead of being soft and friendly, they had turned hard as flint.

"We come up the trail last night using those hand lanterns. That was easy enough. Then the tracks quit on us. I couldn't find none no place. It was like they up and disappeared. I told the lieutenant my eyes couldn't see up close especially with them lights they had. I said we had ought to wait for daylight. He was thinking my idea over when that rider come in and give the lieutenant his orders from Cap'n Miller.

"The Cap'n's orders said that if he didn't find Miss Appleton right off, he was to send somebody back to the post as fast as he could so they could fetch you. The lieutenant done like he was told and sent the corporal back. But that's when the lieutenant decided to keep on looking for Miss Appleton even though it was plumb dark. Him and his three men went riding up and down the canyon, shooting and hollering and building fires. They was at it all night and just now come back."

Monte took off his hat and scratched his head. "Well, that cinches it. Finding her now will be next to impossible."

Looking at Rosa and then me, Monte said, "We might as well turn around and go back."

"Only one thing," said Tin-Pan. "There was something I did notice about those tracks that all of a sudden up and disappeared. The soldiers thought maybe the wind come up and filled 'em in but not me. Even though I couldn't see so good, I got the feeling they had been rubbed out, like somebody had rubbed 'em out on purpose."

With his eyes narrowing in thought, Monte replaced his hat. "I heard somebody found a button. Where'd they find it?"

Tin-Pan turned slightly. Keeping his back to Jones and McIntosh he pointed by sliding his finger across his chest. "Over that a way. And so far, I kept most of the soldiers away from there. Might be there's some sign still left thereabouts."

"We have come this far, Monte," Rosa said, "why don't we stay until sundown? Then we will have done enough to satisfy everyone. If we leave after sundown we can still get back to Señor Slaughter's ranch by midnight, sleep, and be off by tomorrow morning."

"Well," sighed Monte, "let's decide what to do after we get something to eat. Those soldiers dragged us all the way out here, so the least they can do is cook us some breakfast."

"Sounds good to me," I said, eagerly dismounting. "I could use a cup of coffee, strong coffee."

With Tin-Pan following, we led our mounts past the guy lines over to some nearby junipers and tied them off. Several soldiers were already picking up stones and building more fire rings while others were gathering wood. Lieutenant Jones was studying a map and doing his level best to ignore us.

"Alright Tin-Pan, let's take a look at where that button was found," Monte said. "That's a peculiar thing to lose, don't you think?"

Tin-Pan nodded somberly. "Mighty peculiar, I'd say," he answered and then started for a nearby rock face that jutted straight up out of a bed of creek sand, sand that was anything but smooth.

Stopping short of the dry creek, Tin-Pan squatted and pointed as he waved his hand back and forth. "You see where the soldier's walked around some but, thank goodness, only a couple came over. One of 'em found the button right where that rock wall meets the sand."

Monte squatted beside Tin-Pan as Rosa and I stood behind them. "The flashlight picked up the button?" asked Monte.

"It reflected the light like a piece of glass would. Likely we'd never of seen it if was daylight. The button's almost the same color as the sand."

Going to his hands and knees, Monte inched forward and then, bending at the elbows, lowered his head and looked up and down the creek bed. Raising back up, he stood for a moment and peered up and down the rock wall. Then he took two steps out onto the sand and went back down on all fours. Again bending his elbows, he closely studied the grains of sand.

Turning upstream, Monte meticulously repeated the same process twice more. After five minutes he stood up. "Damn," he mumbled, bushing the sand off his pants. "Damn it to hell."

"What is it?" Rosa asked.

Tin-Pan, who had been squatting the whole time, took a moment to straighten up. "Brushed over?"

"Yeah," Monte said, "Somebody used a branch. They even sprinkled dead leaves around when they were done."

"What does that mean?" I asked but, more or less, already knew the answer.

"Spreading leaves and such is an old Apache trick," said Tin-Pan. "But bandits would know that trick, too."

"Then they're in Mexico by now," Rosa said. "The border is not far."

Tin-Pan shrugged. "Depends if them bandits got what they come for. If they did,

I'd say you're right. They'd be way over the border by now. But if they come after something and they didn't have it yet, they might still be around and have Miss Appleton with 'em."

"What would they be after on this side of the border?" asked Monte.

"Gold, silver maybe. Could be they come to rob somebody or they could be after cattle. All them soldiers fighting in the revolution got to be fed. There probably ain't a cow left over there. Beef would be worth a lot of pesos."

Mixing with the jumbled voices of the soldiers, I heard the popping of burning wood. I glanced over my shoulder and saw two blazing fires, each with a coffee pot edged into the flames. "The soldiers are making coffee," I said, then noticed Jones was coming our way. "Never mind, here comes the lieutenant."

"Do you want to tell him," Tin-Pan asked, "or do you want me to?"

"You go ahead," directed Monte. "He'll take it better from you."

Tin-Pan waited. When Jones was a few steps away he said, "We got bad news, lieutenant. Me and Mistah Segundo agrees that Miss Appleton was took by somebody because this place here, where we found the button, has been brushed over to hide what happened."

Jones stopped in his tracks. His eyes narrowed with disbelief and then, a few seconds later, his face flushed red with anger. "Who would dare? Who would do such a thing!"

"Well, Lieutenant," said Tin-Pan, "like I said before, white men wouldn't likely harm a woman, leastwise not a white woman. So I figure the ones that took Miss Appleton had to be bandits, bandits with trail savvy."

Jones shot a contemptuous glance toward Rosa and then spewed, "You mean Mexicans!"

"That's my guess, Lieutenant."

Fuming with rage, Jones struggled to control himself. "So that means it could have been bandits or Villistas or even Carrancistas. In fact it could have been anyone that wanted to cross our border?"

"I suppose," confessed Tin-Pan. "I shouldn't have let 'em go riding off alone like they done. I should'a come with 'em, like it or not."

For the first time since the fight, Jones made eye contact with Monte. "What are the chances of picking up their trail?"

"How long," Monte asked calmly, "did you and your men look around after you got here last night?"

"Until our flashlights burned out. Two or three hours at least."

"Then I would say the chances of finding a brushed-over trail is next to nothing. All you can do now is scout around and hope you stumble onto something. And that could take days . . . if you're lucky."

"Damn this border!" snarled Jones. "It's nothing but a useless line in the sand. This whole country is nothing more than a lawless no-man's-land!"

"Mistah John has done alright for hisself," returned Tin-Pan, his voice surprisingly firm. "But it takes men with the bark on to make a living on the border. And women, too."

Jones snorted. "The sooner I'm away from this Godforsaken country the better. You can have it."

"We will stay until sundown," Rosa said. "That is all the time we can spare."

Regaining his composure somewhat, Jones asked Tin-Pan, "If bandits took Miss Appleton and were headed back to Mexico, what would be the fastest route?"

"The fastest," answered Tin-Pan, "is the way we came in. The mouth of this canyon is split down the middle by the borderline. In fact, back there we was in Mexico for a minute or two when we first rode in. But starting from right here, there's lots of old Apache trails that bandits could use and a good many of them trails lead over to Mexico. The best one, though, is up the canyon a few miles. Right about the New Mexico line the canyon widens out some and a good trail forks off of this one and then climbs up out of the canyon heading southeast. If you follow it for four or five miles you'll cross over a mountain pass and then go between a bunch of rocks called White Gate. Once you're through the gate, you're in Mexico."

"Very well," snipped Jones. "After we eat we'll ride up the canyon. You can show me that trail to Mexico. I'll concentrate my men in that area. We'll fan out and cover every inch."

With her eyes riveted on Jones, Rosa laughed scornfully. "You think Mexicans are fools! But it is you that is *tonto*. You will never find that woman."

Before Jones could react to Rosa's unexpected insult, Tin-Pan hurriedly asked, "Why do you say that, Miss Rosa?"

"Because," Rosa said, "the border is not far from here. If a Mexican was going to return to Mexico with a stolen woman he would not waste time covering his tracks."

Tin-Pan thought for a moment. "You're

right as rain, Miss Rosa. And now that I think on it, I'll wager the most likely way they went was up the canyon toward Animas Valley. There's a spring up that way and over in that valley there's lots of cattle to be had without much trouble."

Jones stiffened. "So that I'm clear, Tin-Pan, you are saying we should continue up the canyon and not branch out toward Mexico?"

"Mostly that's right. But just in case, I'd still send a couple of men to check out that trail to White Gate."

"I would expect you to ride with one of the parties," Jones said.

Tin-Pan nodded agreeably. "Sure enough, Lieutenant. It'd be best if I went with the men riding toward Mexico. I know about where the border is and how far we can go without running into trouble."

"What do you mean," drilled Jones, "you know *about* where the border is?"

"Once you're out of this canyon going south," explained Tin-Pan, "you're in mountains, steep ones, sometimes with rock ledges that are a hundred feet high and a half mile long. Every way you turn, there's draws and bluffs and such. There ain't nothing up that way that is straight enough to mark out a boundary line. It's not like it is when you look out from the post or from Douglas. Up in those mountains a man has to do some guessing about which country he's in."

Jones thought for a moment. "If it's that bad, I doubt they would risk taking a civilized woman up there. I'll send Corporal McIntosh that direction. Tin-Pan, I want you with me."

Jones cleared his throat. He hesitated and then eyed Monte. "And you, Mr. Segundo, what will you be doing?"

"Staying around here," Monte said flatly. "We know for sure that the woman, and at least one other person, was on this very spot. There may still be some sign left that hasn't been ridden over. That's what I'll be looking for."

Ignoring Rosa completely, Jones shifted his attention to me. However, before he could ask the obvious question, I volunteered what he wanted to know. "I'll ride with you and your soldiers if you don't mind. Another pair of eyes might come in handy."

"Very well," returned Jones, suddenly assuming an air of authority, "I'll have Corporal McIntosh handle your assignment. We leave within the hour."

Jones spun on his bootheels and went back

to his men who were now gathering around the cookfires holding metal cups. The sun's rays were creeping down the northern walls of the canyon but had not yet reached the floor. A gentle breeze rattled the leaves in the trees overhead, bringing with it the rich aroma of coffee.

"Do you think they'll loan us some cups?" I asked. "That coffee smells awfully good."

Tin-Pan tipped his head indicating the soldiers. "Them over there ain't made up their minds about you and Mistah Segundo," he said, but then with a twinkle in his eye added, "but if me and Miss Rosa go over there together, I'm guessing them boys will pretty near give us whatever we want."

With a knowing smile adorning her lips, Rosa handed me her rifle. "You hold this, Billy. I don't want to scare them."

I chuckled, "They'll learn soon enough. And, if you would please, have them put some sugar in mine."

Rosa glanced questioningly at Monte. "Sugar?"

Monte, who always took his coffee black, smiled faintly. "Why not?"

As Tin-Pan and Rosa strolled over to the cookfires, Monte and I went back to the junipers where we had tied our horses and found a good place to sit. We hadn't been there long when Rosa brought our coffee. Minutes later, she returned with more bacon and hardtack than we could eat. And by the time breakfast was over, she had every soldier in camp, save the ever-aloof Lieutenant Jones, at her beck and call.

With Jones and Tin-Pan leading and me in the rear behind the pack mules, the patrol of fifteen enlisted men started off at a brisk walk, working our way up the canyon heading in the general direction of the Animas Valley. A half hour later, under a hot sun, we halted in a level field of grass that, perhaps, covered half an acre. The brushy mountains to the south rose sharply, but those to our left were more barren and rolled gently to the north.

After ordering the pack mules to be securely tied off, Jones split his fifteen soldiers into four squads. Two squads were sent to scour the northern hills while McIntosh's squad was to investigate the trail that led south toward Mexico. Jones, reserving the easiest route for himself, took Tin-Pan and four men and continued up the canyon with the goal of reaching the nearest water, which was at the Spring of Contention. Everyone, unless engaged in hot pursuit, was to rendezvous back at the grassy area no later than two o'clock that afternoon.

One of the squads riding north only had three troopers, so I was assigned to it, and with me predictably relegated to ride in the rear, my squad started out of the canyon intending to search the hills to the northeast. However, the moment we bounded over the crusted high-water mark of the canyon our horses became entangled in a thicket of knee-high catclaw, a plant aptly named for its small but vicious thorns.

Skirting that impenetrable barrier, we zigzagged around several others just like it, climbing steadily higher until we reached our first ridge. Pausing to give our mounts a breather, the soldiers clustered together, leaving me to myself. The troopers, all of whom were close to my age, began speaking softly amongst themselves. Occasionally, one would glance back at me, and before the horses had fully caught their wind the voices began to grow louder. I thought I heard Rosa's name mentioned and then a second time I heard it very clearly. A moment later, one of the soldiers turned his drooping head toward me and flashed a lecherous grin.

Realizing the vulgar nature of their conversation, I kicked my horse in the flank, and galloped around them. I didn't stop until I came to the junction of another smaller ridge that branched off to the east. Knowing full well the soldiers would not follow a civilian, I rode up the eastern ridge a short distance all the while pretending to scout for tracks. After a minute or so I glanced back and saw that the three troopers had once again started riding up the main ridge. After they passed the ridge I was on, I retraced my steps and fell in behind them. However, for the rest of our fruitless scouting mission I hung back and kept out of hearing distance.

A little after two o'clock the four of us arrived back at the rendezvous point just as another squad was in the process of dismounting. Off to the south of the pack mules I saw Monte leaning back against a shaded log. Rosa sat beside him with her Mauser across her lap.

Glad to be rid of the soldiers, I rode over to them. As I dismounted, I asked, "Did you find anything after we left?"

"Nothing that made any sense," replied Monte. "What's going on here?"

Tying off my horse, I said, "Me and those troopers over there were divided into two squads of four and sent up into the hills off to the north. Another squad went up a trail that goes into Mexico. The lieutenant took

Tin-Pan and his four men and kept going up the canyon. Everyone was supposed to meet back here at two o'clock, which, according to one of the troopers I rode with, was twenty minutes ago."

Rosa glanced past me. Pointing up the canyon, she said, "Someone is coming now."

I blinked, trying to focus my eyes, but the glare was too much. "It's Jones," Monte said, "and he's still riding stiff as a board."

We watched as Jones rode among the troopers. He asked questions but did not dismount. Finally, we heard him raise his voice, "Has anyone heard from Corporal McIntosh?"

Several soldiers shook their heads. Jones then ordered his squad to dismount, and even though it was almost October, everyone scattered to find some shade.

Tin-Pan started across the grass. Ambling up to us, he stiffly took a seat on the log beside Monte. "We didn't see nothing except some cat tracks. Nothing at all."

I removed my hat and plowed my fingers through my sweaty hair. "Maybe the squad that went toward Mexico found something. They're still out."

"How 'bout you, Mistah Segundo?" asked Tin-Pan. "You find any sign back where that button was found?"

Monte was about to answer but suddenly paused. Then he said, "Here comes that squad now."

We listened but heard nothing. A few seconds later, however, the faint rumble of hoofbeats drifted down the southern wall of the canyon.

"I hear 'em now and they're coming fast," Tin-Pan said. "Maybe they got good news."

The first trooper to appear bounding down the steep trail held the reins of a trailing horse that bore a man wearing a sombrero, clearly a Mexican. The tail of the Mexican's horse was tied to the reins of another horse ridden by a second Mexican. Behind the second Mexican came a third and fourth horse, also tied reins to tail, with two more Mexicans riders. All four Mexicans wore tattered sombreros and were covered with trail dust.

Riding close behind the fourth Mexican came two more soldiers. As the line of men and horses galloped toward Lieutenant Jones, I looked for the fourth member of the squad but none appeared. After realizing the missing trooper was Corporal McIntosh, I turned my attention to the center of the clearing where everyone was gathering.

"Well, look at that!" Tin-Pan said excitedly. "Looks like they caught some bandits."

In seconds Jones and his men surrounded the Mexicans. It was only when they were jerked off their horses that I noticed their wrists had been tied in front of them. "I'm going to see what's happened," I said.

Tin-Pan stood up. "Me, too."

Oddly, Monte seemed disinterested. "I'll wait here."

"How good is your Spanish, Tin-Pan?" Rosa asked.

"I know a few words is all. I can't talk a lot of Mexican and have it come out right."

Rosa sighed. "Then, if the *gringos* need me, they will have to come to me."

Tin-Pan and I hurried over and stopped at the outer edge of the clustered men. Tiptoeing to get a look at what was going on, I was shocked to discover the faces of the Mexicans were grotesquely swollen and crusted with dried blood.

"We tried to get it out of them, Lieutenant," one of the soldiers explained, "but they wouldn't talk. They act like they don't speak any American."

"Where is Corporal McIntosh?" demanded Jones.

"We rode up the trail this morning," explained the soldier, "and the corporal got so tired he said he had to stop pretty soon

195

and get some sleep. He told us how he had to ride all last night to fetch that Segundo fella and how he was plumb wore out. We all kept riding south for a while longer until we got to a place where the trail forked and part of it went east. Corporal McIntosh ordered us to scout a couple of miles up the trail that took off to the east. He said he was going to rest up at that fork for a while and then he'd ride on up the south fork for two or three miles and check it out. We was to meet him on our way back right there where the trail split but when we got back he wasn't there. We saw where he rode on up the other fork though, so we figured he took his nap, like he said he was going to, and then rode on south a ways. Only we figured he hadn't got back from his scout yet.

"Anyhow, when the three of us rode up that eastern trail, we had gone about two miles when we seen these Mexicans riding fast on a ridge across from us. They didn't see us so we crossed down into a draw that was thick with mesquite. When they come riding by us we jumped 'em and got all four without firing a shot. We had 'em dead to rights and they knew it. They give up without a fight.

"Then, figuring that woman was close by,

we decided to question the sons-a-bitches. But they didn't tell us nothing. So, the three of us decided you'd want these kidnapping greasers as soon as you could get 'em. And, anyhow, we knew when Corporal McIntosh got back from his scout he could read our tracks we left there at the fork and he'd know to follow them back here."

"Good enough, Private," Jones said, "and well done."

Jones then looked over the heads of the men and spotted Tin-Pan. "Tin-Pan, we need you to interpret."

Shaking his head, Tin-Pan admitted, "My Mexican ain't good enough. You'll be needing Miss Rosa for that."

Standing a few feet to my left, a soldier waved his arm in the air. I recognized him as one of the three vulgar troopers that had been in my squad. "I'll get her, Lieutenant."

"Very well," snapped Jones. "Go."

The private trotted over to where Rosa and Monte sat and stopped two paces in front of Rosa. Looking down at her, he smirked, "The lieutenant wants you . . . to interpret for him."

"If the lieutenant wants me to interpret," Rosa said flatly, "tell him to bring the prisoners over here to me."

The private chuckled. "You're not in Mexico anymore, little *señorita*. If you know what's good for you, you'll sashay over to the lieutenant and do what he says."

Monte merely cleared his throat.

Rosa grabbed the barrel of her rifle with her left hand and, placing the butt on the ground, hoisted herself to her feet. She casually brushed some debris from the rear of her skirt using her right hand and then grasped the rifle barrel just below her left hand.

"That's it," grinned the trooper.

Rosa glanced at the soldier and without the slightest warning, flipped her rifle upward, slamming the edge of the buttstock squarely in the private's crotch. Folding instantly, the soldier slowly dropped to the ground.

"You have your answer, soldier boy," Monte said to the groaning trooper. "Now before you really get her mad, you best go tell the lieutenant what she said."

Standing where we were, Tin-Pan and I saw the private hit the ground, but no one else seemed to have noticed. "The problem with lots of young folks nowadays," Tin-Pan said blandly, "is they got no manners."

"Amen to that," I seconded and then thinking of the soldier's vulgar behavior

198

earlier in the day, I added, "But what goes around, comes around."

The private rolled over and managed to get up on his knees. He struggled to his feet and then tried to stand up straight but it was no use. Still in agony and hunched over, he stumbled across the clearing, made his way through the other soldiers, and finally back to Jones. Forcing himself erect he said painfully, "She says, Lieutenant . . . to bring the prisoners to her."

Jones clinched his teeth, causing his jaw muscles to ripple underneath the stubble of a day-old beard. He took two deep breaths and then shoved the aching private aside. "Bring the prisoners," he ordered and then began shouldering his way through the men.

The soldiers latched onto the Mexicans and, following their lieutenant, half drug them across the clearing to where Rosa stood waiting. When Jones stopped in front of her, the rest of the men, including Tin-Pan and me, spread out and formed a half circle around the prisoners.

Sneering at Rosa, Jones asked, "How should I address you?"

Rosa glanced at me with a question in her eyes. "He means what should he call you? Miss Rosa maybe or Miss Bustamonte?"

Rosa lifted her chin. "To you, I am Miss

Bustamonte."

"Please, Miss Bustamonte," began Jones, his politeness conspicuously salted with bitterness, "ask these men, if you would, where they took Miss Appleton."

Rosa glared at the swollen faces for several seconds and then spoke to the prisoners in Spanish. The moment she did, all four men began speaking at once, their frantic words voiced at an astounding speed. I had no clue what they were saying but it was crystal clear the men were terrified. Instead of having them slow down or even speak one at a time, Rosa merely listened patiently as each man pleaded his case. A full five minutes passed before the last man stopped speaking, the Mexicans seemingly having exhausted whatever defense they cared to offer.

In the following silence, Rosa took a moment to think. "These men say," she said, choosing her words carefully, "that they are here to buy cattle for their village. They say they are not bandits and they did not deserve to be beaten. Up on the trail, they understood enough to know that your soldiers kept saying 'woman' but they know nothing about any woman."

Without turning to his men, Jones asked, "Troopers, did you search the Mexicans?"

"Yes, sir," came a reply.

"And what did you find?"

"They had one old Winchester, two pistols, a butcher knife, and a good pair of German binoculars. In their pockets all we found was a few extra cartridges and a couple of small silver coins. That's all there was, sir."

"So," announced Jones as if he were in a court of law, "since these Mexicans have no money they are obviously lying about coming across the border to buy cattle."

Rosa spoke again in Spanish. This time the Mexicans did not respond. Rosa spoke again but took more time to formulate her question. There was another long silence and then one of the Mexicans muttered a confession.

"He says," Rosa explained, "they were lying. They did not come to buy cattle but to steal them. They say there is no food in their village and everyone is hungry. The Villistas and Carrancistas have taken everything. They admit to you they are rustlers but they still say they know nothing of a *gringa,* a white woman. Nothing at all."

Jones thought for a moment. "Now that we have established that they are liars and rustlers, ask them if they saw Corporal McIntosh, ask them if they saw a lone rider, an American soldier."

Rosa asked the question, which elicited a silent but agitated response from all four Mexicans. Then, one of the Mexicans mumbled a few words.

"They say no. They saw no one."

"No!" snapped Jones. "Look at them! I don't believe a word of their story. Not one damn word!"

Recovering from the rifle butt to his groin and feeling the security of numbers, the vulgar private called out, "How do we know she's telling the truth, Lieutenant? She's a Mexican just like them."

Monte had been leaning back against the log and watching the proceedings with apparent disinterest. Now, however, he came to his feet. I had seen the smoldering light that was in his eyes on more than one occasion and I knew that if Jones and his men were not careful, the gates of hell were about to be ripped off their hinges.

"Because I say she's telling the truth," Monte said. "That's how you know. And any man that calls her a liar is calling me a liar."

I couldn't see Jones's face but I saw him stiffen and then the back of his neck turn red.

Tin-Pan had lived half his life in the West.

202

He knew what Easterners could not possibly comprehend and that to call a man like Monte Segundo a liar to his face meant there was a better than even chance someone was about to die. Hoping to head off a disaster, Tin-Pan broke in, "There's one way, Lieutenant, to find out if what them Mexicans is saying is true."

With a dozen soldiers standing behind him, Jones was brimming with confidence. "And what would that be?" grilled Jones.

Speaking in an inoffensive tone, Tin-Pan suggested, "We best talk about that in private, Lieutenant. You and us civilians, that is. It just might be that even if there was a kidnapping, that the United States Army don't want to stir up no trouble with the Mexican government."

For all his faults, I will say that Jones was a quick study. He knew we were close to the border and the United States was daily on the verge of armed conflict with Mexico. He also understood that an international incident, perpetrated by either government, could easily instigate an all-out war.

Jones spun and faced his men. "Those that captured the prisoners will take them over by the mules and stand guard over them. The rest of you go back and check your gear and tend to your mounts. Be prepared to move out."

As the men sullenly dispersed, Tin-Pan and I came forward and stood next to Monte and Rosa. When the troopers were far enough away, Jones turned to Tin-Pan. "What is it you have to say?"

Tin-Pan shoved his hat back with the point of his finger. "With Mistah Segundo's help and me knowing the landmarks, we can backtrack up to where your boys caught them Mexicans. Then we can backtrack just them four Mexicans and see where they come from and what they was up to. That won't be no problem at all."

"That sounds too simple," objected Jones. "Why just you and Segundo?"

"Because, from the sound of it your boys was already in Mexico when they caught them Mexicans. That's one problem since they had no right to do that. And the second thing is, we'll most likely be backtracking to the south. That would take us deeper into Mexico all the time we're looking for where them tracks lead. So, maybe it's best only us civilians go up that trail. We can cross the border without no trouble to speak of. But if the Mexicans come up on American soldiers in their country there could be hell to pay. And, to keep everybody happy, it'd be best to get Miss Appleton out of Mexico quiet-like. You know as well as anybody that one wrong move and the whole borderland could go up in smoke."

"No!" Jones said impulsively but then caught himself. He took a moment to think. "Your idea does have some merit. However, under the circumstances, I can see that I am left with no alternative other than to make an in-field command decision. Unorthodox as it may be, I will be coming with you and I'll also be bringing along two of the troopers that caught the Mexicans. They can show us where they overpowered the prisoners and then, as a unit, we'll follow those tracks until we find Miss Appleton . . . no matter how far they go. But it is to be understood that my men and I are going in an unofficial capacity."

"Why do you come, Lieutenant?" Rosa asked. "We can do this without you."

Jones looked directly at Rosa. "Miss Appleton is from a prominent family. I am going to be present in order to assure her safe return to the United States . . . And to make absolutely certain that no one is tempted by the thought of receiving a tidy ransom."

There was an ugly innuendo in Jones's reply but, thankfully, no one took offense. "I'm coming along, too," I said.

"One other thing," Tin-Pan added. "We'll need one of them Mexicans along in case we have some questions we want to ask."

"Excellent idea," agreed Jones. "That makes eight of us that will make the trip so I'll bring along one of the pack mules for supplies. If the soldiers here run out of rations they can send back to the post for more."

"We've got about four hours of daylight left," Tin-Pan said. "We can make good use of it."

"Fifteen minutes and I'll be ready to go," responded Jones. "I'll select my two men and put someone in charge of the rest." Starting back toward the soldiers he said, "We'll all meet at the trail head."

"He sure likes to give orders," Monte said wryly.

I chuckled. "Maybe that's the reason he wants two of his lapdog troopers to come along."

"No," Rosa said, "he only looks for glory . . . and favors from the *gringa pendeja*. He fears that if he is not with us he will get nothing. For this he risks starting a war."

CHAPTER 6

The trail started out in a dry wash that, in the rainy season, would funnel a torrential flow of water down the length of Guadalupe Canyon. Our path then turned up a narrow ravine that was bordered on each side by steep walls of fractured and crumbling rock. Here and there gnarled juniper and oak trees had somehow taken root and then sent their branches, like outstretched arms, arching ominously over our heads. As usual, and especially since the tracks of the horses were easy to read, Jones took the lead. Following close behind was Tin-Pan. One of the Mexicans came next and was followed by the two selected privates, then Monte and Rosa. Assuming my usual position, I brought up the rear, leading our pack mule.

We had not gone far when the ravine veered to the left. Following it, we rode up a short grade that took us out of the shaded wash and into the glaring sunlight. Then, hugging the side of a cactus-covered mountain, we paralleled another ravine and, matching its every twist and turn, gained a foot of altitude with every step the horses took. Eventually we leveled off but, for the next half hour, meandered through a range of low-lying hills. When we reached the base of a steep ridge, Jones called a halt in order to give the sweat-lathered horses a blow.

No more than a mile ahead of us, which was due south, another mountain range abruptly rose into the sky. Many of the peaks were crowned with clusters of craggy, stone pillars, vertical boulders from fifty to one hundred feet high. I found a bit of humor in the fact that the boulders reminded me of huge loaves of French bread, but then a moment later I realized those same boulders formed walls that encircled what amounted to enormous primeval fortresses, fortresses whose many clefts and caves would provide countless places in which to hide. And, too, I quickly surmised that it would be impossible for us to approach any of those hideouts from below without being seen. Understanding the range of mountains I was looking at stretched eastward for several miles, my heart sank. Suddenly, the idea of finding

Marzel Appleton seemed utterly hopeless.

"Halfway up that mountainside it turns into Mexico," Tin-Pan said, pointing at the peak directly in front of us. "Just where exactly, nobody can say. But the top of that mountain, that rocky butte up yonder, is in Mexico for sure."

"Are there trails that lead up to those rocks?" I asked. "That brush looks pretty thick."

"Game trails," replied Tin-Pan. "There're plenty of them but mighty rough to follow on horseback. You can go afoot but you'd need leather leggings up to your thighs. Without them, your clothes would be rags in a few hours. There's mesquite, prickly pear, and catclaw all over these mountains and I ain't said nothing yet about the yucca spines and sharp rocks. That catclaw is the worst, though. From here that catclaw looks like grass but you get up close, Lord have mercy, it can eat you alive."

Jones stood up in his saddle, studying the trail ahead. "It looks like the trail we're on turns east up ahead."

"Southeast," corrected Tin-Pan. "The main trail winds around some, but in a few miles it crosses over a pass and drops down onto the lower end of Animas Valley. But they's little trails all through this country.

This one we're on is just one of the main ones.

"Now that Animas Valley," continued Tin-Pan, "is mighty fine country, mighty fine. It don't look nothing like the San Bernardino Valley where Mistah John settled. No, sah! Beats all I ever saw, how different it is over that way. Best cow country for miles and miles around. But Mistah John, he's got more water than they do. His water comes right up out of the ground on its own."

"Speaking of water," Jones said, "are there any springs up this high?"

"One I know of but only one. Otherwise we'll have to work our way back down to where we was earlier, to the Spring of Contention, to get any water."

Jones turned and eyed the Mexican. "Miss Bustamonte, would you ask our prisoner how much farther it is to where he was captured?"

Rosa said a few words and then received a short answer. "He says," reported Rosa, "he thinks it is not far but he does not know for sure. Fear of your soldiers made him forget." Rosa paused and then added her personal opinion. "Or maybe it was the beating your men gave him, maybe that made him forget, too."

"Desperate times," Jones said flippantly,

"require drastic measures. If we don't find Miss Appleton soon, even more persuasive methods will be employed. I can assure you that one way or the other, I will get the Mexican to talk."

"Como se llama usted?" Rosa asked, and the Mexican replied, "Hernando."

"He has a name," Rosa said. "It is Hernando. And I believe he is telling the truth when he says he knows nothing about the woman. He is no bandit. He is not even a good rustler. If he was, he and the others would never have stumbled into your men. He is nothing but a poor *peón.* And he has a wife and three hungry children."

Jones leaned back in his saddle and sighed. "I am well aware of what you are trying to do, Miss Bustamonte. But it might interest you to know that my father once gave me a pup. I named that dog Major and immediately proceeded to teach him how to fetch. However, despite all of my efforts, at no time did Major ever learn to follow my commands. So, at the end of six months I took Major for a walk in the woods near our home. I shot that dog, Miss Bustamonte, and I can assure you, I shed no tears of sentiment. In fact, I had no regrets whatsoever."

Mexican villages were full of nameless

dogs and quite commonplace to Rosa but, even so, she still found the story of Jones killing his pet quite repugnant. She, however, understood the point of his story, as did I. While Rosa was swearing at Jones under her breath, and I was shaking my head in disgust, the story of Jones killing his pet dog had caused Monte to react in a completely different manner.

All Monte had heard Jones say was, "My father once gave me a pup." After that, the only word that registered in Monte's thoughts, the single word that drowned out everything else Jones said, was a resounding "Buttercup." He heard the word again and again until suddenly he knew that Buttercup was not the name of his family's dog. It was the name of *his* dog. Desperately pursuing that recaptured fragment of memory, Monte suddenly realized that the dog not only had belonged to him personally but that he, and he alone, had chosen the name Buttercup.

Monte briefly shoved the dog's name aside, hoping to recover more of his forgotten past, but try as he might, he conjured up nothing more than a vague, ghostlike image of a smoldering cabin and the corral where his father had died.

Reluctantly, his thoughts returned to the dog. He began to wonder why a six-year-old boy living on the unforgiving western frontier would choose a name like Buttercup. Yellow fur or not, it was at best a sissy name, a name no rough-and-tumble boy would ever think of choosing. And yet that was indeed the name he had selected. Could he, Monte wondered, have possibly been a little sissy boy? And why would any self-respecting pioneer father allow his son to choose such a name? Was it his mother's idea to allow it? Did she convince his father to let their son name his dog Buttercup? If that was the case . . . which was likely . . . what kind of mother did he once have? What kind of mother did the Apaches take from him?

"We best keep moving," Tin-Pan said, breaking into everyone's thoughts. "We ain't got all that much good light left."

To assure everyone that he was in command, Jones deliberately ignored Tin-Pan. Instead, he removed a pair of binoculars from his saddle pocket and meticulously scanned the mountainside to the south. Taking advantage of Jones's stalling tactic, I took a closer look at the two privates, now only a few feet in front of me.

Like most of the soldiers, both were close to my age. One, about my size, was referred to as Trooper Selkirk and the other, quite a bit taller but stoop shouldered, was called Trooper Vogel. Neither seemed particularly enthusiastic about their second ride into the mountains, especially having to take it in the late afternoon heat.

Directing his question toward Tin-Pan, Monte asked, "Do you get many bandits coming through this way?"

"Not too many," answered Tin-Pan. "Most of Mistah John's cattle is on land south of the border and that's where he might lose one or two from time to time. He don't mind that too much. That's because he figures if somebody is taking one or two cows it means they's stealing for food. That's the way he done with the Apaches in the old days; let 'em have one or two. But if bandits come and steal cows to make money Mistah John will go at 'em tooth and nail and then, if he catches 'em, he'll read to 'em from the book.

"Mexicans know about Mistah John and most times steer clear of his range. Mostly the bandits and rustlers ride up into the Animas Valley to do their big-time stealing. They can get in and out real easy. But they got to do it quick 'cause it's hard to hide out in that flatland over there without being seen by somebody. No, Guadalupe Canyon is for them that want to sneak in quiet-like and get away without nobody knowing they come and left."

Looking at Rosa, Tin-Pan pointed at the Mexican. "What do you make of Hernando and his amigos? Do you still think they come for food and not pesos?"

Rosa rolled her eyes and rode up next to the prisoner. She grabbed one of his hands and twisted it toward Tin-Pan. "Look at these calluses. This man is a farmer. The four that were caught are not outlaws." Dropping the Mexican's hand, Rosa frowned. "And look at the fear in his eyes. He's no bandit. Bandits are *muy macho.* They would not have taken a beating like these men. They would have fought back."

After taking a deep relaxing breath, Jones wheeled his horse around. He was facing all of us but focused his attention on Rosa. "You seem to forget, Miss Bustamonte," he said smugly, "that I was at the court-martial of your two friends, here. In the trial I recall that you claimed that you were a captain in Villa's army."

"I was," insisted Rosa.

"And were you not a farmer before that?" Jones asked slyly. "And is it not also true that the majority of Villa's army is composed of peon farmers?"

Jones had made his point but he was not

satisfied. "For your information," he said, waving his hand to include all of us, "I'll have you all know that just five months ago one hundred or more of these so called *farmers* rode across the Rio Grande and attacked the small Texas towns of Glenn Springs and Boquillas. There were only nine soldiers stationed at Glenn Springs and when they were attacked they ran from their tents into a nearby adobe. Even though they were outnumbered ten to one, they held the raiders at bay, fighting for three solid hours amid constant cries of 'Viva Villa and 'Viva Carranza.' Finally, the Mexicans torched the roof of the adobe and when the soldiers ran out, three were killed and four wounded. And one of those killed was a friend of mine.

"Meanwhile, twelve miles to the east at Boquillas, your so-called *farmers* looted stores and kidnapped two hostages, two men that the Mexicans planned on ransoming for thousands of dollars. Then, with the two hostages, all the raiders regrouped and rode back across the Rio Grande and into what they thought was the safety of Mexico.

"However, Colonels Sibley and Langhorne, not the least bit intimidated by the current political situation, rode after the raiders with two columns of troopers. They caught up to the Mexicans and when they did, the raiders scattered like so many roosters and left the two hostages behind.

"Those two hostages were penny-ante storekeepers but still Colonels Sibley and Langhorne received high honors for their courageous rescue."

Jones turned and shoved his binoculars back into his saddle pocket. When he faced us again he sneered, "Now, I'm sure you would all agree that Miss Appleton is far more important than a couple of storekeepers from a town no one ever heard of. And I assure you that I have no intention of allowing her to be held against her will or to be ransomed . . . no matter what I have to do to prevent it."

"So you're saying," asked Tin-Pan, "that you think our Mexicans stole Miss Appleton for money?"

Jones raised an arrogant eyebrow. "I'm sure of it. The same as the Mexicans had planned to do with the two men from Boquillas. Why else would our four take such a tremendous risk?

"I'm not saying," continued Jones, "that our prisoners came here for the specific purpose of kidnapping for ransom. In fact, it's possible they are spies, men sent here to discover how many soldiers we have in our garrison. Or they might have come to see how many men are guarding Douglas and what fortifications we have in place. But when the opportunity to kidnap Miss Appleton presented itself, they took full advantage of it.

"We're on a war footing with Mexico. Every available soldier we have is stationed along the border, and President Wilson has activated our entire National Guard and brought them down here as well, all one-hundred-fifty thousand of them. That's been in the papers for anyone to read and it sounds impressive but if the Mexicans actually knew how poorly prepared we are . . . who knows what would happen.

"I'm only pointing out that these men *could* be spies. But even if they are merely cattle thieves, they sealed their fate when they took Miss Appleton. Their lust for easy money was their downfall."

"Don't you mean," Monte said, breaking his long silence, "*if* they took her?"

Dropping his eyes and gathering his reins, Jones sighed. "Of course they took her," he said and then turned his horse back onto the trail. As he spurred his mount and motioned for us to follow, he added, "Discovering that fact is a matter of simple deduction."

Watching Tin-Pan fall in behind Jones,

Monte said, "I hope he likes the taste of crow."

"You do not think they took her, either?" Rosa asked.

"No, not them. But somebody has her. Somebody that's a lot more trail savvy than those four rustlers."

I hadn't carried a watch in months and, as a result, had grown accustomed to estimating the time almost as well as Monte and Rosa. Glancing at the sun, I said, "We've got less than two hours of good light."

"That fork in the trail those troopers talked about," Monte said, "can't be too far ahead. After we get there I'm guessing we've got another two or three miles to go before we get to where they caught the Mexicans. That's when the trail will start to get interesting but by that time there won't be much light left. If the trail's hard to read we'll have to wait until morning to work it out."

I took a quick look around as the troopers, driving Hernando in front of them, rode up the trail. The craggy mountain range to the south seemed impenetrable, and to the north, east, and west as far as I could see, there was nothing but a rolling sea of stone-covered hills rising out of a labyrinth of meandering arroyos. "Do you think we're still in the states?" I asked. "We've got to be close to the line."

"Who could know such a thing?" Rosa huffed. "This is no-man's-land. Anyone can claim it."

Monte slid the Springfield out of his saddle scabbard, opened the bolt partway, and checked the magazine. "At least it's loaded," he said and then shoved the bolt back into place. "Looks like I've got five rounds but they forgot to give us any stripper clips to reload."

I pulled out my rifle and opened the bolt. "Mine's empty!" I declared.

"Americans," scoffed Rosa. "What do they know of war?"

Monte ejected two of his cartridges and handed them to me. I shoved one into the magazine, one into the chamber, and then flipped the safety. "They might have more ammunition on the pack mule," I said naïvely. "All the lieutenant has with him is his forty-five but both the troopers have rifles and are wearing cartridge belts. Maybe we can get some clips from them."

"You can try," Monte said, sliding the Springfield back into his scabbard, "but I'm guessing Jones won't go for it. He's a man that likes power. Them not giving us cartridge belts was likely his idea in the first place. I'd put money on it that they gave me a loaded rifle by mistake. But tonight, I think I'll even things up a bit. Those boys won't miss a couple of clips."

"So," I said, "you're fairly certain we'll be spending the night up here?"

"Backtracking those Mexicans from that fork will take time and I need good light to do it. And when we get to that fork it'll be near dark. We have supplies on the mule so there's no point in going all the way back to the canyon. And I kind of want to see how good the lieutenant and his two boys are at roughing it in these mountains."

Knowing what lay ahead for the soldiers, I grinned and placed the barrel of my Springfield on the lip of the scabbard. However, as Monte and Rosa trotted after the troopers I hesitated and pulled it back out. Twisting to the left and right, I hefted the weapon to my shoulder several times in rapid succession. Each time, looking down the barrel at the front sight, I aimed at a distant yucca or stunted juniper. I was pleased to discover the rifle was well balanced and not too heavy, even for me.

Satisfied that I had a good rifle and two deadly thirty-ought-six rounds at my disposal, I confidently shoved the Springfield back into the scabbard. Gathering the mule's lead rope, I galloped up the trail, weaving my way up the crest of the ridge until the faint path began to narrow. When I caught up with the others, the trail was barely wide enough for a horse to get through.

With thorns continually scraping across our stirrup hoods and bootheels, we threaded our way up, down, and across the side of the mountain range for the better part of an hour. The trail was finally beginning to open up again when we abruptly came to a halt.

In the amber rays of a setting sun, Tin-Pan turned and looked back at Monte. "Here's the fork where the Mexicans and soldiers met up. You best come and take a look."

Monte maneuvered around a patch of cactus to his left, dodged a mesquite, and rode up beside Tin-Pan. Having to lean to one side in order to see around Jones and his horse, Tin-Pan pointed a few feet up the trail. "What do you make of them tracks there?"

Monte dismounted and without a word walked in front of Jones. The ground where the trails met was relatively level and the junction itself was almost devoid of vegetation. Going to one knee, Monte studied the sandy soil that had been chewed up by horses' hooves and bootheels. A few seconds passed before he stood again and pointed in an easterly direction. "The four Mexicans rode in from that direction," he said, then nodded to the southeast. "Your men came from up that way."

Jones turned and glanced at the troopers behind him. "Is this where you captured the Mexicans?"

Both men glanced around. "It looks right," replied the stoop-shouldered Vogel. "Yes, sir," answered Selkirk. "It looks different coming at it from this direction but this is the place, sure enough."

Monte took a few more steps, then stopped again. Swinging his arm palm down in a low arc, Monte said, "Here is where your soldiers beat the Mexicans."

"Alright then," Jones said, eagerly gathering his reins, "we have plenty of daylight left. Let's see where those Mexicans came from."

Monte turned and looked squarely at Jones. "From here on, I go out ahead and on foot or I don't go at all."

From where I sat, I saw Jones twitch. An instant later he extended his right hand and, with a flick of his index finger, issued a face-saving command aimed at Monte. "Carry on!"

At that juncture, had I been Monte, I would have given Jones a piece of my mind but from what I could observe, it seemed that the lieutenant's pompous antics were about as important to Monte as the price of tea in China.

"Tin-Pan," Monte asked, "how's your eyesight?"

"I can see pretty good as long as we've got the sun but the light's fading fast."

"Then you come with me. Two sets of eyes are better than one and between the two of us, we can cover a lot of ground in the next twenty minutes."

Tin-Pan immediately swung down. Gathering his and Monte's reins, he led the two horses around Jones and then up to where Monte was standing. Handing over Monte's reins, Tin-Pan nodded solemnly. "Let's get to it."

Leading their horses and walking side by side up the crest of the ridge, Monte and Tin-Pan took off at a rapid pace. I couldn't make out what they said to each other as they walked but they seemed to be speaking and pointing every step of the way. Jones, on the other hand, rode in silence, apparently compensating for his subordinate position by assuming the grandiose posture of a conquering hero on parade.

Just as the sun was setting, Monte stopped suddenly. Tin-Pan took one more step, then froze. Monte pointed and kneeled down. Tin-Pan bent low, rubbed his eyes, and stared at something. He rubbed his eyes again and then shook his head.

"What is it?" asked Jones.

Tin-Pan looked out over the brushy ridge we were on, which paralleled a deep ravine and a sister ridge no more than fifty yards to the east of us. "The Mexicans stopped here," Tin-Pan explained. "Two got off and for some reason went into that gully down yonder. Then they come back up the same way they went down."

Jones hastily dismounted. "Let's see where they went. Maybe Miss Appleton is nearby."

Monte and Tin-Pan drew their pistols. Taking a quick look around, Monte eased into the brush with Tin-Pan following. Jones ordered his troopers to stay mounted, and then pulled out his Colt and fell in behind Tin-Pan.

Descending the steep ridge, the sun's rays quickly disappeared and the brush grew thicker. In minutes they reached the bottom of the gully, which was free of heavy growth but choked with melon-sized rocks and a few boulders. A thorough search of the rocks revealed nothing but then Monte caught sight of a broken branch on the far side of the ravine. Seconds later he spotted the Mexicans' tracks where they had left the gully and continued up toward the second ridge.

"What do you make of that?" Monte asked, indicating the deep gouges in the sand and the turned-over rocks.

Tin-Pan worked his way over to where Monte stood, leaned down, and squinted in the dim light. "They went up here alright. But it looks like they went up crawling on their hands and knees."

Jones stumbled around a boulder as he hurried to take a look. "Why would they do that?"

"Must have seen a deer or something," replied Tin-Pan. "Most likely they didn't want to make no sound on the way up. Maybe they were hoping to sneak up and get a good shot."

Monte glanced up the side of the gully. The sun bathed the crest of the ridge in a hazy orange light. "The problem with that is," Monte said as he started climbing, "those two Mexicans were still crawling when they came back down. Something or somebody was on the other side of that ridge up there. The Mexicans wanted to see what was going on without been seen themselves."

Threading his way through the brush but moving quickly, Monte scrambled up the hill. However, when he got near the crest of the ridge he slowed and bent low. He took a few more steps, went down on his belly, and waited for Tin-Pan and Jones to catch up. When they crawled up beside him, Jones cocked and locked the hammer of his Colt. When Monte gave the signal each man began inching his way to the top of the ridge.

As they reached the crest they could see a second deep ravine a stone's throw below them, a ravine whose bottom was dotted with mesquite trees and a few open patches of sand. Monte saw it first, the white color contrasting sharply with a squirming mass of black.

"Oh hell," Monte groaned and then stood straight up, his back catching the last rays of a setting sun.

A flock of ravens instantly exploded off a naked corpse that was sprawled facedown in the bottom of the ravine. "Lord have mercy," muttered Tin-Pan coming to his knees. "Lord have mercy."

Jones sprang to his feet in a rage. "Those

barbarous fiends!" he growled. "They murdered her! They defiled her and then they murdered her!"

Swearing incoherently Jones spun around, stumbled, and then charged down the ridge they had just come up.

"It would be best," Monte said reverently, "to have Rosa come with a blanket. Miss Appleton's family will want the body and they'll take comfort in knowing she was treated decent."

Averting his eyes, Tin-Pan nodded and got to his feet. "I'll go fetch her," he sighed despondently. "Lord have mercy."

Monte holstered his pistol. Looking up at the circling ravens he said, "I'm going down there and read what sign there is. I at least want to know what happened."

From where we sat our horses we saw Jones suddenly bolt back down the hillside as Monte disappeared down into the second ravine. When we heard Jones scrambling up out of the gully, the Mexican burst into a feverish chatter. I didn't understand a single word but I knew panic when I heard it. "What is he saying?" I asked Rosa.

"He says they didn't do it," Rosa answered uneasily. "He says it over and over. And he says they didn't kill anyone."

Out of breath, Jones charged out of the

brush aiming his pistol at Hernando. Wheezing and gasping for air, Jones hesitated and then holstered his sidearm. Going to the blabbering Mexican, Jones jerked him off his horse and threw him on the ground. After kicking him repeatedly, Jones grabbed Hernando by his shirt and jerked him to his feet.

Hernando put up his bound hands to shield his face but Jones buried a fist into his stomach. When Hernando dropped his hands, Jones crumpled him with a brutal blow to his gaping jaw.

Staring down at the unconscious Mexican, Jones bellowed, "They killed her! They defiled her and then they murdered her. Then they left her for the animals."

"You mean," Vogel asked, "they had their way with her?"

"Filthy greasers," spewed Jones.

"They're dead men," snarled Selkirk. "Dead! Let's hang all four of them."

Rosa and I were stunned and had no idea what to say. Jones was catching his breath when Tin-Pan, breathing hard, emerged from the brush. "Miss Rosa, Mistah Segundo says for you to come with a blanket. You men are to stay here until things are made respectable."

Rosa was about to step down when Monte

reappeared on the far ridge and then charged downhill, clearly in a hurry to get back to us.

"Monte is coming," Rosa said. "Something is wrong."

Jones turned and glared at Monte but he was soon out of sight. Everyone froze and in less than a minute Monte bounded out of the ravine. His eyes went straight to Hernando who still lay in a heap at Jones's feet.

His chest heaving, Monte asked, "Did you kill him?"

"No," replied Jones finally catching his breath. "But I'll enjoy watching him hang along with the other three."

"Well, if you do," Monte said, "it won't be for killing Miss Appleton."

"What!" bellowed Jones. "You saw what they did!"

"That's a man down there," returned Monte, "not a woman. And his head is bashed in so bad it's nothing but a puddle of flesh and shattered bone."

Jones blinked several times trying to grasp what Monte had said. "A man? You say that was a man down there."

"You're missing one, aren't you?" Monte asked. "My guess is that's him."

"Corporal McIntosh?" questioned Selkirk.

"I found this next to the body," Monte

said, pulling a cigarette wrapper out of his pocket. "Know anybody that smokes Murads?"

"Damn!" sighed Selkirk. "Corporal McIntosh smokes Murads. Nobody but the corporal smokes those."

Jones still seemed confused. "But what would he be doing here? He's miles from where he was to meet his men."

I thought of how bitterly McIntosh had complained about his demotion and how interested he was in hearing about Mexico. To me, it seemed very probable that the corporal was in the process of deserting when he was killed, but with emotions running high I thought it best to keep my supposition to myself.

"A better question," said Tin-Pan, "is who killed him and why."

Monte stared down at Hernando. "I want to hear what the Mexican has to say. Then I'll tell you what I think."

Jones finally gathered his wits. "Troopers Selkirk and Vogel. You can easily follow our tracks. Go over there and bury Corporal McIntosh in the sand as best you can. Then use rocks to cover the grave. Lots of rocks. I want him buried properly. I don't want the birds to get at him . . . or the coyotes. Do you understand?"

"Yes, sir," answered the troopers as they grimly dismounted and then disappeared into the ravine.

Jones peered off into the sunset and then surveyed the mountains in every direction. "This seems as good a place as any to set up camp."

Tin-Pan eyed Monte, looking for his reaction. Seeing him shake his head, Tin-Pan wisely ventured a diplomatic suggestion. "Up here's a good place to sleep, Lieutenant, but whoever killed the corporal might still be around. Maybe we should make our fires down in that gully we was in, back behind some of those big rocks. I saw lots of deadwood down there and we can roust out any snakes that might be holed up. But up here a fire at night could be seen for fifty miles. And I could sure enough use some hot coffee."

"Excellent idea, Tin-Pan," Jones said smoothly. "Can I count on you to handle the coffee and field rations?"

Tin-Pan nodded agreeably, "Yes, sah," he said and then walked over to where Rosa and I still sat our mounts. Accepting the reins of the pack mule he said softly, "You two keep your rifles close at hand. This don't look good to me."

Hernando groaned and began to stir. Seeing Rosa dismount holding her rifle, Jones stepped away from his prisoner. Passing near Monte, Rosa took his hunting knife from its sheath. Kneeling next to Hernando she defiantly cut the ropes from his wrists. With her back to Jones and holding the blade of the knife, she held it high over her head.

Completely ignoring Jones, Monte stepped forward and took his knife from Rosa's hand and sheathed it. "He's not going to be any trouble," Monte said flatly. "And he's not about to try to escape."

"Of course he won't," snipped Jones. "If he did, he knows what would happen."

Rosa helped Hernando get upright into a sitting position. His lips were swollen and bleeding. His eyes were glazed over.

Taking Tin-Pan's advice, I slid my rifle from its scabbard and dismounted. Joining Rosa, I reached down and picked up Hernando's battered sombrero. He was a pitiful sight and, despite the circumstances, I began to feel sorry for him.

Speaking to Hernando, Rosa asked several questions but he was unresponsive and his eyes had yet to focus. "He does not hear me," Rosa said. "It will take time."

Monte came over and helped Hernando get to his feet. "Let's get him down in the gully, Billy. He'll be hungry like the rest of us when he comes to."

Standing by himself, Jones announced, "I will stay here and assume sentry duty until the troopers return."

I went to Hernando as Tin-Pan and Rosa took a coffee pot and some odds and ends off the pack mule. Grabbing an elbow, Monte and I helped the groggy Hernando down the ravine and over to one of the boulders that was wedged in the bottom of the gully. Strewn around the boulder were several rounded stones that made decent seats and we balanced Hernando on one of them and then leaned him back against the boulder.

After arranging some smaller stones, Monte got a small fire going while Rosa rummaged through some of the supplies she and Tin-Pan had carried down. "There's a side of salt pork on the pack mule," said Tin-Pan. "And a jug of water we'll be needing for coffee."

Volunteering to get the water and bacon, I hurried back up to the pack mule. When I crossed the opening to the mule, a faint glow of yellow clung to the western horizon but stars were appearing in the darkening eastern sky. It was near dark but, even so, several paces up the trail Jones was standing on high ground glassing the hills with his binoculars. Without men to command it suddenly struck me that, all things considered, he was little more than an insecure and foolish man. From the moment we met I didn't like him, and after what he did to Hernando I wanted to hate him, but at that moment I realized it wasn't in me to do so.

"I'll send up one of the troopers as soon as they get back," I said raising my voice.

Not bothering to lower his binoculars, Jones replied. "Vogel would be my choice. Send him to me the instant he returns."

I rolled my eyes and cracked an exasperating smile. "I'll tell him, Lieutenant," I said but then added under my breath, "But only after he gets a cup of coffee."

CHAPTER 7

When Jones stepped into the dancing light, Tin-Pan was frying bacon over a small fire. Off to one side of the flames, steam rose from the spout of a fire-blackened coffee pot. Monte and Rosa sat together on a flat stone. Selkirk sat next to Hernando and I stood beside the two of them, all five of us drinking our ration of coffee from dented metal cups.

Jones took us all in with a sweeping glance, then selected a stone and sat down. "Trooper Selkirk," Jones said stiffly, "in three hours you will relieve Private Vogel and take over sentry duty."

"Yes, sir."

Holding the skillet in one hand, Tin-Pan handed Jones a cup. He then picked up the coffee pot. As Jones held out his cup, Tin-Pan poured the coffee and said, "We got enough water for one cup apiece."

Jones accepted the coffee but sneered at

Hernando. "I see you included the Mexican."

Surprising everyone, Rosa asked sarcastically, "You mean me, Lieutenant?"

Not ruffled in the slightest by Rosa's question, Jones responded blandly, "You know what I mean. And now that he's made himself at home, he can tell us why he murdered Corporal McIntosh."

"He can tell us what he saw," Monte said, "but he never came close to your corporal. The tracks he and the other Mexican made stopped at the ridge we were on. The Mexicans didn't go down into the second gully. They came back down the way they went up. So Hernando didn't have anything to do with what happened to your corporal. But I'm pretty sure he knows who killed him."

With his eyes locked on Hernando, Jones thoughtfully took a sip of coffee and then said, "Alright, let's assume for now that he's only a liar and a cattle thief. You say he knows who killed Corporal McIntosh, so let's hear what he has to say."

Rosa hesitated for a moment and then leaned forward. She spoke to Hernando in Spanish and then leaned back to listen. Hernando took a nervous drink of coffee and then began to speak. At first his words came slowly but once he started, even with his swollen lips, he spoke more freely and then went on for a full minute.

"He says," Rosa interpreted, "that he and the other men were coming over from Mexico when, about noon, they heard a scream. At first, they thought it was a mountain lion since the screams of a big cat and a man sound the same. They stopped and listened until they heard another scream but this one they decided came from a man. And then they agreed that it had come from over the ridge from where they were. So, Hernando and one other went to see what was happening and if the man needed help."

Jones huffed. "I'll bet they did."

Continuing on, Rosa said, "At the ridge they crept up very slowly on their bellies and crawled under the brush so no one down in the other ravine could see them. They didn't like the sound of the man's screams so they were very careful not to be seen. When they peeked down from the ridge they saw six, maybe seven men standing around a man who was on the ground. But he was dead already when they saw him."

Unimpressed, Jones took a sip of coffee and then glanced at Rosa. "And can he describe these six or seven men?"

Rosa asked Hernando a question. When she did, his eyes flared. At that point none of us could tell if those eyes were filled with fear or with guilt.

Hernando didn't answer, so Rosa repeated her question but this time more forcefully.

Rosa got a response. She said something more and then explained, "He is afraid we will not believe him. And then you will think all he says has been a lie."

"Indios," Monte said, confounding everyone but Tin-Pan.

"Sí!" erupted Hernando. *"Sí, sí! Apaches! Usted sabe!"*

"I knew it!" blurted Tin-Pan. "I didn't say nothing to nobody but I knew it! Hot damn, I was right."

Needing no interpretation of the word *Apaches,* Jones leaned back and laughed. "That's even better than I expected. 'Oh no,' he says, 'we didn't do it, it was Apaches!' That's utter nonsense. Is that the best he can come up with?"

Tin-Pan gravely shook his head and muttered, "For their feet run to evil."

"And make haste to shed blood," Monte added, completing the Biblical proverb.

Tin-Pan looked at Monte as if seeing him for the first time. With a knowing smile he said, "Amen, brother. Amen."

Jones's brow wrinkled with incredulity. "Don't tell me the two of you believe this balderdash?"

Sensing the disbelief in Jones, Hernando pointed excitedly at Monte. *"Yo vi El Guerrero Güero."*

"Güero?" snapped Rosa.

"Sí! Un güero!"

Monte frowned and he looked at Rosa. "What did he say?"

Rosa in turn glared at Hernando. *"Un guerrero güero?"*

Hernando responded, all the while emphatically nodding his head.

"He says," Rosa explained, "that one of the Apaches was blond. He called him 'The Blond Warrior.' He says the blond Apache has been seen many times in Mexico."

"Oh, please," exclaimed Jones. "What did you put in his coffee, anyway? Now the Apaches are blonds."

"Lordy, Lordy," proclaimed Tin-Pan, "that would be little Charley McComas all growed up! Everybody wondered whatever come of him. And here he is finally. Land sakes alive!"

"Who is Charley McComas?" I asked.

Tin-Pan poked a fork into the sizzling salt pork and flipped a few pieces. "He was a little blond boy that was took by an Apache named Chato on one of his raids. As I recollect Chato had Benito, Mangus, Naiche, and Tzoe along with him. They killed twenty-six whites in that raid and two of 'em was Charley's folks.

"That was way up near Lordsburg in a place called Thompson Canyon. Little Charley and his ma and pa had stopped for a picnic under a walnut tree when the Apaches come up on 'em. Mistah Mc-Comas got off some shots before they killed him. The wife . . . she died hard, real hard.

"Charley was six at the time and they took him and rode back down to Mexico where they come from. And since Mistah Mc-Comas was a judge and kind of politician he was known all over New Mexico and even back in the Old States. Him being 'somebody,' it got folks riled up for hundreds of miles around and even back East.

"Now, had Mistah McComas just been a regular man like the others that was killed, him and his wife getting murdered and their boy took wouldn't have made nobody back East take notice. But he was a judge, you see, and a high-grade man like that counts for something in the East."

"When did all this happen?" Selkirk asked.

Tin-Pan thought for moment. "Oh, that was back in the springtime of eighty-three.

Now then, Charley was six so now he'd be . . ."

"Thirty-nine," I offered and then I stole a glance at Monte. Even though the McComas story and his own were markedly similar, I could read nothing in his expression that reflected what I knew he most assuredly was thinking.

The two Apache raids had occurred only three years apart. Both he and Charley had been six years old when the renegades struck and both had seen their parents brutally murdered. But instead of being kidnapped, Monte had been thrown into a thicket of cactus and left to suffer a long and agonizing death.

"Tin-Pan," Monte said, "you figured out that the corporal was killed by Apaches before Hernando said they did it. How'd you guess that?"

Tin-Pan slowly shook his head. "When you told me that the man's head had been bashed in, I figured right then and there that the Apaches had done it. That's their way. Bashing in the head is like signing their name. Lots of times they'll cut a body up, too. But they like to kill slow if they got the time, so I'm figuring these Apaches was in a hurry for some reason."

"Do you think," asked Selkirk, "that this

Charley McComas fella remembers who he is? How could he do something like that to another white man?"

Rosa and I knew that Monte had virtually no memory of his childhood, but it was not my place to divulge that fact to anyone. I waited to see if Monte would comment on what Charley McComas might or might not remember; however it was Tin-Pan that spoke next.

"I've seen a few captives come back from being with the Indians. If they've been with the Apaches more than a few years, no matter if they's white or brown, they're all Apache inside. They don't seem to recollect being white at all. And even if they do, they don't want nothing to do with it.

"Back in eighty-three there was a fella named Pitch-Pine-House that was the father-in-law of Geronimo. You see, this Pitch-Pine-House helped General Crook get old Geronimo to surrender back then. Pitch-Pine-House was a great warrior among the Apaches and had killed lot of civilized folks of every color. But he was really a white man that had been captured as a boy. He lived like an Apache, killed like an Apache, and died like an Apache."

Jones finished his coffee but held onto his cup. "Now wait a minute, people. Listen to what you're saying. This is the twentieth century, damn it. We've got telephones and airplanes. Hell, we've got moving picture shows and plays on Broadway. Pancho Villa is using machine guns and in Europe they're fighting with airplanes, tanks, and submarines! And you expect me to believe wild Apaches are still roaming around the West and killing people?"

"You Americans think you know everything!" Rosa said angrily. "You think the whole world is rich and spoiled like you, but you know nothing. Have you ever heard of Oputo, Chuhuichupa, Nacori Chico, Casas Grandes, or Bacerac? Of course you have not. But those are Mexican villages. All of them, and many like them, are still being raided by the Apaches. As long as anyone can remember, the Mexicans have never known peace. Always livestock is stolen and every year people are killed by these Indians, Indians that you pay money to see in your moving picture shows."

"She's telling the truth," Tin-Pan said. "Everybody along the border knows that lots of Apaches still live down in the Sierra Madre Mountains. Some of 'em are left over from Geronimo's band. Some of 'em, you understand, didn't give up with Geronimo. They held out. Others left the San Carlos

244

reservation and joined up with 'em. Mostly they're Chiricahuas, but there's others mixed in, some Warm Springs and even some Navajo.

"Me and Mistah John helped guide General Crook through some of them Sierra Madre Mountains and I swear you ain't seen mountains and canyons until you been in those places. There's places in there a hundred armies could hide and nobody would ever find 'em, much less root 'em out.

"And these mountains we're in now connect to the Sierra Madres. In fact, if you know the trails, you can ride from where we're at and go all the way to Canada and never leave the mountains. And hardly nobody would ever see you, either.

"If you ask a tame Apache up on the reservation what them Apaches down in Mexico are called they'll tell you they're the Netdahe, or 'the ones that never surrendered.' They'll tell everybody that the Netdahe are a bunch of Apaches that just wants to live free. But all that means is there's renegades that want to keep on doing whatever they want, whenever they want, and to whoever they want. That's what freedom is to an Apache."

Monte glanced across the fire and nodded

toward Hernando. "I was waiting to see what the rustler had to say before I told anybody about the Indians, but down in the ravine I saw moccasin tracks. Lots of them. And I saw what had to be horse tracks but they were blunt, almost like they were made by the flat end of a post. Tracks like that would be hard to follow over packed dirt."

"They sure are," agreed Tin-Pan. "I've seen it done many a time. That's what the Apaches do. They sew rawhide around their horses' hooves just for that very reason, to make 'em hard to follow."

Jones thought for a moment. "Let's say, just for the sake of argument, that you're right and those that killed the corporal were indeed some sort of holdover Indians. That still doesn't get us any closer to finding Miss Appleton."

Rosa broke into more Spanish and Hernando supplied more answers. Their conversation seemed intense. Finally Rosa said, "He says that after they saw the Apaches they were afraid. They were too far from their home in Carretera to go back so they started for the Slaughter ranch. They wanted to get to any place safe; it didn't matter where as long as they were safe from the Apaches.

"They were on their way to John Slaughter's when they saw your soldiers. They rode toward them on purpose. They were happy to be captured by Americans and not by the Apaches. But Hernando says they did not see a woman down in the ravine. But he also says they could not see their horses either so there could have been a woman with them. There were too many rocks and mesquite trees in the way and they did not stay long to look."

"The troopers said they found a pair of German binoculars on the prisoners," Jones said. "Ask him if they used them to look down at the Indians."

Rosa relayed the question. The response was surprisingly long.

"He said he was the one that carried the glasses. He said he knew the sun was behind him and there would be no reflection so he used the binoculars. The light was good and he could see very well. The blond Apache had a short beard but long hair down to the middle of his back. He looked very strong but the leader, the one who gave all the orders, was shorter and much older. The others were much younger. But they saw no sign of any woman."

Rosa paused and the moment she did Hernando said something more, something he seemed to have just remembered. As he

247

spoke he ran his finger down the side of his face.

Rosa suddenly leaned forward, her eyes igniting with anger. She spoke again in Spanish but this time she raised her voice, the tone demanding. Then, except for the sound of sizzling bacon, the gulch was quiet as a tomb.

Monte's eyes narrowed with suspicion. "What did he say?"

Turning to Monte, Rosa put her index finger near her temple. Answering Monte's question she slowly drug her fingernail down to her lower jaw. "He said the older Apache has a scar from here to here."

Monte stared at Rosa, but didn't move a muscle.

"And," continued Rosa, "this Apache wore the American's new automatic pistol."

Without thinking I blurted, "Norroso! It has to be!"

"Now what?" growled Jones.

Dumbfounded, I continued to speculate. "It makes perfect sense. Lieutenant Patton said that when Norroso deserted he was headed for the Sierra Madres. He must have met up with some of those Netdahe."

Surprisingly, Monte relaxed. Leaning back against the boulder, he peered at Jones. "Down in Guadalupe Canyon where you found Miss Appleton's button, I told you the tracks had been brushed over by somebody that knew a lot about covering sign. But they missed part of one print. At the time I didn't know what to make of it. Now I know it was the heel of a moccasin. That tells me that if the Apaches Hernando saw don't have Miss Appleton, they're part of a raiding party that does."

No longer the skeptic, Jones said excitedly, "Then we've found her! All we have to do is track those aborigines down and take her back."

Tin-Pan made no comment. Instead he handed a stack of metal plates to me. As I distributed them, he said mildly, "It ain't that easy, Lieutenant. According to Hernando, there's at least six of them warriors, maybe more."

"What did the Apaches get off of the corporal?" Monte asked. "What did McIntosh have with him?"

Jones sighed. "A rifle and forty rounds of ammunition, an automatic Colt pistol with two clips, a pair of field glasses, and the horse, of course."

Tin-Pan stood with the skillet and, stepping carefully over the stones, began forking bacon onto everyone's plate. "That's a good haul. Could be it's enough to satisfy 'em or it might just whet their appetite so they go to lookin' for more booty. There's not much to plunder down in Mexico on account of the revolution and all."

When Tin-Pan got to Selkirk, the trooper shook his head. "I'm not hungry. I keep seeing what they did to the corporal's head. I can't get it out of my mind."

Monte looked across the fire at Selkirk. "Once you caught the Mexicans up on the ridge there, did you all ride back to the canyon easy or did you ride hard?"

"Oh, we rode hard all the way."

"So you kicked up a lot of dust?"

"We sure did."

Tin-Pan set his skillet down, opened a packet of hardtack, and then started passing it around. "Are you thinking them Apaches might have seen the dust?"

Monte took a bite of bacon and then said, "I wouldn't bet my life they didn't see it. And if they did, they'll know about us."

Plucking some bacon out of the pan with his fingers, Tin-Pan took a bite. As he chewed he said, "Then if the Apaches saw us and kept on riding, they'd be looking for us on their back-trail. When we get close they'll lay an ambush for us. On the other hand, they might decide to come after us tonight and hit us at first light."

"Them coming tonight, is more what I was thinking," offered Monte. "Especially if Norroso knows it's me that's after him. And with binoculars, if he saw me and Rosa and Billy riding together, he'd recognize the three of us for sure."

"That's a great deal of speculation," objected Jones. "What are you suggesting?"

"The only way to be sure Apaches won't attack," said Tin-Pan, "is to have more men than they do. And right now we're outnumbered at least two to one. The only good thing we got in our favor is that Apaches don't fight at night. It's on account of one of their superstitions."

Selkirk, still holding his empty plate, sat up and peered into the menacing black shadows beyond the fire. "You think they're out there?"

"Maybe, maybe not," Monte said, "but we've got time to turn the tables on them if they are."

"What do you mean?" asked Jones.

"Rosa," Monte said, "ask Hernando how many times he's come over this way and stolen cattle. Ask him how well he knows the trails around here?"

Rosa asked and then listened to the short answer. "He knows the trails very well."

Monte snapped off a piece of hardtack

with his teeth and glanced up at the stars. "There'll be a half moon this evening, enough light to see by. If we sent Hernando back tonight to fetch the rest of your men, Lieutenant, he could lead them back up here before morning."

Jones's face distorted with incredulity. "You'd trust him to do that?"

"I would if he knew he could save himself and his three friends by doing what he was told."

"He won't go by himself," objected Rosa. "He would fear being taken by the Apaches."

"Well then," Monte countered, "Selkirk and Vogel could go with him. If your troops from down in the canyon get back before first light, the three of them leaving tonight won't make any difference to us here. And if this is all for nothing and the Apaches are long gone, it won't cost us any time in going after Miss Appleton. Whether we get reinforcements or not, it'll be morning before I pick up the Apache's trail. And if we have the extra men there'd be less chance of us riding into an ambush."

For several seconds the only sound heard around the fire was the muffled crunching of molars chewing hardtack and overcooked bacon. What Monte had proposed was quite reasonable and, though Jones had contributed nothing to the plan, it did at least require the lieutenant's stamp of approval. Realizing how serious our predicament was, I crossed my fingers in the hope that his single act of official ratification would be enough to satisfy his sense of self-importance. I also hoped it would distract him from the realization that he would, at least until morning, be in command of absolutely no one.

"The reasoning is sound," Jones said. "But can we convince the Mexican to accept my terms?"

"And what are your terms?" Rosa asked.

Jones sat up, protruding his chin as if he were a judge pronouncing sentence. "The terms are: should he succeed in bringing the troops here by morning, he and his companions will be set free. If he fails, he and the others will be taken to Douglas, jailed, and tried as rustlers, perhaps even accomplices to murder."

Rosa then spoke to Hernando. At first, he adamantly refused, shaking his head from side to side. But when Rosa pointed to Selkirk and also up the ridge where Vogel stood guard, Hernando calmed considerably. Eventually, we heard him voice his approval with a weak but familiar, "Sí."

"Very well," Jones said and then, directing a question to no one in particular, asked, "How soon can they be on their way?"

"I imagine the moon's up by now," Tin-Pan offered. "Only down here in the gully we can't see it yet."

Jones nodded at Selkirk. "Trooper, you and Vogel be prepared to leave in ten minutes. I'll be up forthwith to issue your final orders."

"Yes, sir," groaned Selkirk and then handed me his plate. He was starting to leave when I said, "We could use a few clips of ammunition, Lieutenant. Empty rifles aren't much good." Jones covered his guilt quite well. "Oh, yes," he said smoothly, "That must have been an oversight. Private, hand him four of your strip clips. Have Vogel give you two of his."

As Selkirk reluctantly began unsnapping the pouches of his ammunition belt, Hernando finished the last of his bacon and, after looking around, decided that I was the one to take his plate and cup. He then stood and stuffed his uneaten hardtack down into his trouser pocket. "*¿Vamos ahora?*" he asked.

Selkirk handed me the five-round clips. I dropped two into my vest pocket and tossed the other two clips to Monte.

"Take the Mexican with you," ordered Jones. "Stay close to him, but don't use any flashlights. If he tries to escape, shoot him."

Responding with an emphatic, "Yes, sir!" and a snappy salute, Selkirk and Hernando started up the ridge and soon faded into its black bulk.

We listened as they trudged upward, hearing rocks rattle under their feet. In the distance a coyote howled. Seconds later, faintly and from a different direction, we heard another coyote answer.

Tin-Pan's eyes narrowed with concern. "We all best go up now. I think we've been spotted."

"Why?" scoffed Jones. "Because of those coyotes?"

"Those were not coyotes," snipped Rosa.

"We'll need to move farther up the ridge," cautioned Monte. "About a half mile from our horses I saw a big pile of rocks. We can use that for cover."

"And them horses that are headed back to the canyon," said Tin-Pan, "best have something over their feet so they won't make a lot of noise going over rocks and such. I'm thinking we can cut up some blankets and make some horse moccasins."

In unison, everyone stood but when Tin-Pan began gathering the plates and cups,

Jones waved his hand. "You can leave all that."

"No, sah," replied Tin-Pan, "a body never knows what he's gonna need if he gets in a tight spot. It's no trouble, no trouble a'tall."

"Very well," sniffed Jones and then started up what had now turned into a well-worn trail.

"How many do you think are out there?" Monte asked.

Tin-Pan shrugged as he stacked the plates. "Usually a raiding party runs between five and fifteen. They like to keep the parties small so they can get in and out of the country without being seen."

Monte stepped near the fire and flicked several burning sticks out of the flames with the toe of his boot. Picking them up, he blew out the flame on each. "How good a shot are they with rifles?"

"The Apaches like to get close if they can. I'd say they'll start shooting at one hundred paces. Somewhere in there. Usually they're short on cartridges so they don't like to waste a shot. But you won't be able to see 'em at that distance. You almost never see 'em. An Injun knows how to hide."

Tin-Pan had no idea that, as a young adult, Monte had lived several years with the Kootenai Indians in Idaho. However, like so many others, Tin-Pan had recognized from the outset there was something different about Monte Segundo, something distinctly lethal. "You got an idea, Mistah Segundo?"

"I'm working on it," replied Monte, stuffing the burnt sticks in his back pocket. "But let's get those horses taken care of and then we can talk about it."

When the three of us crested the ridge, Selkirk, Vogel, and Hernando stood holding the reins of their horses. Jones, standing nearby, handed Monte a tightly rolled wool army blanket. "Would you like some light?" asked Jones.

"I don't need it," Monte said, untying the straps that were wrapped around the blanket.

"Monte can see in the dark," I said. "Almost like a cat."

"Is that so?" returned Jones, attempting to sound unimpressed.

After unrolling the blanket, Monte shook it out and then had Rosa and me hold the corners and .stretch it tight. Monte then took his hunting knife and carefully cut several long pieces that were an inch in width. Cutting the remainder of the blanket into four rectangles, he asked for two more blankets.

As Vogel and Jones untied their blankets from the cantles of their saddles, Monte handed the pieces of cut blanket to Tin-Pan, who in turn folded the rectangles into squares. Tin-Pan then covered the hooves of Hernando's mount up to the fetlocks with the squares and then, using the long strips, secured the makeshift socks by tying them off around the pastern.

When all three horses were ready, the men mounted, their forms now outlined by the silver-blue light of a rising moon. "Ride easy," cautioned Tin-Pan, "and those wraps will last quite a while. Be as quiet as you can. Just slow and easy."

"Pistols cocked and locked," ordered Jones. "Just as a precaution."

Silently, the two troopers saluted and then Hernando eased out in front. The only sound we heard was the squeaking of saddle leather, and in seconds, the threesome blended into the dim texture of the mountainside.

Making the sign of the cross, Rosa said softly, *"Vaya con Dios."*

"Amen," seconded Tin-Pan.

"I suppose," Jones said, "since you can see in the dark, you can lead us to those rocks you spoke of."

Monte went to his horse and removed a

small bundle from the saddlebags. "As soon as I get into my moccasins."

"Moccasins?" repeated Jones.

I should have known better but it was only then I began to realize that Monte wasn't going to be with us in the rocks. Monte Segundo was not one to seek refuge and then wait to be attacked. In that respect he was as much like the Apaches as they were themselves. And, too, Monte knew that Norroso was among those that were coming and he wanted that Apache to himself and on his own terms.

"Hard leather soles make too much noise," Monte said, unlacing his boots. "I like to move around. You'll all be up in rocks that are on top of a little hill. With four rifles, you can spread out and cover every approach. The only problem is, there's a good number of junipers up there and a few scattered boulders. That'll give the Apaches some cover."

"So you're giving the orders now, are you?" objected Jones.

"Lieutenant," Tin-Pan said mildly, "all of us except for you has met up with Apaches. And I 'spect they didn't teach Injun fighting in that school you went to back East. That's all we're saying."

"We?"

"Us three," said Tin-Pan, "live along this border. Miss Appleton, Miss Thorndike, and all you soldiers down at the ranch don't know what it takes to live in the borderland. This is a hard country. Things that work back East or even in the army, sometimes don't work down here."

"You mean," scoffed Jones, "things like good manners, good breeding, and respect for authority?"

Monte finished tying up his moccasins. "You can stay here and wait for your men if you want, Lieutenant. You can have the pack mule but we're taking our horses and rifles."

"Those horses and rifles are government property!" Jones said.

Monte untied his mount and swung into the saddle. "Not tonight they're not."

Rosa and I mounted up, but Tin-Pan hesitated. "Lieutenant, if the Apaches come you best put a bullet in your head before they get you. If you don't, they'll likely tie you over an anthill or hang you upside down by your heels and cook out your brains. I seen both them things done to men more times than I want to recollect."

Off in the distance another coyote yipped but this one was not answered.

"I've heard your campfire fables before," scoffed Jones, but then he took the reins of the pack mule and stepped into his saddle. "However, I'm responsible for all this government property and I don't intend to let it out of my sight. And be it known, I intend to make a full report regarding its theft when I return to post."

"Pendejo!" huffed Rosa.

As Tin-Pan mounted I heard him express a barely audible, "Amen."

Monte led off with Rosa behind him. I waited until Tin-Pan moved in front of me and then I took my position. And for the first time, perhaps the first time in his life, Lieutenant Jones was last in line.

Even as arrogant and bombastic as he was I couldn't help but feel a bit sorry for the lieutenant. I felt the same when it came to Ada Thorndike and Marzel Appleton. Perhaps it was because when I looked at each one of them, I saw reflections of myself. Simply put, what we all had in common was snobbery, a character flaw invisible to us but instinctively repugnant to those who had never known a life of privilege.

I, however, had had the good fortune to run into Monte Segundo and then to meet Rosa Bustamonte. In them, I recognized qualities that were lacking not only in me but in everyone I had ever known. My family and those like them had wealth and that cloaked them with enormous power. But what Monte and Rosa possessed, what I had immediately been drawn to, was *strength,* an indomitable trait acquired only by those who had tenaciously endured and prevailed over lives of extreme hardship and tragedy.

In the short time I had been with them I had learned so much about the true plight of humanity that I felt as if I had become a different person, one far removed from William Cabott Weston III. And I knew that if I could change, it wasn't beyond reason to believe that others like me could do the same.

Monte led us to a second ridge that dropped low and then rose steeply to a rocky promontory of boulders that crowned the top of a cone-shaped hill. In the soft moonlight the individual boulders resembled a wall of ten-foot-tall pillars of ice, some having cracked and then collapsed with the remainder leaning ominously to one side as they jutted into the night sky.

We drew up in front of the boulders and looked them over. Then Monte, Jones, and Tin-Pan rode completely around the formation and in half a minute came back to where Rosa and I waited.

"It's no more than forty feet across,"

Monte said, "and that's good. But there's no place for the horses."

Tin-Pan pointed to a lone juniper fifty yards downhill from the rocks. "We can tie 'em at that tree yonder and bring up everything but the saddles and bridles. They won't shoot the horses, at least not at first. They'll be wanting them. And if they try and get close trying to steal 'em, we'll have a chance to pick 'em off."

"Is there no other place we can make a stand?" asked Jones.

"Nothing close by," answered Monte, noticing several piles of crumbled stones near the base of the formation. "We've got time. We can build up some breastworks to shoot behind. And I'm going to leave my rifle here with you, Lieutenant."

"Your what?" demanded Jones. "You're leaving us?"

Monte dismounted. "I won't be far. Just far enough to get behind them."

"That's mighty risky," Tin-Pan cautioned, also stepping down.

"If they come," said Monte, "it'll be the best place for me to be. Your job will be to keep them occupied. The more they're thinking of how to get at you, the better it will be for me."

Rosa dismounted and stood by Monte.

"You will see," she said simply. "But now we will need some long sticks or some yucca poles."

"What for?" Jones asked.

"Snakes," Rosa said. "Snakes live in the rocks. When the sun goes down they like to lay on them for the heat."

Jones shuddered. "Then I'll use my saber instead of a stick."

Rosa and Monte handed me their reins and Tin-Pan handed his reins to Jones. "Tie 'em up good and tight," instructed Tin-Pan. "They might not cotton to lots of shooting."

Jones and I started for the lone juniper. He rode up beside me and lowered his voice. "Is he really going out there alone? At night? And with just a pistol?"

It was dark but I still nodded my head. "He'll have his knife. And I've seen what he can do with it. *El Muerte*, Lieutenant, is not a myth."

CHAPTER 8

On the flat surface of a toppled boulder, Monte and Rosa built up a wall of stone with two shooting portals. When they were finished Monte took the sticks he had taken from the campfire out of his back pocket and sat down. Rosa watched curiously as he rubbed one of the burnt ends over the backs of his hands. When he started on his face, Rosa took the sticks from him. "We are about to be married, Monte Segundo," she scolded, and then began to blacken Monte's forehead. "You can ask for my help."

"That will take some getting used to," Monte said. "I've only had me to think about for a mighty long time."

Rosa worked for several seconds and then spit on her thumb and rubbed it up and down on another of the charcoaled sticks. "Close your eyes," she ordered and then smeared the soot over Monte's eyelids. "I will never forgive you if you get killed."

"Me either," quipped Monte. "But I'm not . . ."

A metallic clank interrupted their conversation. And then we all heard Jones swearing and what sounded like compressed air escaping from an automobile tire.

Rosa chuckled. *"Cascabel,"* she said, but kept working with the charcoal.

I dropped the heavy stone I had been carrying up the hill. Running into the rocks, I scampered over and around some boulders and rushed to see what had happened. I saw Jones wielding his saber and backing up while Tin-Pan, a few feet away, was approaching a dark crevice with a yucca pole extended out in front of him.

"What is it?" I asked.

"Rattler," answered Tin-Pan. "A big one."

"Did it bite anyone?"

"Almost got the lieutenant," Tin-Pan said, poking his pole into the buzzing blackness. "But he's coiled up in here somewhere."

Suddenly Monte and Rosa were behind me. "I see it," Monte said and then stepped over and took the pole from Tin-Pan.

Turning the yucca stalk around, Monte held it by the narrow end and slowly lowered the heavier, wider end into the darkness. With a powerful thrust, he stabbed with the pole and then stabbed again. The third time the rattling stopped. Monte then shifted the pole and, holding the head of the snake underneath the blunt end of the yucca, reached into the crevice and picked the snake up, grasping its neck just behind its venomous jaws.

Holding the mangled serpent high, Monte said, "That's a big one alright."

"A four-footer," added Tin-Pan.

Unsheathing his hunting knife Monte cut off the snake's head and tossed it away. Looking at the rattler's tail, Monte said, "These might come in handy." He then cut off the long set of rattles and stuffed them in his shirt pocket.

"I hate this country," seethed Jones. "I hate everything about it, the wind, the sand, the heat. Everything in it either burns, bites, sticks, or stings!"

Monte laid the dead snake out on a boulder. "If we get hungry you might change your mind about snakes. They taste a bit like a rooster but you can eat them."

"Oh, please!" growled Jones.

Tin-Pan glanced at Monte and then leaned closer for a better look. Tin-Pan's large white teeth suddenly flashed in the moonlight. "Why Mistah Segundo, you are lookin' mighty fine this evening. Yes, sah, mighty fine. You look most as handsome as me."

It was then that Jones and I noticed Monte's makeup. I instantly understood its purpose but Jones was still reeling from the scare imparted by the hostile reptile.

"Are you trying to be funny?" snapped Jones.

Monte merely looked up at the stars and checked the location of the Big Dipper. "It's a good four hours before first light but I have to go." Fingering the two cartridge clips from his shirt pocket, Monte handed them to Jones. "I'll be taking one of the blankets. Just make sure none of you shoot me by mistake."

"One thing you might ought to know," offered Tin-Pan, "is that when an Apache has waited all night and is getting ready to attack, they toss a pebble up in the air. If they can't see it go up and come down, they wait because it's still too dark. Once they toss it and they can see that pebble the whole time it goes up and down, they know it's time. Them pebbles hitting the ground won't make much noise but a body never knows. If you're close enough you might hear it."

"Much obliged," Monte said.

Monte and Rosa maneuvered their way over and around the rocks and back to her breastwork of stones. I had no intention of being nosy but I watched them for a moment as they stood there in the moonlight gazing at one another. I suppose that for them a kiss somehow seemed out of place so they merely embraced. And in that instant, I understood that those few seconds of closeness communicated more than either of them could ever have hoped to express in words.

"Come back to me," Rosa pleaded, as they slowly parted. *"Vaya con Dios, mi amor."*

Monte gently touched Rosa's cheek with the tip of his fingers. *"Siempre,"* he said. Taking off his hat, Monte handed it to Rosa and then picked up a rolled blanket. After a brief pause, he hopped down from the rocks onto the hillside. In seconds, and in total silence, he was gone.

After reaching the first juniper, Monte drew his knife. Then, slowing his every movement, he sank into a crouch. As the Kootenais had taught him, he put all his weight on his back leg, extended his front leg, and then eased his toe down first. Feeling for any hint of a twig that might snap or stone that might roll, he eased the side of his foot down, and finally his heel. Slowly, he shifted his weight to his lead leg easing his trailing leg forward. Repeating the process over and over, he traveled at little more than a snail's pace. Knowing the Apaches would do the same, Monte listened for the slightest sound as he scanned every inch of cover in front of him and, step by step, meticulously worked his way downhill.

Hoping he was hours ahead of the Apaches, Monte looked for a scar in the ground, a ravine where time and the elements had cut a shallow ditch. When he finally found what he was looking for, he checked the stars and realized he had to hurry.

The narrow V-shaped ditch he had selected was only five feet in length but a good-sized catclaw grew at the upper end. The ditch was the perfect depth but a bit short, so Monte dug out the last foot with his hands, quietly setting aside both the sand and rocks. When he was finished he removed more rocks from the remaining five feet, also setting them aside. Then he broke off a small branch of catclaw and placed it near where his head would rest.

Unrolling the blanket, he centered it in the ditch and then draped the edges out over the sides. Lying down on the blanket, Monte folded the lower edges over his feet and then covered that portion of the blanket with the set-aside sand and rocks. In the same manner he worked his way up to his waist. Then he drew his pistol and stuck it between the buttons on his shirt. He also removed the rattlesnake's rattles from his pocket.

Leaning back, Monte tightened his neckerchief and then carefully covered his upper torso with the blanket and more sand. Finally, he placed the branch that he had broken off between his teeth and settled his head between two stones. Under the blanket, with only his face exposed, he palmed the Colt with his right hand. In his left, should he need it, he held onto the snake's rattles. Looking up through the catclaw branches, he could see nothing but stars.

Monte thought of the years he had lived with the Kootenais. They had taught him how to hunt deer and track elk, how to build fires in the rain, and how to make shelters in the snow. But what the Kootenais taught him that was of utmost importance, the thing that set the Red Man apart from the white, was the mastery of patience.

However, Monte was not waiting for a deer to appear or for a snowshoe hare to emerge from its burrow. Now, as both the hunter and the hunted, every thought ceased. Time had no meaning. Monte's world consisted of nothing that he could not see, hear, or feel against his skin. His senses, like that of a common beast, would be what saved his life or got him killed.

The darkness was full of activity, of the struggle of life and death. The pumping wings of an owl cut through the air overhead. Somewhere a mouse was scratching. A rabbit hopped nearby. Sand trickled from an unseen burrow. A coyote yipped, this time a real one. A large insect buzzed by and then a moth fluttered past.

When Monte felt the first tingling prick on his chin, he knew it was too pronounced to be an insect and far too light to be a mouse or snake. When he felt the second and third pokes on his skin, a cold chill ran down his spine. Monte dared not move a muscle, but he did lower his eyes. Even so, he was unable to see what was crawling toward his lip, but whatever it was he could tell it had long legs and was moving slowly. All he knew for sure was that he must not move.

A moment later he saw the arching black legs of the tarantula coming down on the side of his nose. Closing his eyes as the Kootenais had taught him, he then became part of the earth. Blending himself into the desert, he became part of the night, part of the natural order of the desert. In seconds the prickling that covered most of his face moved over both eyelids, then across his forehead. Finally, and with some difficulty, the spider crawled down through the tangled hairs on his head and then continued on its way across the sand.

Monte took a deep breath and silently exhaled as he returned from the oneness he had shared with the earth and again listened to the night sounds. He also watched the Big Dipper as it spun counterclockwise around the North Star. Knowing that dawn was approaching, he rubbed a reassuring finger along the trigger guard of his Colt. He was about to move when he heard an ever so slight rasping. At first, he thought it might be ants working on a mound or a beetle crawling across the sand but the sound was not constant, so he dismissed that possibility.

Seconds passed and then he heard the unmistakable crunch of sand underfoot. Several paces to his left but totally out of his limited range of view, an Apache was making his way up the hill toward the rocks. He was so close that Monte could smell him.

Minutes dragged by. When Monte was certain the Apache was far enough up the hill, he eased his left hand out from under the blanket. With the rattlesnake rattle between his ring and little fingers, he slowly reached for a stone. He was ready to lift it off the blanket when he heard another footfall, but this one was much closer than the first had been. Somehow a second Apache had crept near him without detection.

Monte could feel the Apache's eyes staring at him, staring at the very spot where he lay completely vulnerable to attack. Surely, Monte thought, the Apache had seen the slight movement of his hand when he raised it from the blanket. He certainly had heard a faint rustling coming from the narrow ravine.

At that point, Monte knew he had a chance to leap up and shoot the Apache before the Indian could react. But he also knew that if he chose to do that he would be doomed. Yet, if he did nothing he might be stabbed or shot where he lay. There was no time. He had to do something.

Muttering a silent prayer, Monte shook his hand rattling the buttons of the rattlesnake, duplicating the warning rattle of a viper that had been aroused. However, he only shook the buttons a few times, a signal that the snake was only mildly perturbed.

In the tense silence that followed, Monte did not so much as breathe. Then he heard several rapid and far less cautious footfalls, all of them heading up the hill and away from him.

Monte closed his eyes, took a deep breath, and sighed a silent, "Thank you!"

For several more minutes, Monte remained motionless, waiting for another Apache. He detected no more movement but did begin to hear what had to be pebbles hitting the ground. The Apaches were doing just what Tin-Pan had described, and, luckily, all of the faint popping was coming from up the hill and off to his left. Monte understood that if the Apaches were tossing pebbles, they were already in position to attack and only waiting for more light.

Still clinging to the rattler's buttons, Monte again began removing the stones from his blanket and carefully placing them on the side of the ravine so they would not roll. He had only just begun when he heard the muffled pounding of horses' hooves.

We had divided our fortress up into four nearly equal quadrants, Jones facing more or less south, Rosa west, Tin-Pan east, and me north. The way we were positioned, only Jones was unable to see the two horses charging up our hill. It was still too dark to make use of iron sights and we knew we had to conserve cartridges, but the three of us took aim all the same.

Taking a relatively clear path, two Apaches riding side by side barreled toward us from a distance of two hundred yards. As they closed the distance, we noticed they held something between them, something not quite touching the ground. And when they were almost close enough to shoot with or without our sights, they dropped their bundle, wheeled their mounts, and bounded away, heading back downhill but in two different directions.

A few seconds later they circled, reuniting at the base of the hill. Then, to my utter amazement, a half dozen other Apaches, all on foot, joined the pair. One, holding his rifle in one hand and using it as a pointer, indicated the bundle. He yelled something unintelligible, and then he and the other Indians slowly walked single file down the trail, the same one we had used the night before.

Jones called out, "What's going on. Are they attacking?"

"No," I answered excitedly. "They're leaving. Bring your binoculars and come take a look."

Keeping low but scrambling over the boulders, Jones came over and hunkered down beside me.

I pointed at the bundle the Apaches had dropped. "There, see that dark mound down there? Two Apaches rode up to that spot, dropped it, and rode away. Then a bunch more, all on foot, came out of nowhere. One of them said something and then they all walked off. It looks like they're going to leave us alone."

Jones raised his binoculars and focused them. He took them down, looked downhill, and then raised them again. "It's moving. Whatever it is, is moving."

"What do you see?" Rosa asked.

"I'm not sure," Jones answered. "It looks like a blanket all wadded up. But I think there's something wrapped up in it."

"Should I go and take a look?" I asked.

"You stay put," ordered Tin-Pan. "Apaches don't run off like that unless they got a reason."

"They got a look at my men," Jones said, proudly, "they're on their way. They must be getting close and that's why the Indians left."

"Could be," agreed Tin-Pan, "but it won't hurt to stay here and see for certain. Apaches can be tricky. And they ain't stupid. Not only that, I only counted six that walked off. There could be more of 'em out there hiding and waiting for us to let our guard down."

Jones put the glasses back up and then swore. "That was not a blanket. That is Miss Appleton! I'm certain of it. She's starting to sit up. That's what they dropped. It's her!"

"Could be," Tin-Pan said again. "It could also be an Apache dressed up like her. You just sit tight and wait for more daylight. And besides, if that's her down there she might be able to walk up here on her own if she ain't been harmed."

Not taking the binoculars off the lone figure, Jones said, "I concede those were wild Indians and therefore I admit that I was wrong. But did you see how they ran when the United States Cavalry showed up, the men under my command? What a story this will make in Washington! Just imagine, Apaches in the twentieth century and a well-known aristocrat, a helpless woman kidnapped and then rescued from the savages! It'll make national headlines!"

"Does she know we are up here?" Rosa asked. "She just sits there."

Jones took the binoculars down and stood up, making himself an easy target. "Up here!" he yelled. "Miss Appleton, we are up here. Do you see us? If you see us, wave your hand. Are you alright?"

Still standing in plain sight, Jones took another look with the glasses. "She's not responding and her head is bent low. Her hair is undone and covering most of her face. And . . . and . . . she has no shoes or stockings. She is barefooted.

"I should go down there. Perhaps she hit her head or something. She could be injured or bleeding."

Seeing no necessity to burden himself with an excessively large vocabulary, Tin-Pan repeated for the third time, "Could be."

Jones almost dropped his binoculars. "Why do you keep saying that?" he roared. "Could be, could be, could be."

Tin-Pan took a moment to answer. When he spoke his tone was subdued but firm. "Because me and Mistah Slaughter fought Apaches for more years than I want to recollect. And I know how they are and what they can do. Like I said, they ain't stupid, not one bit. They learn quick. And thinking on what *could be* is what keeps a body alive in Apache country.

"Now maybe they took off 'cause of the army's coming like you said and that does make sense. But it might be they're using Miss Appleton for bait, that there's two or

279

three sharpshooters down there waiting to pick off whoever goes down to get her. And maybe them same sharpshooters told Miss Appleton that if she tries to make it up to us, they'll shoot her, too."

"They wouldn't dare!" snarled Jones.

Suddenly, it dawned on me that Jones had abandoned his position in the rocks, leaving us defenseless should any Apaches approach from that direction. Knowing it was useless to point that fact out to Jones, I said nothing to him and climbed over the rocks as quickly as I could to protect our southern exposure.

I could not see Tin-Pan from my new position but I could easily hear him. "Good thinking Billy," he said. "Don't let 'em flank us."

When Monte heard the galloping horses he stopped removing the rocks from his blanket. Motionless, he listened as the hoofbeats halted and an Apache called out. Once more he heard the sound of thundering hooves, but then he could tell they were heading northeast away from the crest of the hill. He had just begun to move again when he heard Jones foolishly calling out to Miss Appleton.

Swearing silently and taking a chance,

Monte began to move more quickly. He knew from the direction of the sound that the mounted Apaches had ridden toward Rosa's position in the rocks but had stopped far short of it. And, listening to Jones, it was obvious the Apaches had left Miss Appleton out in the open where she could be seen. But it was Jones that called out to the kidnapped woman. That meant Jones had left his position, and his attention, and likely everyone else's, was focused on Miss Appleton. If that was the case, no one was covering the southern approach to the boulders.

Having no other choice, Monte quickly slid out of the blanket. Easing out of the ravine, he stopped briefly to study the ground around him. Had it not been for the urgency of the situation, Monte would have taken more time before moving again but there was no time. The Apaches would have anticipated the momentary distraction Miss Appleton had provided and at least one of them would be set and ready to take advantage of their ploy.

Bending low and angling for the south side of the boulders, Monte stepped swiftly yet softly from one juniper to another, then from a spiny yucca to a patch of beavertail cactus. From the cactus he dropped into a tall stand of dry grass. From there, he crawled uphill on his belly, angling toward the rocky pinnacle of the hill.

He had not gone far when, through the blades of grass, he spotted movement not twenty feet in front of him. Seeing the slow but rhythmic motion of two moccasins, he paused. However, in the same instant so did the moccasins. Then to his shock, a brown hand emerged and motioned to him in what had to be a type of sign language.

Realizing the warrior had mistaken him for another Apache, Monte drew his knife and crawled directly for the moccasins. But this time he crawled quickly. When he was within an arm's length, Monte came to his knees, coiled, and sprang on the unsuspecting Indian.

I took up Jones's position behind the breastwork he had built and raised my head just high enough to be able to see the hillside below me. The sun had not yet crested the mountain peaks but it was getting brighter by the minute. Eighty yards away, I could see several small boulders scattered about, and for a frantic moment mistook one for a crouching Apache.

Once I was over that scare, I studied a few yucca plants to make certain they weren't moving. Then, a bit closer to our fortress, I carefully looked over a patch of beavertail cactus that was growing near a tall stand of dead grass, grass that reached all the way to the base of the boulder I was hiding behind.

Once, out of the corner of my eye, I thought I saw something move in that patch of grass. My heart racing, I spun and focused my full attention on that one small area. However, concentrating was very difficult with Jones continually calling out to Miss Appleton and pleading for her to come and join us.

About the time Jones gave up, I decided that my eyes had merely been playing tricks on me and I resumed searching everything else that I could see from my station.

I heard Tin-Pan say, "Sun's coming up." I glanced to my left and caught a blinding splinter of the sun's rim rising above the gray fringe of a distant mountain range.

"Your men," I said, slightly raising my voice, "should be here soon, shouldn't they, Lieutenant?"

"Within the hour," replied Jones, his voice now vibrating with a tone of authority that had been absent throughout most of the night. "As soon as they're sighted, I'm going to march down there and rescue Miss Appleton."

"That's brave of you," I muttered and continued to look for Apaches.

Lying flat in the grass and not wanting to be shot by mistake, Monte shifted only his eyes as he inspected the rifle next to the dead Apache. It was an old Winchester. Its stock was decorated with brass tacks and it had a roll of wire holding the forestock onto a rusted barrel. Gambling the rifle would be more trouble than it was worth, Monte chose to leave it beside the Indian. When he saw me finally look away he began, inch by inch, backing down the hill the same way he had come up. Twenty minutes later, he was able to get off his belly and crouch behind a deadfall. From that vantage point he could see the top of the juniper tree where our horses had been tied.

The Apache Monte had killed was young, twenty years old at best, and Monte was keenly aware that others like him could be anywhere nearby. However, knowing the horses would be a prize that would tempt any young buck on a raid, Monte decided to move in the direction of the juniper.

Nothing was moving except the sun, which had cleared the mountain range an hour earlier. The morning coolness was gone and it was deathly quiet. The air was still and I could already feel the rays of the sun burning into the side of my face. A half hour earlier, Jones had again begun calling out to Miss Appleton but had since given up. And still, there was no sign of the soldiers.

"There's nothing moving down there," Jones said, almost whining. "Not a single thing. If the Apaches are down there, why haven't they at least taken a shot at us?"

"You don't see Monte either," Rosa said, "but he is also down there. If there were no Apaches, he would have let us know by now."

Jones, unable to argue with Rosa's assertion, fell silent for several minutes. What I heard next I assumed was the sound of an Apache signaling to the other warriors using some sort of animal call. That thought, though, was shattered by the bellowing of Lieutenant Jones. "Up here, Miss Appleton!" he shouted. "Up here!"

When Jones finished, I heard the sound again. This time I recognized it for what it was, a weak female voice uttering one dreadful word. "Water!"

"Yes," Jones called out, "we have water. But you have to come to us. Please, Miss Appleton, come to us."

"If she could come," Rosa said scornfully,

"she would have come already. They're out there telling her not to move or they will kill her. Anyone can see that."

"You can't be sure of that!" retorted Jones. "Like I said, we've seen nothing all morning. Your man probably hasn't seen anything either."

"She's right, Lieutenant," said Tin-Pan. "And besides, Miss Appleton is a long way from dying of thirst. For now, we all best be patient and see what happens. You know, Lieutenant, you know down deep that things ain't right."

The wiry Apache that Monte saw fifty feet away from him had risen without a sound and seemingly out of thin air. He wore only a headband, breechcloth, and pair of moccasins. He carried no weapon but instead held a coiled, braided leather lariat in his left hand. In a crouch, he was gliding cautiously toward the horses, no doubt confident his approach was hidden from view to anyone in the rocks above.

Monte, lying next to a mesquite trunk, waited until the Indian turned his head and looked away. Then, Monte slowly drew his pistol, swung his arm around, and took aim. As he raised his thumb to cock the hammer a shot exploded to his right, blasting splinters of wood into his face.

Monte rolled on his back in time to see another Apache, rifle in hand, charging toward him. Firing instantly, Monte cocked and fired a second time, hitting the charging Indian with both slugs and spinning him sideways. Rolling again, Monte lunged to one knee and fired again at the first Apache, who was now running downhill and away from the horses. Monte saw the Apache stumble and then drop his lariat but he kept running. In seconds, he was gone.

Staying low, Monte ran downhill, taking a dozen strides before dropping behind a yucca. There, moving only his eyes, he listened.

Despite the repeated shots fired right below us, the only movement we saw was our horses jerking at the branches of juniper and the frenzied stomping of their feet. Soon, even that commotion ceased and then, once again, all was quiet. It was as if nothing whatsoever had happened.

"Three of those shots was pistol shots," said Tin-Pan. "I counted four shots all together. All of 'em down by the horses."

"Me too," I said. "Four shots. The first one was from a rifle."

"Billy," asked Tin-Pan, "how good is Mistah Segundo with that pistol of his?"

"He can hit a five-gallon bucket at one hundred yards if he has time to aim," I answered. "Up close, when he doesn't have time to aim, he's even better."

Tin-Pan thought for a moment. "That Norroso you talked about, how old do you figure he is?"

Having been a reporter for the *Chicago Tribune* when I was in Columbus, I had interviewed the officer in charge of the Apache scouts and knew a great deal about each of them. Two of the scouts had worked with General Crook during the Geronimo campaign thirty years before and one of them was Norroso. "He would be close to sixty by now."

"Sure enough," said Tin-Pan. "That's about how old Geronimo was on his last raid, fifty-seven I think it was. And I recollect you saying Charley McComas would be nigh on to thirty-seven."

"What difference does that make?" asked Jones. "That shooting means the Apaches are here! They're actually out there and they have Miss Appleton."

"Yes, sah, Lieutenant. That's what that means alright. But I got to thinking that Miss Appleton is the plum, she's what we all want. And so I figure the head men are the ones closest to her so they can get the best shots and the most glory when they get back to their stronghold and tell their stories around their campfires. That sort of thing is big medicine to an Injun, getting the glory, I mean."

"So, what is your point?" Jones asked.

"Just thinking," said Tin-Pan, "that's all. But if Mistah Segundo is still alive, I'm thinking he's figuring things the same as me. And if he can kill those two older bucks, the rest will hightail it back to Mexico."

"I do not care about Charley McComas," Rosa said. "I want to kill Norroso."

"Why?" Jones asked but then said derisively, "Oh, that's right. You claim he stabbed you in the back. Is that it?"

"No. That is why Monte wants to kill him. I want to kill him for what he did to two Mexican wire cutters. To kill is one thing, but anyone who tortures men in that way deserves only to die."

"Amen," said Tin-Pan. "Amen to that."

"What was that?" Rosa asked excitedly as she pointed to the northwest. "I saw a flash."

"Where?" demanded Jones, leaning his rifle against a boulder and raising his binoculars.

"Two ridges over," Rosa said. "It had to be metal or glass reflecting the sun."

"Two ridges!" blurted Jones. "Two ridges over?"

"There!" said Rosa. "I saw it again."

"I saw it, too," said Tin-Pan. "About three miles off, I'd say."

"I see them, damn it," said Jones. "That's them. But what the hell are they doing way over there?"

"Americans," sneered Rosa. "They are lost."

Jones grabbed his rifle, fired off a shot, and then checked the ridge with his binoculars.

"That's way too far away, Lieutenant," said Tin-Pan. "They can't hear that shot and even if they did, nobody could tell where it come from."

"They're about to go over the ridge," exclaimed Jones. "They're going the wrong way!"

Rosa swore and jerked off her jacket. She faced a boulder and then jerked her blouse over her head. Before anyone noticed she slipped her jacket back on. Holding her jacket closed with one hand she grabbed her white blouse and a yucca pole. Snagging her blouse on one end of the pole, Rosa hopped up on the top of a boulder and waved the makeshift signal flag back and forth.

Jones glanced up at Rosa and if he saw more of her than he should have, he hid it well. He threw his binoculars back up. Ten seconds later, a rifle shot sent a bullet whizzing past Rosa's ear and she instantly jumped down off the rock.

As Rosa struggled back into her blouse, Jones exclaimed, "It worked! They stopped. By damn, it worked. They saw it."

Monte was lying prone and within pistol range of Miss Appleton when he heard the rifle shot that narrowly missed Rosa, which caused him to flinch badly. Realizing he had not been hit, he tried to guess precisely where the shot had come from. The best he could tell, however, was that it had been fired from somewhere very near where Miss Appleton sat but on the far side of her. Unfortunately, he could detect no cloud of smoke so he knew the shot had come from a newer, smokeless rifle cartridge, likely a Mauser taken from a murdered Carrancista soldier.

A long minute passed with no additional shots from the Mauser or any return fire from the rocky fortress. With his eyes on Miss Appleton, Monte moved forward an inch and then paused. He was about to slide again when a black loop of braided leather flew through the air and dropped over Miss Appleton. Encircling both her shoulders, the lariat was jerked tight, toppling the woman onto her side. Then, with her offering no resistance, she was dragged toward the brush.

Monte was directly in line with both Miss Appleton and whoever was on the other end of the lariat. Even if he had seen who was reeling the woman in, a shot would have been far too risky. Instead, assuming he had not been discovered, Monte stayed where he was, watching as Miss Appleton silently disappeared into the brush. Then he listened to the multiple heavy and hurried footsteps that followed.

The Apaches, Monte knew, were leaving and they were leaving in a hurry. Realizing the soldiers were finally on their way, Monte relaxed. However, not wanting to be mistaken for an Apache and shot by mistake, he chose to stay where he was until it was safe.

When the lariat tightened around Miss Appleton, Jones suggested we blindly shoot into the brush with our rifles in hopes of hitting whatever Apache was dragging her. Tin-Pan, though, advised against it, saying it would only get her killed and that it was better to wait for another chance. I wasn't so sure that Tin-Pan was right, but we all held our fire. A few minutes later, Rosa caught sight of some movement far out on our back trail.

Jones peered through his binoculars. "It's them, damn it! It's them! Finally!"

"That's why them Apaches took Miss Appleton and run off," Tin-Pan said, standing up for the first time in hours. "Now they know they're outnumbered and out-gunned."

Rosa stood as well, but she was not interested in the distant column of soldiers. She was searching for Monte. My nerves were frayed to say the least so I sat where I was. Protected by the rocks, I decided that I, for one, was going to remain vigilant. And I did not leave my post until I heard the welcome rumbling of cavalry hooves charging up the base of our hill.

When I got over next to Rosa, I glanced to my left and saw Jones standing on top of a boulder gallantly holding his drawn saber and fiercely staring into the morning sun. Had I not known better, I undoubtedly would have been impressed with the dashing figure he presented. As it was, I paused to watch the approaching troopers, shaking my head as they slid to a dusty stop and then gathered in a tight bunch, looking up in awe at their commanding officer.

"Trooper Vogel," Jones said angrily, "what took you so long? We've been holding our position for hours!"

"Sir," replied Vogel, "on our way down the trail last night, the Mexican heard a coyote and panicked. He took off running and one of the blankets on his horse's feet came untied. His horse tripped and threw him. He busted some ribs when he landed and his horse kept on going.

"So, we had to double up with him behind me. Only, then we got lost. When we finally got back into Guadalupe Canyon we had to wait for daylight to figure if we should go up or down the damned canyon in order to find the men. Then we had to make a stretcher for the Mexican and send him with two men back to the post.

"After that the rest of us, along with the three other Mexicans, started up the trail. The Mexicans were leading and got out in front of us. Then all of a sudden the three of them took off in different directions and we couldn't see good enough to follow after them. But we could still see your old tracks, so we followed them until they up and disappeared."

"What do you mean 'disappeared'?" demanded Jones.

"I mean the tracks were all of a sudden gone, sir. We looked but couldn't find any so we kept on going the best we could until daylight. That is when we saw your signal flag."

Rosa and I heard a voice behind us. "Whose idea was that?"

Startled, we both turned to see Monte. "Monte!" scolded Rosa. Then throwing her arms around him she said, "Don't sneak up like that!"

Ignoring Jones, who continued to interrogate his men, I asked, "You mean the signal flag?"

"Yeah."

Blushing a bit, I said, "It was all Rosa's idea."

Still holding onto Monte, Rosa shrugged. "There was no time. The soldiers were going out of sight. I used my *camisa*."

"You don't say," Monte replied, flatly.

Rosa let go of Monte. Studying him closely, she smiled up at him. "I was careful. No one saw me. Not too much of me, anyway."

Monte frowned but half in jest said, "Maybe next time I should stick around for the show."

And, as simple as that, we turned our attention back to Jones, who had finished haranguing his troops and was now putting on quite a performance.

Gesturing with his saber, he declared, "As hard as it is to believe, men, the ones that kidnapped poor Miss Appleton, are honest-to-goodness wild Apaches. They are every bit as cunning and dangerous as those that raided thirty years ago with their famous war chief, Geronimo.

"We held them off all morning but now we're about to engage in hot pursuit. Anyone not on guard at all times is risking his life. From here on out . . ."

I saw Tin-Pan skirting his way around the rear of Jones's granite soapbox and coming our way. His old eyes were steady, his expression grim. When he got close he spoke softly, not wanting to distract the troopers. "Them two mounted Apaches are likely decoys so we don't want to go after them. The ones that are on foot will be headed for wherever they hid their horses. And to get to them horses they'll go through places no horse could ever follow. Then, as soon as they get mounted up again they'll light out. After that, even if we find their trail and are lucky enough to get close, them Apaches will, sure enough, split up and take out in all different directions. But later on, they'll meet back up at some place they all know. That's how they done it years ago and it makes catching them nigh on impossible."

"Clever," I said.

"If they do that," Monte advised, "all we can do is hope there'll be a way to tell which one of them has the woman."

"And which one is Norroso," added Rosa.

"It's a little simpler," Monte added, "because there are two, maybe three less of them."

"Is that what those shots were about?" Rosa asked.

"I knifed one," Monte offered. "Shot two others. One dropped, the other ran off with a slug in him."

Tin-Pan eyed Monte for several seconds. "Lord, have mercy!"

"All three were young bucks," Monte said, "and none of them were blond."

"I was thinking on that being the case," said Tin-Pan. "This being a raiding party, there'd be some young ones, maybe on their first raid, and some older ones. Chances are good them two older Apaches, the one with the scar and the blond, will stick together and keep the woman. She's most likely the property of one of them two bucks and one of 'em is for sure the leader. But if them older Apaches get pressed too hard, they'll split up too. And then's when they might decide to kill Miss Appleton."

"We've got no other choice," Monte said. "We can pick up the trail right where they dragged her off."

"We all agree, then," asked Tin-Pan, "that we got no choice but to go after 'em and go hard?"

I nodded and so did Rosa.

"Alright then," muttered Tin-Pan, "I guess it's up to me to tell the lieutenant. He ought to know if he gives the go-ahead that the odds are stacked are against him . . . and Miss Appleton."

Jones was winding down his speech. After ordering that our horses be brought up from the juniper, he glanced around and, seeing Tin-Pan coming toward him, hopped down from the boulder. For a moment, the two men spoke softly and then Jones stared over at us. Of the three of us, I was the only one that nodded in confirmation.

Jones sneered and then sheathed his saber. Working his way around the rocks and, seemingly determined to charge after the fleeing Apaches, Jones swung into his saddle.

"The lieutenant still doesn't get it," complained Monte. "Tin-Pan's got to make it clear that he and I have to work out the

Apaches' trail before anybody goes any-where. That's got to be done on foot. Until we do that, Jones has got no place to go."

Watching the lieutenant mount up, Tin-Pan also realized Jones was confused. So, once again he approached him, quietly explaining a second time that the trail of the Apaches would go through terrain too rugged for mounted troops to follow.

Jones, realizing his mistake but thinking quickly, issued a face-saving command. "Spread out, men," he shouted, "and search this entire area for hostiles. Report back in half an hour."

The troopers eagerly bounded off in every direction. Watching them scatter reminded me of a swarm of children scampering about in a disorganized game of hide and seek. Jones, though, methodically rode in a circle around the crest of the hill and then came back to where we were standing by the rocks.

Paying no attention to Jones, Monte glanced from Rosa to me. "I think it's best if the two of you come with me and Tin-Pan," he said. "Billy, when we find where the Apaches left their horses, you'll need to come back and tell the lieutenant where we are. It'll be up to you and the troops to find a way to get back to us on horseback."

Still mounted, Jones said emphatically, "I'll be coming with you as well. I'll leave one of my men in charge here."

Tin-Pan glanced uncertainly at Rosa, then at Monte. "Are you thinking they'll leave Miss Appleton along the trail somewhere?"

Understanding the undertones of Tin-Pan's question, Monte said, "No, I don't. I want Rosa along because I've seen her shoot a rifle at long range. And, unlike those wet-behind-the-ears troopers, she's battle-tested. And she knows how to walk without making a lot of noise."

Rosa looked up at Jones. "Why do you come with us, now?"

Jones immediately soured. It was the second time Rosa had asked such a question and the lieutenant was not used to being second-guessed, especially by a peon woman. "This is now a military operation and it will remain a military operation. Therefore, I will accompany you in my official capacity."

"Suit yourself," Monte said as he gazed down the hill, studying the lay of the land where Appleton had been sitting. "But there won't be any need to bring your sword along."

With an insulting snort, Jones said, "This is a saber. The navy uses swords. And for your information, I had no intention of bringing it. Sabers are only used when on horseback."

"How about a rifle, then?" countered Monte. "Do you use one of them?"

"If you were indeed in the National Guard, Mr. Segundo, you would know perfectly well that officers don't carry rifles into battle, only pistols."

"Alright then," Monte said, "I'll take back the Springfield I left with you."

Feeling the tension rising between Monte and Jones, I offered, "I'll get it, Lieutenant. Is it near where you stood guard this morning?"

"No. It's leaning against the boulder where I addressed my men."

"Let's go down and have a look at where they dragged off Miss Appleton," Tin-Pan suggested. "Let's see how much sign they left us."

I found the Springfield easy enough but quickly realized that carrying an eight-pound rifle in each hand while climbing over rocks was no simple task. By the time I reached the drag marks, Jones had dismounted and was standing alongside Rosa. In front of them, both Monte and Tin-Pan were several paces into the brush. Tin-Pan was bending low, studying the ground at his feet, and a few feet away, Monte was on his knees pulling something from a branch of mesquite.

Monte came to his feet and crossed over to Tin-Pan. "What do you make of this?" Monte asked holding up a tuft of something between his thumb and index finger.

Tin-Pan squinted and then shoved Monte's hand farther away so that his eyes could focus on what Monte held. "Blond hairs," said Tin-Pan.

"But are they Miss Appleton's or the blond Apache's?" Jones asked.

Reaching for the strands of hair, Tin-Pan carefully took them and then rubbed them between his fingers. "It's too fine, way too silky to be the Apache's."

Nodding thoughtfully, Monte took the tuft of hair from Tin-Pan. Tucking it into his pants pocket, he asked Tin-Pan, "What did you come up with?"

"An Apache was dragging Miss Appleton. He's got to be strong but his feet ain't all too big. And his right toe points out more than his left. I'd guess he's about one-hundred-sixty pounds, a little heavy for an Apache with feet that size."

"Yeah, I saw some of those tracks, too," agreed Monte, "but mixed in with them were tracks of another Apache, one that has big feet. He's heavier than your man so I'm guessing he's the big blond."

"So, there were two Indians down here?" asked Jones. "And you think one was Charley McComas?"

"Looks that way," answered Tin-Pan.

"In that case," Jones said enthusiastically, "we should make every effort to capture McComas alive. Can you imagine what it would mean to his family? Just think of it! After thirty years among the aborigines. And then to rescue him along with Miss Appleton . . . what a sensational story!"

I could see the wheels turning in the lieutenant's head. Appleton was from an influential family and so was Charley McComas. And I had to admit, the story of their rescue would make headlines from coast to coast. Lieutenant Jones would become famous overnight and then he would unquestionably skyrocket in rank.

"One thing I can't figure," said Tin-Pan, "is why the Apaches didn't kill Miss Appleton right here. They know'd the cavalry was coming and it was time to run off. That's when they tend to kill their captives. They don't want to give 'em back but they don't want to be slowed down either. That part's got me stumped."

We were suddenly distracted by a

mounted trooper barreling down toward us. In seconds, he slid to a dusty stop, barely missing Jones. "Sir, we found three dead Apaches! Two were shot and one had his throat cut . . . cut clear down to the bone!"

Jones, in his own way, was a rare one. He reacted as if what the trooper had reported was yesterday's news. "Very well," he said matter-of-factly. "Have the men regroup by those rocks. I'll be along momentarily."

With an excited, "Yes, sir," and a crisp salute, the young trooper bounded up the hill.

"We best get on our way, Lieutenant," Tin-Pan said. "You can go and give your orders and come back. We won't have gone too far."

"My thoughts, exactly," replied Jones and then swung up and into his saddle. Before spinning his mount and galloping up the hill, he grunted an authoritative, "Carry on, gentlemen."

Watching Jones ride away, Rosa laughed. *"¡Que gilipollos!"*

"That man," lamented Tin-Pan, "shore puts me in mind of that Lieutenant Bourke that rode with Crook back in the eighties. He shore 'nuf does."

CHAPTER 9

Following the trail left by the Apaches, Monte took the lead and, as expected, Tin-Pan was right behind him. They had only covered fifty feet when Jones returned, this time on foot. Rosa and I were standing and observing Monte and Tin-Pan but Jones, without a word, walked past us and plunged into the brush.

Rosa rolled her eyes and shouldered her Mauser. "No use to wait here," she said, and then trailed after Jones.

In times past, being last at anything would have been a source of considerable irritation, but I had been around Monte Segundo long enough to learn that such things were of no importance to him. What mattered most was how one behaved when the pressure was on. And I had recently come to understand that only the foolhardy and the dead were eager to attain fame and glory. So, shouldering my rifle and content to bring up the rear, I did just that.

Before we had gone far, Monte instructed me to continually be looking back, not for Apaches but to study the trail and the surrounding land formations from a different perspective. He assured me as did Tin-Pan that no trail ever looked the same going east as it did going west.

For the better part of an hour we followed the tracks left by the Apaches and whenever Monte stopped and went down on a knee, I would come up close to see what he had discovered. But many times, Monte would point out slight disturbances in the ground or leaves that none of us, not even Tin-Pan, could see. However, both Monte and Tin-Pan agreed the Apaches were in too much of a hurry to conceal much of their trail. Their intent was to get back to their horses as fast as they could and then use them to make their getaway.

The trail led us through three deep gorges, two of which were choked with boulders and the other lined with steep rock walls. Shortly after clearing the third gorge we came upon a small bench on the far side of a hill. It was devoid of brush and covered with the tracks of horses, moccasins, and one very distinct set of small bare feet.

Turning to me, Monte again explained

how critical it was that I quickly retrace our trail back to the troopers. Then, using the landmarks I had studied, we were to find a way to get back to the bench as soon as possible.

With those simple instructions but loaded with doubt, I started back. However, to my relief and thanks to Monte's advice, I easily recognized the terrain we had just come through. Hardly needing to even look for the tracks we had left, I made it back to the troopers in twenty minutes. Hastily, I explained the situation to Vogel, whom Jones had again left in charge, and in mere moments we were mounted and riding.

This time, though, I was in front of the column with Vogel. I pointed out the landmarks but also explained the location of the two gorges we had to avoid. By going farther down the ridge and angling to the northeast, we were able to work our way around the three gorges. We then started up a likely looking ridge, which, as it turned out, branched in the wrong direction. Crossing down a narrow drainage, we came out on the right ridge, and in the glare of the noonday sun, rode up to the bench.

Jones had heard us coming and was standing in the small clearing as we approached. "Excellent, Private Vogel!" complimented

Jones. Another private brought up the lieutenant's horse. Stepping into his saddle, Jones added, "You made good time getting here, Private. I'll make a note of that in my report."

Admittedly, at that moment, I did feel a bit like a piece of wallpaper but, then again, I reminded myself that whether or not I received recognition for what I had accomplished really didn't matter. I glanced at Monte who was sitting next to Rosa and Tin-Pan, all three in the shade of a juniper. Monte gave me a nod. And that simple gesture meant far more to me than any pat on the back Lieutenant Jones might have doled out.

Monte, Rosa, and Tin-Pan got to their feet. Rosa went to her horse, mounted, and then rode up beside me. Tin-Pan, beginning to feel his age, also saddled up, but Monte again started out on foot.

Allowing a head start, Tin-Pan waited until Monte had taken ten paces before he fell in behind him. Jones was next, followed by Rosa, but then, instead of bringing up the rear, I cut in behind Rosa and in front of Vogel. It wasn't because I was tired of being last. It was due to the fact that we were closing in on the dreaded Apaches, and Rosa, Tin-Pan, and Monte were my friends.

And being positioned to fight alongside them was vitally important to me and therefore something that mattered a great deal.

With the sun beating down on us, we had followed a side-hill trail for less than a quarter of a mile when Monte stopped and turned. Taking off his hat and shading his eyes, he looked to the north. "Half of them, I'd say four or five, left this trail and cut down that way," he said. "Looks like they're headed back toward Guadalupe Canyon."

"Four or five," repeated Jones. "So half of the horses are still heading south."

"Looks that way," Monte said.

"Then doesn't it make sense," Jones asked, "that Miss Appleton is with the Apaches heading toward Mexico, and she is on one of those horses?"

"Unless," Tin-Pan said, "she's riding with them that's headed north. Apaches is tricky that way. What seems right can be plumb wrong. They know how we think sometimes. But you never know what an Apache might have up his sleeve."

"Then we have no choice," Jones said. "Tin-Pan, can you follow those tracks to the north?"

"The best I can, I will," Tin-Pan said. "But the ones going south might be heading for the buttes. If they go for them rocks up yonder, they'll take off on foot. But first they'll cut their horses' throats and slice off chunks of meat to take along with 'em. Then it'll be a foot race between them and you. And if the woman slows 'em down too much they'll kill her, sure enough."

Jones stewed for a full minute and then stood in his stirrups. Turning, he faced the troops. "Half of you men will accompany Private Vogel, and trail to the north. The other half will stay with me. Private Vogel, Tin-Pan will be your guide. If you lose the trail, mark that spot and then come and find us immediately."

"Yes, sir," Vogel said with a salute.

As Vogel selected his six troopers, Tin-Pan hung his head for a moment and then looked sad-eyed at Monte. "I'll be praying for you, for all of you, and 'specially for Miss Appleton. 'Specially for that poor woman. Only maybe it's best she be dead. I seen too much in my life, too much evil for one man to see. Lord have mercy."

"We will pray for you, too," Rosa said. *"Vaya con Dios, amigo."*

"Amen," Tin-Pan said gravely, and then turned his mount and angled off to the north. Vogel and his men followed close behind in single file, their fatigued horses sending up a cloud of dust as steel shoes clattered noisily over a bed of broken rock and loose sand.

Monte once again started off, but Jones hesitated and glanced at Rosa and me and then at his six troopers who were lined up behind us. I could see that he didn't like the arrangement. He was about to protest when he took a second look at Rosa and the rifle she expertly held across her lap. Then, with nothing more than a disapproving scowl, he turned and nudged his horse forward.

We moved very slowly but had gone less than a mile when Monte stopped and stared at a branch of juniper that was eye level and just to the side of the trail. Carefully, he reached up and pinched his fingers at what appeared to be thin air.

"What is it?" Jones asked.

Monte held his fingers up into the sun, examining what he held. "More of Miss Appleton's hair."

"Then we are on the right trail," declared Jones as he wheeled his horse and faced his men. "Private Selkirk, ride to where the trail forked off to the north. Find the rest of our patrol and bring them back. You'll find us farther down this trail."

Watching Selkirk gallop away, Rosa said,

"Maybe she is not so stupid after all."

I was a bit confounded by Rosa's back-handed compliment. "Why do you say that?"

"Because," Monte answered, "Miss Appleton may be marking the trail for us."

"You mean she's pulling her hair out?" Jones asked.

"If we find another piece, we'll know for sure. It makes sense, though. The Apaches might see a thread or a piece of cloth if she dropped something like that. But they likely wouldn't notice a few hairs, especially being in a hurry like they are."

"Very smart," I said. "She must have remembered what we talked about around the fire the other night. Tin-Pan told us a lot about the art of tracking, how good trackers see even threads and bits of hair."

"Let's hope that's it," Monte said. "That would mean she still has her wits about her."

"Of course, she has her wits about her," Jones said. "Why wouldn't she? Miss Appleton is not the naïve, hysterical type. She's an educated, well-traveled, and sophisticated woman. I'm certain this experience has not been pleasant for her but she knows full well that the might of the United States military will soon descend upon her captors and she will be rescued."

"If it weren't for Monte, Tin-Pan, and the four Mexicans," Rosa said dryly, "the might of the United States military would still be wandering around the bottom of Guadalupe Canyon. Do you think she knows that, too?"

"Captain Miller," Jones said snidely, "had the strategic foresight to request civilian help. Otherwise, you would be miles from here, doing what? . . . Herding cows? Make no mistake, this mission is following standard operating procedures for a military operation."

Rosa's eyes flickered with cunning satisfaction. "So then, everyone will understand that you and your captain are the ones to blame if the woman is found dead."

Jones was taken aback. Apparently, he had not considered such a bleak outcome. "Obviously," he said weakly, "she is not dead."

Not being one to waste words arguing, Monte glanced up at the sun and then studied the dull imprints left by the rawhide shoes of the Apache mounts. Feeling suddenly uneasy, he started up the trail, only now he moved much more rapidly. Somehow, almost as if he'd had a premonition, Monte sensed that time was running out for Marzel Appleton, that if we did not find her soon, she would be dead before the sun set.

The country we passed over opened up on three sides but a half mile to our right a steep range of mountains, all crowned with vertical walls of stone, pierced a cloudless sky. At the higher altitude, the junipers clinging to the mountainsides were larger than down below but they were spaced farther apart. Between them grew scattered yucca, prickly pear, and carpets of grass mixed with hidden stands of the ever-present catclaw. And as we rode beneath those stone fortresses, it was obvious to everyone that we were completely visible to anyone who might be hidden in those buttes.

The hairs on the back of my neck prickled. My senses were on edge, yet sharp and clear. I was filled with what I can only describe as a macabre blend of exhilaration and anxiety. I was at once the predator and prey. And to my surprise, instead of being filled with fear, I felt an inexplicable eagerness stirring deep within me, a primitive desire to charge headlong into whatever danger lay ahead.

We had ridden close to two miles when Monte paused. He said nothing, only pointed. Two ravens, a few hundred yards ahead of us but a bit farther up the side of the mountain, were circling erratically. "Those birds spotted something," Monte said simply and then continued following the tracks, which now angled toward the ravens.

Private Selkirk's description of what the Apaches had done to McIntosh immediately came to mind but then the vivid memory of what I had personally witnessed while in Mexico flooded my thoughts. I could see the two dead Mexicans that Norroso had tied up and then disemboweled, a torture that was designed to kill a man slowly. However, repeatedly assuring myself that Miss Appleton was more valuable to Norroso alive than she was dead, I managed to shove all thoughts of such a death aside. No, I was certain he would not kill her. At least not the way he killed the Mexicans. But then another thought came to me, a thought that sent a chill down my back.

Norroso almost certainly knew that Monte Segundo, the man who shot off part of his ear and then ultimately forced him to flee the comforts of army life, was following him. And, too, the Apache would know that Monte was also *El Muerte,* the legendary hunter of Apaches. If Norroso killed Monte, he would not only exact his revenge but

315

would become a big man among the Sierra Madre Apaches. Tin-Pan said he couldn't understand why the renegades hadn't killed Miss Appleton instead of dragging her away but now it all made sense to me. The thought that occurred to me, the reason Miss Appleton was still alive, was that Norroso was using her for one purpose only, to kill Monte Segundo.

I was about to inform Monte of my revelation when he suddenly stopped. Looking past him, we all caught sight of a horse's legs. They were stretched out across the trail with the body of the dead animal concealed by a stunted juniper. Riding closer, we then saw blood splattered in every direction as well as the contorted bodies of four more lifeless horses. Each had had its throat severed and a foot-long slab of meat cut from its flank.

Before anyone could react to the grisly scene, we heard the other troopers galloping toward us. Instead of turning to watch them approach, every eye began searching for hidden Apaches, Apaches that might be lurking behind any innocent-looking rock or in the meager shade of a nearby juniper or mesquite tree.

The soldiers drew up next to their comrades but Tin-Pan rode on up to Jones.

Studying the dead horses, Tin-Pan somberly shook his head. "That's what they do, alright. They'll scatter, now, some going one way and some another. If Miss Appleton is with these bucks, it don't look too good for her."

"She's with them," Jones said. "She's been helping us by dropping bits of her hair along the way."

Tin-Pan considered what Jones said for a moment. "Well, even if they give her back her shoes she'll slow 'em down too much. Then they'll kill her for certain. Fact is, I'm surprised they didn't kill her right here."

"Why do you say that?" demanded Jones.

Tin-Pan shrugged. "Well, for one thing, with Miss Appleton dead, the Apaches would know there'd be no reason for us to keep after 'em. And, two, them Apaches know that we're in Mexico and have been for a while. I think they figured, with all that's going on along the border, we'd turn back once we got to the Mexican line. But now they see we didn't do that."

"I don't think they'll kill her just yet," I interjected.

"And why is that?" snapped Jones.

"By now," I answered, "Norroso knows Monte is the tracker leading us to Miss Appleton. But unlike you, Lieutenant, Norroso knows Monte for who he is, *El Muerte,* the white man who hunts Apaches. He also knows Monte as the one that shot off part of his ear while he was hiding behind Rosa. And, also, he wouldn't have forgotten that Monte was the reason he deserted the army scouts and ran off to Mexico.

"I'm convinced he'll keep Miss Appleton alive, at least long enough to lure the unsuspecting *El Muerte* into a trap. She's his bait. That's why she's still alive."

I glanced at Monte and saw him looking at me. Monte was not one to show emotion and I could count on one hand the times I had seen him smile, but there it was, a smile so faint that most would not even have noticed. "You're learning fast, Billy. I was thinking along those same lines."

"Sir?" came a voice from behind us. It was Vogel, who was mounted next to Selkirk, the only two troopers who had seen first-hand what the Apaches could do. "Don't we have standing orders not to cross into Mexico?"

"Who told you we were in Mexico?" Jones asked, but his question was a thinly veiled threat. "I have no way of knowing our precise location and neither does anyone else. The borderline in these mountains is, at best, vague."

318

Glaring at Tin-Pan, Jones said, "Isn't that true, Tin-Pan?"

Tin-Pan had been with General Crook, and knew how the army worked. He was also familiar with young lieutenants hungry for promotion. "If you say that's so, Lieutenant," replied Tin-Pan, "I can't say nothing against it."

"There, you see?" said Jones addressing, and at the same time, warning his troopers. "No one knows that we are not still in the United States."

With that declaration, Monte motioned to Tin-Pan. "Let's work out this trail."

Dismounting, Tin-Pan said, "If these here Apaches split up, the ones we'll be wanting will head for them boulders up ahead." Pointing up at an expansive rock fortress perched on top of a mountain, he added. "They'll go for that big butte there, the one sitting all by itself. You can bet your bottom dollar on that."

Jones was suddenly in an awkward position. He had just contradicted Tin-Pan in front of the men and his eye was still black from Monte's fist. He didn't know what to do but was too proud to ask for advice. However, like a fool, I stepped into the void.

"Monte," I asked, "what about the rest of us?"

"Bring any water you've got and follow me and Tin-Pan on foot," Monte said. "But somebody needs to stay here and guard our horses."

"Better leave at least three soldiers, Lieutenant," suggested Tin-Pan. "Right this minute, I'll wager them Apaches are watching us from up on that butte. They need to see the horses are guarded real good or they'll send a couple of braves to try and steal the whole lot of 'em."

Jones reached into his saddle pocket and took out his binoculars. Looping them over his neck, he looked over his men until his eyes settled on Vogel. "Private Vogel, select four men to remain here and guard the horses. You and seven others will bring your rifles and follow me. And be prepared for a long day."

Vogel's "Yes, sir," was less than enthusiastic.

Rosa was the first to step down, which seemed to confuse everyone in uniform, including Jones. It wasn't until she had opened the bolt of her Mauser and slammed a cartridge into the chamber that anyone made a move. The troopers then slid their rifles from their scabbards and, almost in unison, dismounted.

I, on the other hand, stayed in my saddle,

savoring the once-in-a-lifetime moment. Monte and Tin-Pan were seasoned frontiersmen and Rosa was a veteran of the Mexican Revolution. Lieutenant Jones was an ambitious and pompous officer leading a dozen wet-behind-the-ears soldiers in pursuit of a band of renegade Apaches, remnants of a bygone era thought to exist only in the pages of history books.

And there I sat in the middle of it, William Cabott Weston III, on the back of a sweaty horse in the uncharted Guadalupe Mountains, about to shoulder a Springfield rifle and help rescue a damsel in distress. I knew I was naïve and I accepted the idea that I was being a fool, but at that moment, God help me, I was in seventh heaven.

As Vogel selected his four troopers, I took my rifle and stepped down beside Rosa and then watched Monte and Tin-Pan start working their way through the grass, following what appeared to the untrained eye to be an invisible trail. Jones naturally stepped out in front of Rosa and she, as usual, registered no complaint.

For some reason, I hesitated. Glancing over my shoulder, I saw Vogel and Selkirk huddled together with several of the troopers. Vogel and some of the others were speaking but their voices were too low for me to hear what was being discussed. An instant later, the gathering dispersed and, thinking nothing of the meeting, I quickly caught up to Rosa. However, when I happened to look back a second time, I noticed the soldiers were already lagging several paces behind.

"Look here, Monte," Tin-Pan said, halting where he stood. "What do you make of this?"

Monte took a few steps over to Tin-Pan and went to his knees to get a closer look. Bending until his head was only a few inches from a swath of bent grass, Monte said, "It's a shoe print. Moccasins won't crush the blades that way."

"Then Marzel has her shoes!" said Jones. "They gave them back."

"That goes along with what Billy was thinking," said Tin-Pan. "They want her alive. At least for a little while longer."

Monte was still bent over but he had moved a foot to his left. "It looks like she's with Norroso," he said, leaning back and placing his hands on his knees. "And I don't think he cares that we see her tracks. Else, he wouldn't have led her up this way where she would leave a good print."

"We are almost in rifle range of anyone in those rocks," Rosa said, surveying the butte.

322

"And there is lots of open country between here and those rocks. How do we get from here to there?"

"Only way I know of," said Tin-Pan, "is, when we get close, we run dodging and weaving from cover to cover as fast as you can. That's what them Apaches do and it's mighty hard to hit a target that's moving like that."

"I'll have the men form a line three hundred yards out from the face of that butte," offered Jones. "I'll space them one hundred or so paces apart, in sight of one another. They can cover us as we work our way to the base of the butte and then, when we're climbing over the rocks, they can give us cover fire if they see any Apaches."

"If the Indians have Mausers," Rosa said, "there will be no smoke from the rifles. And it is very hard to see an Apache, even in plain sight. Your men will have to look hard or they will have nothing to shoot at."

"I'll be no good in them rocks," admitted Tin-Pan. "I'm too old and some of them walls on that butte are forty feet high. But I can still shoot good with my rifle."

"Alright," Monte said, coming to his feet. "I'm going to the butte. Rosa, you're most likely the best shot with a rifle that we have so I want you to stay with Tin-Pan. Find a safe spot to shoot from, one where you can cover the face of the butte."

Rosa looked around. Seeing a chest-high boulder up ahead, she pointed and said. "We will be there."

Jones took off his binoculars and handed them to Tin-Pan. "I'm coming with you."

My blood was up and before I knew it, I blurted, "Count me in."

Monte looked at me with a trace of uncertainty in his eyes. "Are you sure, Billy? With a rifle?"

I grinned confidently. "I've been practicing at the ranch in Sasabe. While you were out building fence, Angelina and I did a lot of shooting and she's a good teacher. Standing and with no rest, I can hit a pie plate at one hundred paces four out of six times."

Monte nodded his approval. "Well, me and the lieutenant can climb a lot better with our hands free. Lugging that rifle, you won't be able to keep up with us, Billy, but you and that Springfield could come in handy."

Rosa stepped forward and gave Monte a hug. Then, without a word she stepped back and allowed Tin-Pan to shake hands with Monte, Jones, and then me. "You boys be mighty careful up there," Tin-Pan said. "I'll be praying for you."

"As will I," Rosa seconded and then she added sincerely, "I will be praying for *all* of you."

At the time, I wasn't much of a believer but, even so, suddenly realizing I could get myself shot or even tortured to death, I heartily welcomed their righteous intercessions and, had there been opportunity, would have converted right there on the spot.

Monte pulled his pistol and opened the loading gate. From his belt he took a cartridge and slid it into his empty sixth cylinder. Jones checked his chamber and then cocked and locked his Colt automatic.

Not to be caught unprepared, I drew my thirty-eight caliber from my shoulder holster and inspected it, making certain the cylinder spun smoothly.

Jones gave me a curious glance. "Have you always carried that?"

"Yes."

Shrugging, Jones quipped, "It's rather small, isn't it?"

Rosa huffed. "I saw him kill a man with it. It is big enough."

Jones studied me closely for several seconds. Then, glaring at Rosa, his eyes filled with skepticism but he said nothing.

Grouped together, the troopers finally

caught up to us but instead of eight troopers there were only five.

Jones looked them over. "Where are Privates Vogel and Selkirk?"

A lanky trooper with a baggy uniform and prominent Adam's apple spoke up. "Vogel said he busted his ankle, sir. He had Privates Selkirk and Wright help him get back to the horses. Private Vogel said he'd send Selkirk and Wright up here after they got him back."

Swearing under his breath, Jones fumed for several seconds and then gave his orders. In minutes his men had spread out and moved into position. If Jones's plan was carried out properly, I found it comforting to believe that they would be able to cover about a quarter mile of the butte, almost the entire length of the rock formation that faced us. However, I knew only too well that what we saw in front of us was only one wall of the natural fortress, the bulk of which likely covered at least ten acres.

Monte pointed to a narrow cleft in one of the pillars of stone that was a good three hundred yards from where we stood, three hundred yards over broken country that held a few scattered boulders and only a sprinkling of juniper. "We're going to try and make it to that black shadow at the base of the butte. If there aren't any tracks there, we'll go around the base of the rocks until we find some. Then we'll know where they went in.

"But to get to that shadow we're going to have to run and drop, run and drop. Drop behind cover whenever you can. Run zigzag if you can but don't run more than three or four seconds at a time. And after you drop, try and roll a little bit so that when you get back up you're not in the same place you dropped. Make them guess where you'll pop up next."

"Do we go one at a time?" I asked.

"That's best," Monte said, as he tightened his gun belt and shoved his Colt down tight into its holster. "I'll go first."

Jones hesitated for a split second, and I immediately pounced. "I'll go second."

Monte nodded and, without warning, took off running at full speed. His first run was a full five seconds if not longer but his next burst was much shorter as he dove behind a small boulder. When he jumped up from the boulder, I made my first run and then, making sure to protect my rifle, dropped flat on the ground. My face was pressed into the dirt and I couldn't see Monte or Jones. I took a few breaths and then rolled over twice, ending up on my belly. Holding my rifle in my left hand, I got ready to make my next run. To lift myself off the ground, I shoved my right palm squarely into the needles of a prickly pear cactus. Jerking back from the searing pain, I used my elbows to get up and then made my next run, zigzagging to a boulder not much larger than my head but enough to hide behind when I laid flat.

Once when I was running I got a glimpse of Monte. But I didn't see him again until I reached the shadow, which was actually a huge crack in a wall of solid rock. I was breathing hard when I ducked into the opening but Monte, standing in the shadows of the crack, had already caught his breath. I looked at my palm and saw that it was filled with broken needles and beginning to drip blood.

"You better pull those out or they'll fester in no time," Monte said.

We both watched Jones making his way to us. And I must say at that moment, his athleticism was on full display.

"He's pretty good, isn't he?" Monte admitted. "Runs like a damn deer."

"That he does," I agreed, leaning my rifle against a rock wall and then picking at a cactus needle with my fingers. "Imagine what he could do," I chuckled, "if he were dodging bullets?"

Jones came running at us and instantly darted into the crack alongside us. His chest was heaving, however, not so much as mine had been. "No shots," he managed between breaths. "No shots."

"I didn't see any tracks around here," Monte said, "so we'll have to work our way around the base of the butte. If we don't find tracks but see a way in, I say we take a chance and use it."

"Agreed," said Jones, suddenly sounding nothing like an army lieutenant.

The sharp pain in my hand had subsided somewhat but it was already beginning to swell and throb. I licked the blood off my palm and then used my front teeth to pull out the rest of the needles, at least the ones that weren't buried beneath my skin.

"Once you get the needles out, keep working your hand," Monte advised, "it'll hurt but if you don't you may stiffen up."

Jones noticed what I was doing. "Can you still shoot?"

I opened and shut my hand. It felt like someone had hit it with a hammer. "I can shoot the rifle but I might have some trouble with my pistol."

"Remember," cautioned Monte, "don't look for an Apache. Only look for a little part of one, just a small piece."

Monte went down on his belly and slid into the sunlight but only far enough to see to his left and right. When he was satisfied, he stood up and drew his forty-five. "Billy, you look for long shots and cover me and the lieutenant the best you can but stay within ten steps. Me and the lieutenant will be looking for anything that might be up close."

Unsnapping his holster, Jones inspected his pistol and then blew some sand off of the slide. "Ready."

"One more thing," Monte said, "if either of you see that blond Apache don't think of him as Charley McComas. He's an Apache now just the same as the others. So, shoot him if you have to and don't think twice about it. Thinking too much can get you killed."

Easing out into the blazing sun, Monte stayed close to the rock wall as he scanned every conceivable place an Apache might hide. Monte had only taken a few steps, when Jones lunged into the light and then hurriedly leaned back, flattening himself against the stone and holding his pistol across his chest.

After taking a deep breath, Jones shoved himself a few inches away from the boulder and started down the wall. Then, after a slow count to ten, I shouldered my rifle and slowly backed out of the shadows until I could see up and down the rock face for one hundred feet.

It was then I noticed that what from a distance had appeared as a solid walled fortress was nothing of the sort. The entire butte was composed of tightly fitting, though somewhat cylindrical-shaped, boulders stacked side by side and one on top of the other. In the cracks and spaces between them, creosote bushes flourished and even some weather-beaten juniper had taken root. All of which, to my dismay, drastically increased the number of places an Apache might hide.

I felt the sun's heat radiating off of the boulders. The air was thin and dry and I could hear nothing but the crunch of sand under my boots. With my head constantly swiveling and beads of sweat forming on my temples, I took a few cautious steps to my left in an effort to keep up with Jones and Monte. I paused and then I took a few more.

The three of us continued maneuvering around the base of the butte but had not gone far when Monte signaled and then pointed. The next time I glanced in his direction, Monte was gone and Jones had turned to face what had to be a gateway into the heart of the butte. As soon as he saw me looking his way, Jones motioned for me to follow and then he too stepped out of sight.

Hurrying to the entrance, I saw Jones carefully making his way up a narrow, winding passageway where fallen stones had formed a virtual staircase between two towering walls of stone. Searching the crest of the walls for any sign of movement, I entered the shadowy passage. However, I soon discovered that in order to climb I also had to watch my step. And, in attempting to keep an eye out for Apaches while trying not to stumble, I quickly fell behind. As a consequence, I soon lost sight of Jones, who, I am quite certain, never lost sight of Monte.

At the top of the passageway, I came out on a diminutive bench of sand no larger than the back of a horse. In that sand, though, I saw the heel print of an army boot, and from that track I deduced the direction Jones had taken. But from where I stood, all I saw was a maze of boulders and more climbing. I was in the process of deciding what to do next when a rifle shot rang out from somewhere inside the butte.

With so much rock, there was no way Monte could follow a trail. He was going on pure instinct when a bullet smashed into a slab of stone only inches over his head. Ducking instantly, he silently slipped around another boulder and then between two more before he stopped. Knowing the Apache that had taken the shot would also change positions, Monte listened for any hint of sound, any mistake the Indian might make.

All he heard was a faint metallic clank behind him and knew at once that Jones had just banged his pistol against a rock. Then he also detected a faint grating noise. Jones was moving and the thick leather soles of his boots were grinding sand against stone.

Ten minutes slowly passed. Then the silence was interrupted by a distant whisper. At first Monte could not understand the words but soon realized it was Jones foolishly calling out to him. In that same instant, another thundering shot shattered the stillness. It was followed immediately by the wicked whine of a ricochet and a surprised yelp. Jones had been hit.

With a better idea of where the shooting was coming from, Monte holstered his pistol and painstakingly crept through the boulders, swinging in a wide arc in hopes of getting behind the shooter. Moving silently, it was late afternoon before he reached the back side of the butte. He found a narrow ledge and was halfway across the ragged face of the fifty-foot-high boulder when an angry black wasp flew out of a deep fissure in the stone, its wings brushing past Monte's ear.

On a hunch, Monte stopped and clung motionless to the ledge. In moments, two more wasps buzzed overhead, this time on their way into the interior of the butte. Marking the direction of their flight, but unable to see over the top of the ledge, Monte continued inching his way along. However, he had not gone far when he a detected a low-pitched hum, the telltale sound of wasps hovering around water. Somewhere nearby, Monte knew there had to be a tank, a natural stone basin that had collected and held rainwater. He also guessed that the Apaches had known about the existence of the tank and had retreated to this particular butte for that very reason. And it was also likely they would cluster near the water just like the wasps.

After making his way to the far side of the ledge, Monte crawled onto the slanted side of a leaning boulder, a boulder that reached almost to the lip of the butte. Wanting to get a look at the tank of water, Monte lay flat on his stomach. Using his toes to shove and his hands to pull, he painstakingly advanced up the leaning boulder until he was confident that by lifting his head he would be able to see over the rim of the butte.

Monte paused to catch his breath. Hoping not to find himself looking into the barrel of a gun, he slowly lifted his head. He did so just in time to catch a fleeting glimpse of blond hair disappearing around the sharp corner of a fractured boulder.

Glancing quickly to his left, he saw a cloud of wasps hovering over a crystal clear pool of water. The stone tank was roughly six feet across and the entire water's edge was lined with scores of pulsating, thirsty black wasps. Off to one side, and of no interest to the wasps, lay a coiled rawhide lariat, some bridles, and a pair of women's high-top shoes.

Lowering his head, Monte grasped the walnut grips of his Colt but then realized that he would need both hands free in order to vault himself up and onto the top of the butte. Letting go of his pistol he decided he must move quickly and, if at all possible, make it over the edge of the butte in one continuous movement. Monte understood all too well that if an Apache should appear at the wrong time all hell would break loose before he could even hope to get off a shot.

Once again, Monte cautiously peered over the lip of the butte and, seeing no one, raised his arms and placed both palms on the butte's jagged rim. Gritting his teeth, he shoved with his legs and pulled hard with both hands, but instead of sailing onto the top of the butte, his thighs scraped on the sharp edge, jerking him to a sudden stop. However, he had at least managed to get his hips up and over the rim. With his legs extended in midair he reached out with both arms, desperately searching for a fingerhold, anything he could grasp to keep from sliding backwards.

Feeling a faint lip of stone with his left hand, he curled his fingers into a claw and locked his fingernails behind a tiny ridge. All he could do with his right hand was lay it flat on the rock and pull the best he could. All he needed was to slide forward a few inches and then he could roll sideways, that is, if an Apache didn't blow his brains out first.

Monte pulled with all his strength and gained a precious half inch. Taking a breath he pulled again but his right hand was starting to sweat and it slipped. Wiping the sweat off on his pants, Monte tried again and this time gained a full two inches. On his third try he added another inch. At that point he thought about trying to roll but, discovering a meager depression with his right hand, decided against it. Instead he pulled himself forward one final time and was then able to bring up a knee, gain a hold, and finally crawl full-length onto the top of the butte.

Coming to his knees, he drew his pistol. Puzzled that no Apaches had appeared, the thought suddenly occurred to him that any noise he might have made climbing onto the butte had very likely, and very luckily, been masked by the constant buzzing of the wasps.

Rising to his feet, Monte crept forward in the direction in which, only moments before, he had seen the patch of blond hair vanish out of sight. Looking down into a narrow crevasse, he saw a passageway that led to a descending stairway of broken boulders. The steps led underneath a toppled boulder that formed a short tunnel. Beyond the end of the tunnel and in bright sunlight, Monte could see a few creosote bushes and some tufts of grass, which indicated the presence of another bench.

The rocky floor of the passageway was six feet below him and Monte was searching for a way down when he heard a woman scream. It was a long, hair-raising screech, not of pain but of abject fear. The scream was continuous, only stopping when the woman gasped for more air.

Having no other choice, Monte jumped down onto the rocky floor, managing to land solidly and not break an ankle. Cocking his Colt, he hurried through the tunnel and came out onto a level bench that was forty feet long and half as wide. It was walled off on three sides with vertical boulders but the northern rim of the bench dropped off in a sheer cliff.

At the base of the rearmost stone wall, the fallen trunk of a dead juniper tree was sliding, inching toward the cliff in erratic jerks. Tied to the weathered trunk, stretched tight and disappearing over the edge of the cliff, was a rawhide lariat.

Realizing he had no choice, Monte swore and then ran to the cliff. Looking over the edge, he saw Miss Appleton hanging upside down with the lariat tied around one of her ankles. Trying to be heard over the woman's screams but at the same time watching for Apaches, Monte yelled, "Stop moving, damn it, don't move! The more you move, the worse it gets."

Miss Appleton continued to scream and the log continued to slide. With his eyes searching the boulders surrounding him, Monte felt for the lariat with his left hand. He grabbed it but swore again. The lariat had been coated with grease and no matter how hard he squeezed, the rope oozed across his palm. He needed two hands to stop the sliding but the moment he holstered his pistol he knew he would be as good as dead.

He yelled at Miss Appleton again and again but she was panicked beyond hope. The juniper trunk was sliding faster and faster and at any moment might let loose entirely.

Feeling the lariat slipping through his grip, Monte sighed and shook his head. "God help me," he muttered and then holstered his pistol.

Turning his back to the juniper trunk, Monte dug his feet in and grabbed the lariat with his right hand. With Appleton flailing wildly, the lariat continued to slip so he looped his right arm under and over the rope, coiling it around his forearm. The sliding stopped. He leaned backward, took a breath, and then reeled in a good six inches.

He was digging in with his feet when he sensed a presence looming over him. Then a shadow crept across the ground next to him. A few heartbeats later, a figure appeared in the corner of his eye. Before he turned his head, Monte knew it was Norroso.

Wearing the traditional headband, breech-cloth, and moccasins, the scar-faced Apache triumphantly raised his rifle, leveling the barrel even with Monte's rib cage. "You fool! You hunt Apache, now you find. I, Norroso, kill Monte Segundo, kill *El Muerte*. Then, I Netdahe chief."

Norroso had no sooner uttered his last word when he suddenly flinched as a rifle shot roared from some hidden place deep inside the butte. Looking down at a small black hole in the center of his chest, Norroso staggered from side to side. His eyes narrowed into slits and then he fell backward, landed with a thud, and did not move.

"Nice shot, Billy," grunted Monte and then, straining with all his might, pulled again on the slippery lariat but made little headway. He continued to struggle as Miss Appleton's screams grew weaker. Finally, he heard footsteps behind him.

"Billy," warned Monte. "The rope is greased. Get a hold on that log and pull."

Instead of hearing my voice, Monte saw the end of the lariat that had been tied to the log fly through the air and land by his feet. He saw no knot or loop tied on the end and knew instantly the lariat had been cut with a knife.

"Billy," snarled Monte, "what the hell are you doing?"

"I chief now," came the reply.

Monte craned his neck the best he could and, looking over his shoulder, got a glimpse of the blond Apache. He was easily six feet tall, with well-defined muscles from head to toe. He wore a knife and held a Winchester rifle.

Monte was desperate. With both hands holding the lariat, he knew he had only one hope. "Charley McComas!" he blurted. "Charley McComas! Do you remember? That's who you are. You're not an Apache."

The blond eased up behind Monte. Reaching down, the Apache jerked Monte's Colt out of its holster. Then, stepping over the body of Norroso, he stood in plain view and began inspecting the pistol and calmly admiring his new weapon.

"You can come with us, Charley," Monte said, and taking a chance, pulled in more of the lariat. "Come back where you belong. You can get your life back."

The blond turned the pistol upside down and stared at it for several seconds. Walking behind Monte and around to the opposite side, the blond took a second long look at

Monte. "You *El Muerte*," he said but his tone was more that of a question.

Continuing to reel in the lariat little by little, Monte grunted, "Some call me that."

The blond huffed scornfully and shoved the barrel of the Colt behind his breechcloth. "You big medicine, now. Many speak your name. I kill you now, I be big medicine."

Monte saw the bare foot of Miss Appleton rise above the cliff. To get her any higher he knew he would have to walk to the edge of the cliff and pull her straight up. However, if she continued to struggle she might very well pull them both over the cliff.

"Miss Appleton," Monte yelled, "you're almost up but if you don't stop moving I can't get you over the edge. You have to trust me and be still!"

The screams slowed and then ceased altogether. Monte worked his way down the rope until he was within inches of the ledge. He could see that Appleton had been tied by her right ankle, the left leg hanging free. "Miss Appleton, bring your left leg in and put it next to your right leg. Put your legs together and turn your back to the cliff. That way your legs can bend toward me when I pull you up."

Appleton's legs came together. "Don't

drop me. Dear God, don't drop me."

"Put both hands to your sides and be still. When your legs are over, bend at the waist as far as you can and reach for me with both your hands. I'll grab one and pull you in."

When Appleton's heels were facing Monte, he gave one final pull and lifted her up. As soon as the back of her knees cleared the edge of the cliff, Appleton folded her legs, helping to support some of her weight on the butte.

"Now, Miss Appleton, give it all you've got. Bend up toward me and reach out!"

A hand shot up. Monte immediately let go with his left hand and snatched Appleton's wrist with an iron grip. In one desperate jerk backwards, Appleton flew up and over the ledge as Monte fell flat on his back. Appleton landed at Monte's feet but then frantically clawed her way up his legs and then clinched his sweat-soaked shirt with both her fists.

The blond huffed again and then stepped back two steps. Holding his rifle at the hip, he kept it aimed at Monte.

Monte caught his breath, as did Appleton. "You can let go now," Monte said. Prying the woman's fists loose from his shirt, he shoved her aside and sat up.

Glaring at the blond man, Monte repeated, "Do you remember, now? Charley. Charley McComas."

"You know me," was the reply from the blond. "You know. And I know you, *El Muerte.* I know you. You big medicine now."

Appleton pushed herself off the sand and up onto her knees. Her face twisted with hate as her eyes settled on the blond. "You filthy, vile beast," she spewed. "You're not a white man, you're worse than a beast!"

"She's still scared, Charley," Monte said, coming to his feet but watching the barrel of the Winchester. "Don't listen to her. Don't listen to anything she says."

The blond slammed a fist on his chest. "I Apache! No more white, forever. No Charley! Ah-toe-nay. Ah-toe-nay. By this name, you know me. I Apache! I go to be chief, now."

At that moment, Monte was expecting a bullet but to his astonishment, the blond took the Colt from his breechcloth and tossed it at Monte's feet.

Thinking the gesture to be some sort of challenge, Monte glanced at the Winchester still aimed at his chest. Then he looked long and hard at the blond Apache, trying to read what was in eyes.

"Kill him!" demanded Miss Appleton. "Pick up the gun and kill him!"

"Ah-toe-nay," Monte said. "That is your name?"

"Now, you know me," said the Apache, slowly lowering the barrel of the Winchester. "No white man, now. Not ever more. Ah-toe-nay is big medicine now."

Ah-toe-nay walked across the bench, heading for the stone staircase. "Now's your chance," screeched Miss Appleton, rising to her knees and pointing at Ah-toe-nay, "Kill him! Shoot him, you coward! Shoot him!"

As Ah-toe-nay entered the tunnel, Monte slowly bent his knees. Making no sudden moves, he reached for his pistol. Half expecting the blond Apache to spin around and shoot, Monte picked up his Colt. But instead of aiming it at Ah-toe-nay, Monte holstered his pistol and started after him.

With Miss Appleton's shrill, hate-filled rants filling the air, Monte followed after Ah-toe-nay. A moment later, she reconsidered her situation and staggered after Monte. It was then, at the base of that stone staircase, Marzel Appleton saw Monte approach Ah-toe-nay. She saw them face each other. She watched as they spoke one to one another and then, to her horror, she saw Ah-toe-nay simply turn and walk away.

CHAPTER 10

After hearing the third rifle shot rumble down from the butte, it was impossible for Rosa and Tin-Pan not to at least consider the grave implications. Monte, Billy, and Jones were somewhere in those rocks and there had been no return fire. And, after the last shot, when the troopers started running toward Rosa and Tin-Pan, it was clear the soldiers had also assumed the worst.

Resting his rifle against the boulder in front of him, Tin-Pan glanced at the approaching troopers, all of them clustered together. "I'm surprised they stayed out that long," said Tin-Pan. "The lieutenant had 'em spaced too far apart. With nobody to watch a man's back, it makes a fella feel like a sitting duck. In times like these, most folks naturally like to be close to other folks."

Rosa grunted but, rifle in hand, did not take her eyes off the butte. "They think the lieutenant is dead. Now they will want to run. I have seen the same thing many times in the revolution."

The lanky private with the Adam's apple was in the lead as the group of five dropped down behind Rosa and Tin-Pan and then crawled up to the edge of the boulder. Breathing hard he said, "I think the Indians got them all. We're going to get back to the horses and get the hell out of here."

Tin-Pan half turned toward the soldiers and immediately noticed the wide-eyed uncertainty that was tattooed on every face. Singling out the lanky private, Tin-Pan asked calmly, "What's your name, boy?"

"Hall, Private Hall."

Nodding, Tin-Pan studied the other men, all of whom at that moment looked more like frightened boys. "We got lots of time, yet. Let's stay put and keep an eye out. It looks bad but that don't mean nothing. Why, I can't count the times me and Mistah John were in scrapes just like this one here. And it always turned out alright 'cause we didn't never give up, not 'til the very last minute."

Rosa suddenly grasped the binoculars that Jones had left behind. Looking toward the butte, she exclaimed, "It's the lieutenant! He's getting ready to run back to us."

"You men," ordered Tin-Pan, "spread out

a little. Lie down so you can get a bead on that butte. If you see anything moving up in them rocks, anything at all, let loose with all you got."

The troopers took up positions six feet apart and then dropped on their bellies, aiming their Springfields at the wall of stone. They had barely steadied their rifles when Jones, holding his right side, broke into a full stride. Zigzagging down the incline with amazing speed, he reached the clustered group in less than a minute.

Scrambling around the rocks next to Rosa and Tin-Pan, he collapsed and laid on his back, gasping for air.

"We thought you were dead," explained Hall. "All of us did."

Jones, waved his left hand. "Only . . . wounded."

"How bad are you hit?" asked Tin-Pan.

His chest heaving, Jones removed his bloody left hand. "I . . . don't . . . know."

Rosa handed the binoculars to Tin-Pan and then turned her attention to Jones. "Unbutton your shirt," she ordered. "I have seen many wounds."

Jones nodded and, with a slight tremor in his hands, untucked his shirt and then released the buttons up to his chest. Gingerly, he pulled his undershirt up past his bloody side but then anemically turned his head away. "How bad is it?"

"Who has a knife?" Rosa asked.

"Oh, God!" moaned Jones. "I need a doctor! Get me back to the garrison!"

Tin-Pan handed Rosa an open jackknife. She took it and cut a square out of Jones's undershirt. Folding it, she wiped the blood off of the wound and then, after examining it closely, she leaned back. "This was only a ricochet," Rosa said, handing the knife back to Tin-Pan. "You were only hit with pieces of the bullet. The bleeding will stop soon."

"How deep are they?" Jones asked. "How deep are they in me?"

Rosa sneered. "Not deep enough to kill you. And not deep enough to keep you from running all the way here and leaving Monte and Billy. Where are they?"

Jones looked at Rosa and somberly shook his head. "The three of us were going through the boulders. Segundo was in the lead with me not far behind. First, I looked behind me and saw that Billy had disappeared. Then I heard the first shot and saw Segundo go down. I tried calling out to him several times. And then I was shot. I was lucky to have made it out alive."

Rosa gazed back at the butte for several seconds. Then she said, "Monte is not dead.

If he was I would know it."

"We'll have to go in and find out," said Tin-Pan. "You don't never take a chance on leaving a man for the Apaches. And the same goes for Billy. We got to find out about him, too."

Jones was too distressed to be aware of the guilt in his eyes but he was quick to respond to Tin-Pan's gallantry. "Yes, of course. I'm wounded but I'll send in all the troopers. It's like a jungle of boulders up there with countless places to hide. You'll need to make a show of force in order to flush the Apaches out."

"And what about Miss Appleton?" Rosa asked. "They might kill her."

Sitting up, Jones took the folded piece of undershirt from Rosa and pressed it against his side. "We've done all we can for her. Perhaps we can recover her body."

Jones pointed at a private. "You, trooper. Go down and bring Private Vogel and the others back up here."

"But sir," said the trooper, "Private Vogel busted his ankle."

"Make him a damned crutch," snapped Jones. "He can still shoot."

Hall stood suddenly. Pointing at the eastern end of the butte he asked, "What's that?"

Rosa lifted the binoculars. *"Gracias a Dios,"* she said softly. *"Gracias a Dios."*

"What is it?" demanded Jones.

"It is Monte," Rosa said, "and he has Miss Appleton with him."

"Is she alright?" Jones asked.

"Thank the Lord!" sighed Tin-Pan. "It's a miracle, sure enough."

Rosa took a better look as Monte grew closer. "Miss Appleton is walking behind Monte," said Rosa, her voice reflecting some confusion, "and she is shaking her fist at him. Now she . . . she is throwing sand at him!"

Jones got to his feet and, with his free hand, snatched the binoculars from Rosa's gasp. After squinting through them for several seconds he muttered, "She seems uninjured."

Tin-Pan cringed. "Then she's probably done lost her mind. Lots of women that's been captured do. What happens to 'em is too much and their mind goes off someplace to find comfort."

"Is there any sign of Billy?" Rosa asked.

"None," returned Jones, regaining his bravado. "But we've rescued Miss Appleton. That's was my mission and now it's been accomplished."

"We still have to go in there and find

Billy," Rosa said.

Jones took the binoculars down. "I could ignore my wound for the time being, but we have to get Miss Appleton to a doctor as soon as possible, and she'll need to be protected along the way. The situation has changed, now. I don't have enough men to guard Miss Appleton *and* go looking for someone that most likely is already dead."

"In that case," Tin-Pan said sternly, "me, Monte, and Miss Rosa will go after Billy our own selves."

"You," Jones said impudently, "are free to do as you wish. I, on other hand, am an officer in the United States Army. I have my orders."

Handing the binoculars to Trooper Hall, Jones ordered, "You men stay here." Holding his side, Jones stepped around the boulder and started for Miss Appleton.

Rosa stood up but Tin-Pan took her by the wrist. "Just to be safe, Miss Rosa, we'd best wait until they're a little farther from that butte. They're still in easy rifle range and I don't put nothing past an Apache."

"It is good," Rosa said thoughtfully, "to have you with us."

"The same goes for you and your friends," replied Tin-Pan. "I can't say as much for that shavetail lieutenant."

352

Taking long strides, Jones moved quickly. When he neared Monte, Miss Appleton, who lagged thirty paces behind, burst into a rage. "He's a coward!" she ranted, pointing at Monte. "A worthless coward. He's no better than the damned, filthy Indians. I want him arrested, do you hear? I want him to spend the rest of his life in a stinking prison cell!"

Rushing past Monte, Jones went to the woman. Grasping her arm and giving her some support, he asked, "Are you alright, Miss Appleton? Are you well?"

"Well?" seethed Appleton. "Well? I would be if that horrible brute would have done what any real man would have done! But he was afraid, afraid of a primitive savage."

Helping her along, Jones asked, "What are you saying, Miss Appleton, that Monte Segundo is a coward?"

"Of course, he is! Look at him! Big and strong and full of himself. But he allowed the savage to get away, the same one that murdered your trooper, the one that captured me. The one that took me and then gave me to . . . that, that . . ."

"I'm sorry, Miss Appleton," Jones said. "I'm having a difficult time understanding you."

Appleton could not keep her hate-filled

eyes off of Monte. "He could have killed that vile creature but he refused. He let him go when he could have killed him."

"You mean Charley McComas?" questioned Jones.

"I mean the blond Indian!" snapped Appleton. "He was as bad as the scar-faced one, the old one. All of them are nothing but filth."

When Monte was far enough from the butte, Tin-Pan gave Rosa a nod and, leaving her Mauser behind, she broke into a run. When she got to Monte, she threw both arms around him. And to her surprise, Monte put both of his arms around her and then lifted her off the ground.

Leaning her head on his chest, Rosa beamed, "I knew you were alright. I just knew it. God is merciful to us, Monte."

"More than you know, Rosa," agreed Monte and then gently set her down.

Rosa looked up at Monte. She blinked and looked again. "You are smiling. Monte, you are smiling. Why do you smile?"

"I guess maybe I am," Monte said. "I'll tell you why later. But now you might want to see what you can do for Miss Appleton. Not that I blame her, but she's gone off her rocker."

"She's what?"

"She's not right in the head."

Rosa stepped to the side of Monte, her eyes sweeping over Miss Appleton as she approached with Jones at her side. Appleton's hair was frayed in places and twisted into knots in others. Her face, almost unrecognizable, was smudged with layers of dirt and dried sweat. Her filthy blouse was untucked and had no buttons left on it. However, it had been tied together with thin pieces of string, the ends having been threaded through the buttonhole and then back through a hole poked in the other side of the blouse. Her riding pants were comparatively clean but torn in several places and she was wearing her shoes but with no laces.

Monte continued on toward Tin-Pan, but Rosa waited where she stood. When Miss Appleton was two steps away, Rosa went to her. Opposite Jones, Rosa began walking alongside her.

"Perhaps, Lieutenant," Rosa said compassionately, "Miss Appleton would like the company of a woman. She may wish to talk to someone who can better understand what she has been through."

Glaring hysterically at Rosa, Appleton clutched the front of her blouse, holding it tightly together. "What do you mean 'what

I've been through'?" she snapped. "Is that all you Mexicans think about? I don't need anyone's sympathy, especially not from a whore like you.

"You can't possibly understand someone like me but I can easily understand you and your kind. You are thinking those awful brutes violated me, aren't you? Of course you are! That's what you've been thinking, that's what all of you have been thinking, isn't it? Isn't it?

"Well, I hate to disappoint all of you but not one of those lecherous beasts so much as touched me. Not one, do you hear me? I wouldn't let them near me.

"Now, get away from me and go back to your coward of a man. I can't stand the sight of either of you."

Rosa studied Jones for a moment, but he merely stared straight ahead. When he refused to even make eye contact, Rosa stopped walking. Allowing Jones and Miss Appleton to proceed by themselves, Rosa felt a white-hot surge of anger boiling up inside her. But then, thinking of her own ordeal in Las Palomas, the rage slowly melted away. She knew Marzel Appleton had been through a living hell but clearly had chosen to deal with it by denying that anything had happened.

Watching her walk away, however, it occurred to Rosa that the poor woman might even *believe* nothing had happened. If that were the case, was she so very different from Monte who, as a child, had blotted out every detail of his parents' murders, effectively erasing them from his memory? Was it better, Rosa wondered, for a woman to talk about such an atrocity as they both had suffered or, as Rosa herself had chosen to do, lock the nightmare in the darkest closet of her soul, then move on and try not to look back?

Rosa was searching for the answers to questions of her own when she heard someone far away call her name. Facing the butte, Rosa saw me trotting toward her with my rifle. As I neared she could see that I too was smiling.

Slowing to a stop in front of her, I grinned. "I saw from up there," I said and then took a deep breath and started again. "I saw Monte and Miss Appleton. He got her!"

"Where have you been?" Rosa demanded. "Jones thought the Apaches got you."

"I got separated from Jones and Monte so I picked a good spot and looked for Apaches. I heard some shots but that was it. After a while, I snuck over to the edge of the butte and looked for you and Tin-Pan.

That's when I saw Monte and Miss Appleton out in the open."

"Come, Billy," Rosa said, "we are done here. It is time we get back to Sasabe. Angelina and Señor Cruz will be waiting."

Walking beside Rosa, I asked excitedly, "What happened? How did Monte get her away from the Apaches?"

"You know as much as me," Rosa answered. "Jones got peppered with a few pieces of lead from a ricochet but they barely broke the skin. He was the first one to show up. He thought you and Monte had been killed by the Apaches. He was so afraid of his little wound that he was ready to leave Miss Appleton to the Apaches and run back to the garrison."

I huffed. "There was a time I thought the lieutenant wasn't all that bad. I guess I was wrong."

"That's not all," Rosa added. "I looked at his wound and told him it was little more than a scratch but after he saw that Monte had rescued Miss Appleton he decided it was time to leave. He said me and Monte and Tin-Pan could look for you if we wanted, but he was taking his soldiers and the woman and going back."

I was shocked and appalled that Jones would abandon me but all I could manage was a mild, "You don't say."

When we got to where everyone was gathered, Monte and Tin-Pan were standing together and talking while Jones and his men were several paces away, hovering intently around a raving Marzel Appleton.

"Now there's a sight for sore eyes," grinned Tin-Pan. "We was about to go in and get you, Billy."

"So I hear," I replied, as Rosa hurried over to Monte and put her arm snuggly through his.

Tin-Pan pointed at my rifle. "I hear you shot that Apache you all were after. The one called Norroso."

I was confused. "What?" I stammered. "I shot who?"

"You sure enough saved my bacon, Billy," Monte said. "Norroso had me dead to rights. Another second or two and he would have put a slug into me or cut my throat."

"I didn't shoot anybody," I protested, leaning my rifle against a large rock. "I didn't fire a shot."

Monte gave me a queer look. His brow furrowed in thought and then I could see his mind was racing. "But it was a rifle shot that killed him," said Monte.

"I heard three reports," I admitted, "all rifle shots. But none of them were mine."

I had seen the look of wonder on Monte's face twice before and each time it had been when some event or sound had triggered the return of one of his buried childhood memories. And this was no exception.

Ever so slowly, Monte began to shake his head. "I'll be damned," he muttered. "I'll be double-damned."

Staring curiously up at Monte, Rosa asked, "What is it?"

Before he could answer, Jones strutted over to where we were standing. Miss Appleton was at his side and the five troopers, armed and scowling, were close on his heels. "What's this about you letting McComas escape?" Jones demanded. "You made no attempt to stop him, to detain him?"

"That's right," Monte said. "I didn't."

"Miss Appleton informs me that he was the one that murdered Corporal McIntosh, killed him and then, along with the others, smashed out his brains. And McComas was also the one that kidnapped Miss Appleton. She also informed me that she told you all of this up on the butte, told you this while you were in the presence of McComas. And yet you refused to do anything about it, that you could easily have shot him, but you simply let him walk away."

"Miss Appleton is confused," Monte said flatly. "That happens to some folks when they've been hung upside down over a cliff. The blood all runs to their head and clouds their thinking."

That revelation stumped Jones for a moment but he quickly resumed his line of questioning. "So, you don't deny that you had the opportunity to apprehend the blond Apache and failed to act. Then, do you also admit that you are a coward as Miss Appleton has reported. Or are you calling her a liar?"

Monte pulled a half step away from Rosa and at that point I knew the time had come. Monte Segundo had had his fill of Lieutenant Jones. Monte's eyes darkened and all expression vanished from his face. It was a look I had seen before and when it appeared, there was a better than even chance men were about to die.

"If Monte let him go," I said, attempting to head off a disaster, "he had a good reason. Maybe it was a difficult decision . . . something like the one you made to leave me stranded up on the butte."

"You stay out of this!" demanded Jones.

Six months earlier I would have cowered to such a man but, surprising even myself, my response was instantaneous. "I don't

361

take orders from you, Lieutenant."

My unexpected and icy rebuttal stunned Jones, leaving him momentarily speechless. Or perhaps it wasn't so much my newfound courage as it was the fact that he knew I carried a hideout gun under my vest, a pistol Rosa had told him warranted a notch on the grips.

Miss Appleton angrily inserted herself into the tense pause. "Aren't you going to do anything to him, Lieutenant? Are you just going to stand here and do nothing? He's an accomplice to a crime."

Rosa took a step toward Tin-Pan and he casually handed her the Mauser. He then turned to face Jones.

"Careful now, Lieutenant," cautioned Tin-Pan, "you ain't back East no more. Out here the wrong word said at the wrong time can get a man killed. And, as things is sizing up, if it comes down to root hog or die, I'm siding with Monte Segundo."

Jones glanced incredulously at Tin-Pan. It wasn't until he noticed Tin-Pan's hand resting on the butt of his pistol that the lieutenant realized what was happening.

"Don't be ridiculous!" huffed Jones. "You're all living in the past."

"And you're a slow learner," Monte said. "How about I give you another lesson about fighting, one you'll carry with you . . . as long as you live anyway?"

Jones looked into Monte's blazing, black eyes, and then, as if a plug had been pulled from his throat, the color instantly drained from his face.

"And you soldier-boys remember," Monte added savagely, "I'll have five slugs left in my Colt after I finish with your lieutenant."

"Too bad they will all die so young," Rosa said, leveling her Mauser at the troopers and fingering the trigger.

Consumed in the heat of the moment, my eyes locked on the nearest soldier to me, Trooper Hall. My rifle was out of reach but my thirty-eight was close at hand behind my vest. "I'll take the tall one," I said and meant every word.

"Don't none of you boys move a muscle," warned Tin-Pan. "We'll shoot if you do."

Jones's eyes flared wide as the troopers behind him did exactly as they were told. Jones did not blink for several seconds, but then somehow, he managed to swallow. "Don't be absurd," he scoffed, but the bravado in his voice now harmonized with the tinny notes of fear and panic. "I'm simply asking why you let McComas go?"

Monte glared at Jones for what seemed like an eternity. Finally, satisfied that Jones had no fight in him, Monte said, "I let him go because he could have killed me and he didn't. Not only that, he shot the Apache named Norroso just as he was about to shoot me."

"He did what?" questioned Rosa.

"You expect me to believe that?" Jones said, doing his best to sneer, but failing miserably. "Why would he do such a thing?"

"Because," Tin-Pan offered, "he's still got some Charley McComas left in him. Maybe he didn't want to see another white man get killed."

Realizing the crisis had passed, I breathed a sigh of relief and glanced at Monte. Even though he made no comment regarding Tin-Pan's assertion, I knew there was more to the story, something Monte was keeping from the rest of us.

"Did you at least attempt to get Mc-Comas to come with you?" Jones asked. "To come back to civilization, to the white race?"

"The what race?" questioned Monte.

Jones glanced uneasily at Tin-Pan and then at Rosa. "You know what I mean. To his people, his relatives. To civilization."

"I said his name, Charley McComas. I said it lots of times but he didn't seem interested. Instead, he kept calling himself Ah-toe-nay, his Apache name. That's about all he said."

Deflating like a hot-air balloon, Jones tentatively turned to the woman Monte had rescued. "Miss Appleton, under the circumstances all I can do is make out a report. Captain Miller will have to sort this out. I, well, I . . ."

"Enough of this!" shrieked Miss Appleton. "You're all cowards! Every one of you! Take me back to the ranch! Hopefully, you can at least manage that."

Miss Appleton spun on her heels. The troopers scattered immediately, giving her a wide berth as she stormed off. Jones hesitated and then hurried after her.

I glanced at the troopers and noticed Hall staring at me with an obvious question in his eyes. Understanding his confusion, I pulled my vest open. Seeing my pistol for the first time, he merely grunted in surprise. Then lethargically scratching his neck, he turned his attention to Monte.

"I don't get it," Hall said. "You saved her life and she hates you, hates you with a passion. You should've heard the things she was saying about you."

Monte nodded. "Yeah, but she hates that blond Apache a hell of a lot more. She wanted him dead. She wanted him dead more than she's ever wanted anything in her life, and she's a woman that's used to getting what she wants."

"But why?" Hall asked. "She don't look too worse for wear and he's a captured white man after all."

"The reason she hates him," said Tin-Pan, "is the same reason she hates all of them Apaches that took her. And that particular reason ain't decent to talk about. Ain't decent for nobody to be talking about, 'specially back at the garrison."

Hall squinted thoughtfully. "You don't mean those Apaches . . ." Glancing at Rosa, Hall stopped in mid-sentence. "Hell, no!"

"Like I said," affirmed Tin-Pan, "it ain't decent to talk about."

Hall hung his head and swore. Then he and the rest of the troopers followed after Jones.

"Tell us what happened up there on that butte, Monte," I said. "None of this adds up. There's something you're not telling us."

"There is," agreed Monte, "a whole lot. To start with, the first shot you all heard missed my head by a few inches. The second shot was the one that ricocheted into Jones. I'm thinking those two shots had to have been fired by Norroso. He knew he missed me so they set a trap using Miss Appleton for bait. And a damned good trap it was.

"Up on a piece of dirt, they tied a leather rope around one of Appleton's ankles and hung her over a cliff headfirst. Then they tied the other end of the rope around an old dead juniper log that was lying up there. Then they greased the rope."

"I heard of Apaches hanging people like that," said Tin-Pan, "but greasing the lariat is a new one."

"They knew you would try and pull her up," said Rosa.

"Pretty smart," I said. "And the grease was so you'd have to use both hands, right?"

"You got it," nodded Monte. "And that's just what I did because Miss Appleton was screaming and jerking around so much that the log was sliding closer and closer to the edge."

"But you had to know it was a trap," said Tin-Pan. "And you grabbed hold of that rope anyhow?"

"If she'd have quit squirming, I could have waited but she didn't. Anyway, while I was trying to pull on that rope, Norroso showed up. He was a foot away and ready to kill me when Ah-toe-nay shot him."

"But you still had hold of the lariat," said Rosa. "How do you know it was Ah-toe-nay that shot Norroso?

"He shot him, alright. He told me as much."

"Then you talked to him?" asked Rosa. "You saw *El Guerrero Güero*?"

"Not right off. I was still trying to get Appleton up when he came up to me carrying a rifle. Then he cut the rope free of the log it was tied to. That way he knew I couldn't let go and make a try for my pistol, something Norroso didn't think about. So, then, with my hands on that rope, he just walked up and took my pistol, pretty as you please."

"What did he look like?" asked Tin-Pan.

"He was taller than me, maybe two inches. He had seen some hard work because he had muscles on him. In fact, he was about the size of Jones. He wore a headband, moccasins, and a breechcloth, just the same as Norroso. His skin was almost as brown as Norroso's but he had the blond hair, of course. It reached halfway down his back and he had a short beard. It had a little bit of red mixed in it. And his eyes were brown."

"Brown?" questioned Tin-Pan.

Monte nodded and said, "All I could do was keep on pulling that greasy lariat."

"But what if the rope would have slipped out of your hands?" I asked.

Monte snickered. "You've seen Marzel

Appleton. I don't think Norroso or Ah-toe-nay were too awfully worried about losing her."

"So, what happened once you got her up?" asked Tin-Pan.

"Well, she was acting crazy as you might expect, spouting off all sorts of things that I can't remember. Ah-toe-nay ignored both of us. He just looked over my pistol, looked at it like a man would if he was fixing to buy it. He even seemed to be interested in the serial number. All the while he had me covered with his rifle."

"But you've got your pistol," Rosa said. "How did you get it from him?"

Monte shrugged. "I didn't. He threw it down at my feet."

"You mean," I said, "he unloaded it and then tossed it?"

"No. It was loaded. At first, I thought it was a game, that he wanted me to try for it so he could have some fun shooting me. At the same time, Miss Appleton was screaming for me to grab the pistol and kill him. She didn't care if I got killed in the process, she wanted him dead right then and there."

"But Miss Appleton said the blond just walked off," Rosa said. "Did he walk off with the pistol at your feet? A loaded pistol and he turned his back on you?"

369

"Sounds crazy doesn't it?" Monte admitted. "It struck me that way, too. But before he walked away he kept looking at me in a peculiar sort of way, really peculiar. Somehow, I got the idea he wasn't going to kill me. And he didn't seem to want Miss Appleton either . . . which, at the time, was something we both had in common."

"So," I asked, "he just walked away? Just like that?"

Monte paused for a moment. "He did. But then I went after him. I wanted to try one more time to tell him to come back with me, to tell him he was Charley McComas. And I did get to talk with him one more time. And that's when I found out he wasn't Charley McComas."

"He told you that?" asked Rosa.

"Not in so many words. But when he told me he wasn't Charley, I knew he was telling the truth."

"He wasn't lying," agreed Tin-Pan. "Little Charley had blue eyes, not brown."

"Did he?" questioned Monte. "I didn't know that."

I was totally bewildered. "Then how did you know he wasn't Charley McComas?"

"Because," Monte said, "he told me everything I wanted to know and he put it all in one word."

Monte gazed at Rosa and began to smile.

"What is it, Monte?" Rosa asked. "What did he say?"

Monte took a breath. He let it out slowly and then said, "Buttercup."

...aid, Buttercup."

CHAPTER 11

When Monte said the word *Buttercup,* my
mind went completely blank. In a state of
mental paralysis, all I could do was stare at
him. Rosa, equally stunned and disoriented,
was also speechless.

Tin-Pan glanced at Monte but then carefully studied Rosa and me. "I take it
'Buttercup' means something special to you
folks."

Recovering from the shock, Rosa asked,
"But Monte, how would he know that
name? How could he? That was the name
of your dog, the one the Apaches killed
thirty years ago."

"She's right, Tin-Pan," Monte said. "Buttercup was a dog that belonged to me and
that was the name I gave her."

The wheels in my head sluggishly started
to turn again. "Then, Ah-toe-nay was a
neighbor? A friend of yours?"

Monte shook his head. "We had no

neighbors."

Rubbing the side of my head, I confessed, "I don't see how that's possible. How would he know your dog's name?"

Glaring wide-eyed at Monte, Rosa asked excitedly, "How do you know that you had no neighbors?"

Monte didn't answer. He merely looked at Rosa and smiled.

Rosa gasped and put a hand over her lips. *"Madre de Dios,"* she whispered. Slowly taking her hand away, she said softly, "You remember, don't you? You remember it all."

"Ah-toe-nay," Monte said, "was taken the same day Ma and Pa were killed. All these years I didn't remember him or anything about another boy being kidnapped. But up on that butte today, when I followed after Ah-toe-nay and he turned around, we were standing eye to eye. For just a second, I thought he looked familiar. That's when he said 'Buttercup.' He was telling me who he was."

"Who is he, Monte?" pleaded Rosa.

"Ah-toe-nay is my brother."

At first we were all too bewildered to react but then Tin-Pan blurted, "I'll be a hog-tied son of a gun! Your brother! If that don't beat all I ever saw! Wait 'til I tell Mistah John about this! He's gonna bust a gut."

"But wait," I said, trying to make sense of it all. "When did you realize he was your brother? He knew you were his brother and yet he was walking away? That doesn't make any sense. None of this does."

"It didn't come to me until he was out of sight," Monte said. "I was just as stumped as you and Rosa when he said 'Buttercup.' But then . . . but then it started coming back to me. All of it. Ma and Pa. Buttercup, the cabin, the cows, the stories Pa told, the pies Ma baked for Christmas. And last of all, I remembered Anthony. He was eight and I was six when all of it ended.

"Anthony was out looking for our milk-cow when they came. They got him first. I remember that they had him tied and sitting behind an Apache up on a big bay horse. He was yelling at me, trying to get me to stop crying. Somehow, he knew they would kill me if I didn't stop crying."

"But he walked away?" Rosa asked. "Why would he walk away from his brother?"

"God only knows," Monte sighed. "I guess we both changed that day, changed forever. I guess that's why he kept pounding his chest and saying 'Ah-toe-nay!' He knew who I was but he wanted me to know he wasn't Anthony anymore."

"That's the way it usually was back in the

old days," admitted Tin-Pan. "Hardly any captives ever come back to live like they used to. It's hard to understand why."

"How did he know who you were, Monte?" asked Rosa. "Do you think Norroso told him?"

"I wondered about that," answered Monte. "Norroso had binoculars and figured out who I was, who all three of us were. That was easy enough for him. But Apaches like to tell stories and brag about what they're going to do. And I'm thinking . . . Ah-toe-nay . . . listened to Norroso's story about me shooting off his ear and how he's going to kill me for it. Then Norroso likely told about how he and I first met, how he was with the army when they came to our place right after the raid. And Norroso likely bragged about how he left me in the cactus to die, the cactus that Anthony saw them throw me into.

"It wouldn't be hard for Ah-toe-nay to figure out Norroso was talking about his brother. But you have to remember, Norroso was not a Netdahe. He had lived on a reservation since the days of Geronimo. When he left Columbus and joined with the Netdahe, he had no clue who Ah-toe-nay was and, I'm thinking that Ah-toe-nay never told him."

"And so you think he killed a fellow Apache to save your life?" I said. "Wouldn't that cause trouble with the rest of the band?"

"Oh, that don't mean nothing to an Apache," said Tin-Pan. "I knew an Apache buck once that brought in the head of his own father that he'd killed and then gave to General Crook. Killing to an Apache ain't the same as killing is to civilized folks. And besides, this Norroso was a reservation Apache. The Netdahe prided themselves on being the ones who never gave up. They looked down on all the others."

"What will you do now?" Rosa asked. "Will you try to find your brother?"

Monte thought for a moment and then said matter-of-factly. "No. There's nobody forcing him to stay with the Apaches. That's his choice. And he made it clear to me that he doesn't want to be Anthony anymore."

I was a bit unsettled by his answer and a bit curious as well. "You remember your brother's name. Do you remember yours?"

"I do," Monte answered. "But it's going to stay, Monte Del Segundo. That's who I am now just like my brother is Ah-toe-nay. It's the hand that we were dealt."

"Your mother," Rosa asked, "she was Mexican. But was she a *guera*?"

376

Monte nodded. "Yeah, but not as blond as Ah-toe-nay."

"It's the sun down here," Tin-Pan said. "Apaches ain't big on wearing hats and if a body don't wear one the sun'll bleach out your hair right quick."

I glanced at Rosa. Her eyes were glazed over. She was deep in thought but seemed to be troubled, almost frightened. Raising her head, she couldn't bring herself to look into Monte's eyes. "Monte," she said softly, "now that you have your memory . . . do you feel any different, any different about us?"

Monte thought for a moment. "Now that you mention it, I do feel kind of different."

"You do?" questioned Rosa, her voice pitched with anxiety. "How?"

Clearly perplexed, Monte replied, "Not about you and me, not on your life. But different somehow . . . in a good sort of way."

It was after sundown when we got back to the Slaughter ranch and, as tired as he was, Tin-Pan went right to work building a fire in the kitchen stove. On one side he heated water and on the other started boiling a stew that he and Rosa had hastily thrown together. Monte and I went to the large pen where the cattle had been corralled days earlier and threw them a half ton of hay. Miss Appleton had arrived a few minutes before the rest of us civilians and had gone straight to her room and locked the door, even refusing to speak to Miss Thorndike.

An hour later, the stew was done and Tin-Pan had filled the Slaughters' bathtub with hot water. All of us, including Miss Thorndike, were sitting down to eat in the dining room when Marzel Appleton passed by on her way to the tub wearing an elegant full-length robe and carrying a small but ornate toiletry case.

Monte, Rosa, and I sat on one side of the table and Ada Thorndike, with a small bandage on her forehead, sat on the other side but not across from us. Other than having that bump on her head, Thorndike seemed to be in perfect health.

"How are you, Miss Thorndike?" I asked. "The last time I saw you, you were unconscious and on a travois."

"I am well," Thorndike answered stiffly. "But I am quite concerned about Miss Appleton. She seems ill."

"She has had a rough time," I said, choosing my words carefully. "When she feels better I'm certain she'll tell you all about it."

"The men that attacked us," Thorndike said, "looked like Indians. Is that what they were, real Indians?"

"They were Netdahe, holdouts from the days of Geronimo," I answered, assuming that bit of information was no secret. "There were about a dozen of them here to make a raid."

Tin-Pan, with an apron around his waist, came in from the kitchen and placed a steaming metal pot of stew in the center of the table. "Miss Appleton will feel lots better after her bath. She's gonna be fine, Miss Thorndike, you'll see."

"I'll put some coffee on. That might help her some, too."

"Is anyone going to tell me what happened?" asked Thorndike.

Tin-Pan wiped his palms on his apron. "That's up to Miss Appleton." On his way back to the kitchen, he added, "We kinda figured it was best to let her tell what she might want anybody to know when she feels up to it."

Miss Thorndike frowned knowingly. "My God. How utterly dreadful. Poor Marzel."

We filled our bowls with stew and had only begun to eat when a knock came at the front door. Assuming it was Jones, I got up and offered to let him in. It was dark outside but when I opened the door I was surprised to recognize Captain Miller. "Come in, sir.

We're just sitting down to supper. Would you care to join us?"

"I've eaten, but I would be pleased to have some tea or coffee."

"Tin-Pan's putting some coffee on now. Come in."

Seeing the seating arrangement at the table, Miller took a seat on the same side as Miss Thorndike and directly across from Monte. "Good evening, everyone," he said as he scooted up his chair.

Not even Miss Thorndike responded to Miller's greeting, so once again taking my seat I asked, "What brings you here tonight, Captain? Is this a social visit or are you conducting army business?"

"Some of each, I suppose," Miller answered politely. "I've just finished reading Lieutenant Jones's report on the goings-on up in Guadalupe Canyon. I've also heard some of the misleading rumors that are spreading through the garrison. It appears that certain facts contained in the report need to be, shall we say, clarified."

"Like what for instance?" I asked.

Miller lowered his voice. "Is Miss Appleton expected at the table this evening?"

"She is bathing at present," snipped Thorndike.

Miller nodded but keeping his voice low

he said, "The first issue that needs clarification is that Lieutenant Jones, at no time, crossed the border and entered Mexico."

Monte and Rosa both glanced at Miller but kept eating. I, on the other hand, did not miss the innuendo in Miller's point of "clarification." "And what is the second issue?" I asked.

His face flushing red, Miller said flatly, "That Miss Appleton was on a ride in the canyon and got separated from Miss Thorndike. Miss Appleton was then thrown from her mount and eventually became lost. Learning of this, Lieutenant Jones immediately formed and led a search party of troopers into the canyon. And after searching day and night, he and his men rescued Miss Appleton. And Miss Appleton, though suffering a bit from exposure to the elements, was returned to the Slaughter ranch completely unharmed and in good health."

Rosa stopped eating and raised an eyebrow. "So there were no Mexican rustlers?"

"That is correct, Miss."

"And there were no Apaches either?"

"Yes, Miss."

Understanding somewhat the purpose of Miller's visit, Rosa snorted derisively. "And your Corporal McIntosh, did he fly away like a bird?"

Miller shrugged. "The report asserts that the corporal deserted and then escaped into Mexico."

"And what about Monte and Tin-Pan," Rosa continued, "were they not there either?"

"The report states that Lieutenant Jones saw fit to hire civilian scouts and that they were of some use in locating the general whereabouts of Miss Appleton."

"Your report," Thorndike said, coming to her feet, "seems perfectly accurate, Captain Miller. I must compliment you on your thoroughness. You seem to have established all the facts quite nicely. I'll go and inform Marzel. I'm certain she and her family will be pleased when they hear how well this incident was handled."

No one spoke until Miss Thorndike was out of sight. We heard the door of the bathroom open and close. At the same moment, Tin-Pan returned to the table with a pot of coffee and some cups.

Miller, trying to maintain his dignity, sighed heavily. "You must understand, the Appleton family, not to mention the Thorndikes, both have a great deal of influence in Washington. That influence extends to the War Department, and even to the Commander in Chief."

Breaking his silence, Monte asked glibly, "And who would that be, the Commander in Chief?"

"Why, the President of the United States. President Wilson."

Monte took a bite of stew. Chewing while he talked, he asked, "Is that the same Wilson that double-crossed Pancho Villa, pissing him off so much that he raided Columbus and killed eight soldiers and nine civilians? The same Commander in Chief that stirred up this border mess and almost got us into a war with Mexico?"

"That's politics," Miller said humbly. "And so is this report Jones gave me. Now, he'll no doubt get transferred back East. And he'll get promoted, likely to colonel."

"Why are you telling us this?" Rosa asked. "We have nothing to do with army reports."

Miller's brow wrinkled with concern. "The lieutenant and Miss Appleton are covering all the bases. The four of you are loose ends they wish to tie up."

"Loose ends to what?" asked Tin-Pan.

"We can control the troopers," Miller admitted, "but Miss Appleton wants to make certain the truth of what happened in Guadalupe Canyon never gets out. I think we can all understand why.

"However, she has made certain threats,

threats that concern me as well as all of you. Basically, she says she will ruin any one of you should you ever tell what you know."

"Now, Captain," protested Tin-Pan, "it wouldn't be Christian to go and spread a story like that about poor Miss Appleton. We don't need no threats to do what's right."

"Well," Monte said, "I'm not as good a Christian as Tin-Pan because when it comes to 'poor Miss Appleton,' I don't give a tinker's damn about her. We're leaving here tomorrow morning and I'll be glad to be rid of her. And if she thinks her threats would have any effect on us, you can tell her she's wrong, dead wrong."

"I'm just the messenger," Miller said, "but I will be more than happy to personally deliver your message . . . word for word."

Miller reached for the coffee pot and filled his cup. "Mister Segundo, I owe you an apology. Once Lieutenant Jones is transferred, I will set the record straight with the troopers. We have done you a great disservice."

"How's that?" asked Monte.

"By believing and behaving as if you were a traitor."

"That's General Pershing's doing," Monte said. "I can't fault you for that."

"I don't know exactly what happened in Guadalupe Canyon," Miller said, "and the less I know the better. But I do know that Lieutenant Jones did not get his black eye by running into a tree branch. And I know that he never would have found Miss Appleton on his own. Like a lot of young lieutenants, he's a glory hunter."

"He'll have to steal it, then," said Tin-Pan. "I seen lots of fighting men in my time, Captain, and your lieutenant ain't got what it takes. He'd be better off staying back East with Miss Appleton where he belongs."

"The lieutenant," Miller said, "has developed a sudden romantic *disinterest* in Miss Appleton . . . I can only guess why."

"Then he is no man," Rosa said bitterly, "he is a pig, a *cabrone*!"

Miller took a sip of coffee. "Now, his interest in her is strictly based on *quid pro quo.*"

"What's that mean?" asked Tin-Pan.

"It means Lieutenant Jones will bury the truth if Miss Appleton will see to it that he gets what he wants in return. And it means that what happened in the canyon, as fantastic as it sounds, will never make it to the newspapers. A few local rumors might surface but other than that, the story of what occurred in Guadalupe Canyon will be buried."

EPILOGUE

How rumors spread so quickly throughout
Mexico and along the border is still a
mystery to me but by the time we had
driven the cattle to the outskirts of Douglas, word of an Apache raid was already on
everyone's lips. There was, however, no
mention of a blond Apache or of a woman
captive. I suppose that the Mexican rustlers
who had escaped from Jones's men could
have ridden to the sister city, Agua Prieta,
to spread the alarm, or that some of the garrison troopers had beaten us to town and
started talking.

At any rate, what we heard as we passed
people from town sounded more like folk-
lore than anything substantial. And a week
after we left Slaughter's ranch, we pushed
sixty head of prime breeding cows into the
corrals at the Rancho de la Osa.

The following week, Monte and Rosa
walked down the aisle of the centuries-old

San Xavier Mission. There was standing room only inside the mission. All the guests except for Señor Cruz, Angelina, and myself were Rosa's friends and relatives from Mexico. Outside the mission, hundreds of curious Papago Indians had gathered to watch the festivities and to get a look at the man many of the guests claimed was *El Muerte.*

When the priest, dressed in his ornate liturgical vestments, entered and took his place in front of the church, it took several seconds before Monte or I recognized that it was our friend Padre Marco, his participation being a secret Rosa had been guarding for weeks.

As I sat next to Angelina and her father in the old Spanish mission and watched the ceremony, I could not help but think of how Monte had changed the entire course of my life. Six months earlier, I had been in a similar situation but instead of watching a wedding in Arizona, I was sitting next to my Harvard classmates listening to a commencement address.

But that day seemed ages ago. Since that time I had packed my bags and gone west, ridden through the heart of the Mexican Revolution, been in a gunfight, fought rustlers, and, now, even chased after wild renegade Apaches. However, had I not stumbled into Monte Segundo on that fateful day in Columbus, I would, no doubt, be living a mundane life behind a desk in Chicago or some other crowded eastern city and never have known what life was actually about.

I looked up at the ceiling of the church. After years of neglect the frescoes were being restored. Everywhere, there were saints peering down at us. It was as if their eyes were silently watching our every move.

It was then it hit me just how much Monte's life resembled a three-act play, a tragedy with a happy ending that had been scripted and then set in motion by the unseen hand of fate. As I glanced back at Monte and Rosa, though, I knew this was not to be the final act to his incredible story.

After all, Monte and Rosa had decided to make the borderland their home, a country that was filled with soldiers ready to go to war, bandits eager to rob anyone they could find, rustlers wanting to steal cattle, and even wild Apaches making raids. The borderland was still the frontier, the last of the untamed and wide-open West. And as strange as it may seem to some, from the very moment I met Monte Segundo, I knew the rough and tumble life on the borderland was a life tailor-made for a pampered city slicker like me.

Except from *The Apache Diaries*, Goodwin and Goodwin, page 48:

"A small band of perhaps a dozen Apaches crossed the border and entered the Animas Valley in the fall of 1924 . . . Local ranchers began missing cattle and blamed each other until the haltered cattle mentioned by Bill Curtis were discovered . . . The Apaches' camp on Animas Mountain was soon discovered, but the band slipped away east into the Alamo Hueco Mountains, with twenty-eight head of stolen horses and mules. They were soon discovered again, and they vanished, leaving behind all the livestock, shod with rawhide; a quantity of hides; grass mats; bags of acorns; and thirteen hand-made saddles."

Excerpt from *They Never Surrendered*, Meed, page 14, 15:

"Back in the 1920s trying to patrol this

section of the border was less than futile. The ranchers knew it and so did the Apaches still operating from their bases in the Jaguar Mountains. In those days for all practical purposes the Big Hatchet country was still a frontier where the horse maintained a fading ascendency over the truck and car. In 1924 the Apaches were restless.

Their war chief was a tall, strapping man with white skin tanned by the blistering western sun, and a long mane of blond hair that streamed behind him like a scarf as he rode north at the head of the band."

Excerpt from *The Cochise Quarterly*, Willis, volume 14, Spring 1984 page 17, 18:

"I have also heard that this group of Indians were believed to be the fiercest warriors of the Apache tribe; and when Geronimo surrendered, this group escaped into the Sierra Madre Mountains in Mexico.

Listening to some of the old-timers' stories of the 1924 incident, the Diamond A cowboy was close enough to see the scout or leader of these Apaches. He was a white man with a red beard. It is believed he was the little white boy kidnapped near Safford, Arizona. Some say his name was Mc-Comas."

ABOUT THE AUTHOR

Paul Cox was born in rural Arkansas. When he was ten years old his family moved to California. There Paul attended college at Cal State Fullerton, competing at the national level in the decathlon. After college he attended graduate school in San Francisco, earning a doctorate degree. Paul is an avid outdoorsman and presently lives on a small ranch just outside of Sandpoint, Idaho.

The employees of Thorndike Press hope you have enjoyed this Large Print book. All our Thorndike, Wheeler, and Kennebec Large Print titles are designed for easy reading, and all our books are made to last. Other Thorndike Press Large Print books are available at your library, through selected bookstores, or directly from us.

For information about titles, please call:
  (800) 223-1244

or visit our website at:
  gale.com/thorndike

To share your comments, please write:
  Publisher
  Thorndike Press
  10 Water St., Suite 310
  Waterville, ME 04901